THE .... HANNAH

Nick Alexander grew up in the seaside town of Margate, UK. He has travelled widely and lived in the UK, the USA and France, where he resides today.

Nick's first five novels – the *Fifty Reasons* series – were self-published from 2004 onwards and went on to become some of the UK's best-selling gay literature.

His crossover titles, *The Case of the Missing Boyfriend* and its sequel, *The French House*, each reached #1 in Amazon's UK chart.

The Half-Life of Hannah, Nick's ninth novel, has sold more than 260,000 copies to date and a hotly anticipated sequel entitled *Other Halves* is due out at the beginning of 2014.

For more information please visit the author's website on www.nick-alexander.com.

Available now

OTHER HALVES
the sequel to *The Half-Life of Hannah*

ebook (ISBN 978 1 84502 767 4)
available for download now

print (ISBN 978 1 84502 764 3)
available April 2014

THE HALF-LIFE OF HANNAH

Nick Alexander

BLACK & WHITE PUBLISHING

First published 2014
by Black & White Publishing Ltd
29 Ocean Drive, Edinburgh EH6 6JL

1 3 5 7 9 10 8 6 4 2   14 15 16

ISBN: 978 1 84502 719 3

ALBA | CHRUTHACHAIL

A CIP catalogue record for this book is available from the British Library.

Typeset by Iolaire Typesetting, Newtonmore
Printed and bound by Grafica Veneta, S. p. A. Italy

ACKNOWLEDGEMENTS

Thanks to Rosemary – without your constant encouragement nothing would ever never get finished, and without your friendship this planet would be a much darker place. Thanks to Allan for his eagle-eyed copy-editing skills and to Jerôme for his help with the French text. Thanks to my family for being there, and to all my readers for sticking with me and showing so much enthusiasm about every new project – you make it all worthwhile. Finally, thanks to Black & White Publishing for making this physical book a reality.

ONE

"I'm sorry," Hannah says, aware that she doesn't sound very sorry at all, "but that's what it says. It says to go straight down this track."

The Mégane slithers to a halt on the gravel. Cliff sighs. "How can it be up there?" he asks. "I mean, seriously, how?"

They have spent fourteen hours in the car since they left Farnham, of which seven already today. Tempers are getting frayed. Hannah peers along the gravelly farm track to where it vanishes into the trees. "Maybe it's at the end of the track," she offers, both unconvinced and unconvincing. "Maybe it's in the middle of the forest."

Cliff pulls on the handbrake and wrenches the GPS from her grasp. "Only it isn't. And we've still got seven miles to go," he says. "It can't be seven miles down a track, can it?"

Hannah rubs the bridge of her nose and turns to look out of the side window at the rolling fields, at the pine forests in the distance. It's stunning scenery, but she can't enjoy it. Not yet. She discreetly takes a deep breath. She doesn't want Cliff to think it's a confrontational sigh. Not at a time like this.

"That is what it says, though," Cliff admits, jabbing at the screen. "I don't know what you've done to it."

"Cliff, I haven't done anything to it," Hannah says quietly, struggling, now, to hide the exasperation in her voice.

"If we had just left it where it was, stuck to the windscreen, I could have followed it myself," Cliff says.

"If you were able to look at a GPS without veering onto the wrong side of the road every time, that would be a good idea," Hannah points out, forcing a false laugh into her voice to mask her rising anger. "But you can't. And anyway, we *have* followed it. Right up this track."

"Veering onto the *right* side of the road," Cliff corrects her. "Not the wrong one."

"The *left* side, not the right side," Luke offers from the rear seat, laughing at his own wit.

"Well, the *correct* side then," Cliff admits. "You know what I mean. And anyway, it's not my fault if the frogs all drive on the wrong side of the road."

Luke undoes his seatbelt and leans forward. "We're the ones who drive on the wrong side, Dad," he says. "The English swapped sides so that they could stab people better with their swords." He demonstrates this by wielding his phone – Cliff's old iPhone – with a flourish.

Aware that in some way, Luke, by contradicting Cliff, has sided with her, Hannah feels a bubble of warmth for him. She reaches back to ruffle his hair. "Is that true, sweetheart?"

"Yes," he says. "I saw it on the telly-box." The term 'telly-box' came from his uncle Tristan, and because it's cute, they all use it now.

"Well, if you saw it on the telly-box!" Cliff says drily, still stabbing at the buttons on the GPS.

"It was on *QI*," Luke tells him.

"That's all very interesting, I'm sure," Cliff says. "But it doesn't much help us here."

Stephen Fry is revered in the Parker household as the font

of all knowledge. So Luke has won. Even Cliff isn't going to argue with The Fry.

"But what do we do?" Cliff continues. "Do we carry on up here until we get stuck, or . . ."

"I'm hungry," Luke says.

"Have one of those biscuits," Hannah tells him a little abruptly – her tone a coded warning – then to Cliff, "It does look a bit muddy."

"So I turn back," Cliff says. "That's what you're saying now?"

Hannah shrugs, still angry about the implication that this is somehow her fault. "We should have bought a map," she says. "I said we needed to buy a map back in that petrol-station."

"This *is* a map," Cliff replies, tapping the top of the GPS. "It has a map of every bloody road in France."

"I'll tell you what then, darling," Hannah says in her special faux-kind voice. "Why don't you look at your map of *every-bloody-road-in-France*, and work out how to get there?"

Cliff fiddles with the box for another minute or so and then sighs. "I don't know how," he admits. "It keeps coming back with the same bloody route."

"You just have to go back to the main road and drive," Luke offers. "It will recalculate a new route."

"Will it?" Cliff asks. "Or will it just keep telling us to turn around?"

"It will for a bit, but then it will recalculate," Luke says. "That's what happens in *Drive Apocalypse* anyway."

"Only this isn't a game. We're not in *Drive Apocalypse*," Cliff says.

"Well, we kind of *are*," Hannah points out, wittily, she thinks, not that anyone notices.

3

Luke's phone makes a honking noise. He checks the screen. "Jill and Tristan have arrived," he says. "So it must be possible."

"Maybe they have *a map*," Hannah suggests. "Maybe they have a proper actual map printed on a bit of dead tree."

"Dead tree! You're funny, Mum!" Luke says, laughing at her wit, and she loves him even more.

"Are you *sure* that isn't costing a fortune, sweetheart?" Hannah asks him. "I saw *Watchdog* and they said that you have to be really careful about . . ."

"Not to receive," Luke says, interrupting. "It costs to send. But they were on about Internet anyway and I've switched it off. Can I send a text back saying we're lost? Maybe Tristan can come and find us. It's only fifty pee to send an SMS."

"No! There's no point," Cliff replies gruffly, imagining the shame of having to be saved by a gay guy. "We'll be there in a minute anyway."

"In a day, more like," Luke says, sarcastically.

Hannah shoots him a warning glance, and he sinks back into his seat and pulls the biscuits from the seat pocket.

"So we turn around?" Cliff asks, then, after a pause, "Anyone?"

Hannah shrugs. She's no longer in the mood to be helpful. "You're the one with maps of the whole of France, darling," she says. Because she feels bad for repeating that same dig twice, however, she adds, "But yes. You're right. We probably should, shouldn't we?"

Cliff sighs deeply and hands the GPS not back to Hannah, but over his shoulder to Luke. She grinds her teeth at the betrayal.

"OK, I'm gonna reverse back and then turn around. In the meantime, see if *you* can work it out, son, OK?"

"If anyone can solve it, Luke can," Hannah says with apparent generosity, yet praying secretly that Luke, too, will fuck it up.

TWO

Cliff

I met Cliff when I was twenty. I was a late-starter, romance wise, so Cliff was only my second boyfriend.

I got back from that oh-so disastrous holiday in Amsterdam with anarchist boyfriend Ben, and met Cliff on my second night back.

I was in a wine bar with my friend Shelley telling her all about splitting up with Ben when Cliff sent us both drinks. It seemed old-fashioned and chivalrous, and after three weeks of Ben's selfishness, exactly what the doctor ordered.

Cliff was three years older than I and already working as an accountant. He was well dressed and polite and an almost mirror opposite of dope-smoking, unpredictable Ben. He seemed much older than I, much older than Ben, and I found that maturity attractive.

I often think that if I hadn't been rebounding from Ben, I never would have given Cliff a second glance. That's not to say that Cliff was unattractive – he wasn't. He was a tall, well-built young man who played squash and tennis and had two-weekly appointments at the barber's to keep his new-romantic mop in shape. It's just that I had been more attracted by the goths and the bikers up until that point.

But glance, I did, and by the time he had bought both Shelley and me a couple of rounds of rum and Coke, given us a lift home in his Ford Sierra and had treated us to chips and curry-sauce on the way, he had pretty much snared me.

Shelley declared him 'boring' even back then, and I suppose that if there was one criticism that could be levelled at Cliff, boring would be it. But excitement, I reckon, is overrated. Kindness and generosity, an ability to provide, a stable temperament . . . I think these qualities are underrated in these days of unbridled individualism.

So, though I suppose life hasn't exactly been a roller-coaster with Cliff, it has been fine. It has been perfectly *fine*. And I know plenty of women my age – my sister included – who would give their right arms for a bit of 'perfectly fine'.

THREE

When they get to the villa, there are no signs of Tristan's car at all.

"Are you *sure* this is the place?" Cliff asks, apparently, *inexplicably*, directing his question at Hannah.

She shrugs. "Luke has the GPS," she reminds him.

"This is *it*," Luke says, demonstrating his conviction by climbing down from the car and pushing open the heavy forged-steel gate.

"But what if it isn't?" Hannah says, releasing her own seatbelt. "What if there's a guard-dog?" She opens the car door and extracts herself from the seat, noting, as she does so, that after an eight-hour car journey, this isn't as easy as it would have been even ten years before. "Luke!" she calls out, nervously heading past the gate. "Wait!"

"Hellooo!" A voice to her right. "Sweetie!" Hannah spins to find Jill's head peeping over the edge of an orange cotton hammock suspended between two trees.

"See!" Luke declares gleefully as he runs over to his aunt. "I told you."

"Hi Luke," Jill says brightly.

"I told them this was the right place but they didn't believe me," Luke tells her.

Hannah spins and beckons towards the Mégane, then, nodding exaggeratedly at Cliff's questions, silently mimed behind the windscreen, she shouts, "Yes. Yes! This is it! They're *here*! I don't *know* where Tristan's parked, but Jill's here."

"Tristan and Aïsha have gone food shopping," Jill tells her, waving what looks suspiciously like a joint in the air.

As the car crunches up the driveway, Hannah crosses the lawn and ruffles Luke's hair. "Can you go help your dad?" she asks.

"Sure," Luke says, then, already distracted from this idea, "Hey, where's the pool? They said there was a pool."

"It's around the other side," Jill says, her joint leaving a fragrant trail in the air as she gestures. "It's . . ." But Luke is already out of earshot.

"It's empty," she tells her sister more quietly, reaching out now with her left hand to take Hannah's fingers between her own.

"Empty? What, dry?"

Jill nods and pulls a despondent face. "'Fraid so," she says. "How are you, Sis'? How was the drive?"

"Is that a joint?" Hannah asks her.

Jill smiles and shrugs as if she sees no reason for embarrassment. "You want some?" she asks, proffering the joint.

Hannah pulls her hand away and frowns at her. "I do hope you didn't bring that with you through customs," she says. "Not with Aïsha in the car."

"Of course," Jill says. "We put it in Aï's teddy bear."

Hannah opens her lips to express fury, but Luke has returned. "The pool's empty," he says breathlessly. "It's got a dead bird in it. A pigeon I think."

"Well, don't touch it," Hannah tells him. "They have all sorts of diseases."

"I can't *touch* it, Mum!" Luke says, now starting to rock Jill's hammock. "It's at the bottom of the pool."

"I'm sure Dad'll get the pool sorted," Hannah tells him. "Now go help him, will you?"

Once Luke has run off, she nods at Jill's joint again. "You're out of control, Jill," she says quietly. "You and I will have words about this later when the kids are in bed."

Jill grins at her and shrugs. "I don't doubt it," she says.

The Mégane parked, Cliff climbs out and places one hand in the small of his back. "Jees!" he says.

"Long drive?" Jill asks him.

"Endless," Hannah says quietly, so that only Jill will hear her. "Absolutely bloody endless. I came close to ramming the bloody GPS down his throat."

Cliff crosses the scrubby lawn to join the women. "Nice place," he says, and Hannah realises that she hasn't properly looked yet. She looks around now, taking in the pink stucco villa, the olive orchard, the hammock, the shady patio, the wooden pergola, the sound of cicadas. She takes a deep breath of the baked, earthy air. "It is," she says. "It's gorgeous."

Jill attempts to extract herself from the hammock, then reaches out again for her sister's hand. "Help me," she says, then, "It's lovely."

Once she has been pulled upright, she keeps her sister's hand and tugs her towards the villa. "The inside is pretty funky too. Come see," she says.

The interior of the villa is dark, and cool. It feels, in fact, almost cold after the scorching Mediterranean sunshine outside. The tiled floor shines and the rooms smell rich and waxy from furniture polish. As Luke runs echoing from room to room, Jill leads them on a guided tour, announcing, as if

10

it weren't obvious – as if this were *her* villa – that *this is the bathroom*, and *this is the kitchen*.

Cliff is struggling to restrain himself from commenting, *"Really? So that's a kitchen, huh?"* He finds Hannah's sister endlessly annoying – unreasonably so. And rarely do they spend time together without some flashpoint being reached. Generally it's a conflict between Cliff's cartesian logic and Jill's random new-wave spirituality that's at the origin of the disaccord. But he has promised himself (and Hannah) that she will not get to him on this trip. He's determined to be nice to her. He will rise above it all.

"So where's Tristan?" he asks her, mainly to stop her listing things – cupboards, shower, washbasin – that they can all see, and identify, perfectly well for themselves.

"They've gone to get food," Hannah informs him.

"He's a shopaholic," Jill says. "He got excited when he spotted the hypermarket on the way in."

"Well, we do need food," Cliff points out.

"Yes, but you know what he's like," Jill says. "He'll come back with one each of every most expensive food item on sale. It's an absolute obsession with him."

"Yum," Hannah says. "I love Tristan's food."

"Well, he is a chef," Cliff says as Jill opens another door revealing a blue bedroom. "My room," she declares, then, "and it's got nothing to do with his being a chef. He's the same whatever kind of shop it is. Clothes, food, gadgets, men . . . It's just consumerism with Tris. It's just *more, more, more.*"

Cliff thinks it's unfair to criticise the guy for going to buy food for them all, but Hannah catches his eye and shoots him her doe-eyed look – a plea – so he asks instead, "So where's our room?"

When the bags have been carried in, Hannah heads for a shower, Jill returns to the hammock and another joint, and Cliff and Luke head off to search, in vain, for the filler valve for the pool.

By the time Tristan returns, techno blaring, his red Wrangler Jeep slithering to a halt on the gravel, they are all installed on the patio drinking – for want of anything else – glasses of tap water.

The silence when Tristan cuts the engine, and with it the music, is total. Even the cicadas have been stunned into silence.

They all stand and move towards the car. Luke runs straight to the passenger door. "Hi Aï!" he says enthusiastically as his cousin climbs out. "The pool's empty, did you see?"

"Yeah," Aïsha replies. "There's a dead bird in it too. I put a photo on Facebook."

Of course you have, Hannah thinks, checking out her niece's black Dr Marten boots, her black fingernails, her purple lip-gloss.

Luke frowns. "Mum says Internet's too expensive in France," he says, to which Aïsha just shrugs. Aïsha's Mum doesn't worry about such things, and Aïsha wouldn't care if she did.

Cliff watches as Tristan hugs Hannah, and then holds a hand out in front of him to preclude any idea that he and Tristan might do the same thing. It's not that he doesn't like Tristan (though he's never quite sure that he does) nor the fact that Tristan is gay (though he has confused feelings about that too). It's just that Cliff doesn't hug men. Ever.

The two men shake hands. "So we have food!" Cliff says, glancing at the bags piled on the back seat of the Jeep. "Well done."

12

"We do," Tristan replies, starting to lift the bags from the car and to hand them out.

"We have wine, more to the point!" Jill laughs, swiping a bottle of rosé from a passing bag, and heading off towards the kitchen with it, without, Hannah notices, carrying anything else.

"Cool car, Tris," Luke says, taking two bags from his adopted uncle.

"Thanks, Luke," Tristan replies. He's genuinely pleased that someone noticed. "It's brand new. Only three-thousand miles on the clock. Actually not even that. Lovely to drive."

Hannah takes two bags to carry in and notes that Aïsha is already slinking behind the villa. She thinks, *Like mother, like daughter.* She feels a little jolt of pain for her little boy who, though only two years younger than his cousin, won't, she knows, understand that this growing chasm between them has nothing to do with him and everything to do with the fact of Aïsha's adolescence. For the next five years, being cool will trump everything else for Aïsha, whether it be love, friendship or even fun. As a parent, you just have to pray they get over it. Because Hannah has known a few people who got stuck that way, and they were unbearable.

By the time the bags have reached the kitchen, Jill has a glass of wine in her hand.

"You might like to offer everyone else a drink, too," Tristan tells her – his voice polite, without judgement. Both Hannah and Cliff are thankful that it was he, not them, that said it.

Between sips of her own, Jill has served everyone with drinks. The kids have Cokes, and the adults have dewy glasses of fragrant rosé with ice-cubes that clink against the sides of the glass every time they gesture.

Tristan appears with a plate of salmon toasts. "Wow," Hannah says.

"Those look gorgeous," Jill agrees.

"I spreaded the cheese," Luke tells them.

"He's a very good spreader," Tristan says, smiling. "Very precise. No corners were missed."

"Cheese?" Hannah questions, taking a slice and lifting one corner of the salmon.

"Yes. There's cream cheese underneath," Tristan tells her. "Saint Moret."

"And this is rocket, right?" Jill asks.

"Yep."

"Love rocket," she says.

There's something cloying in everyone's tone that vaguely irritates Cliff. He thinks that everyone is making just a little bit too much fuss. They are, after all, just slices of toast with salmon on. But he's glad that Tristan is cooking. Hannah only has about five recipes which she rotates so religiously that you can pretty safely bet what you'll be eating each day based on what came the day before. Salmon toasts make a change.

"This is the life," Hannah says, nibbling at a slice, and then sipping at her wine. "I thought we'd never get here at one point, I swear."

"If it had been up to her, we wouldn't have," Cliff says.

Hannah shoots him a glare. The argument is on the tip of her tongue. But she can't quite decide whether to put it out there and get it over with or say nothing and hope to forget.

Thankfully, Cliff gets it. "Only joking, sweetheart," he says, putting down his glass so that he can squeeze her knee.

"We had some trouble with the GPS," Hannah explains. "It directed us up a farm track."

"We got that too, didn't we?" Jill says, addressing first Aïsha, who shrugs, perhaps because she doesn't remember, or perhaps because with her earphones in she can't hear what anyone's saying. Jill turns to Tristan instead.

"We had to use Google maps instead," he says.

Hannah nods discreetly at Cliff in a *you see?* manner.

"Anyway, just relax now," Tristan says. "We're all here safe and sound, and I'm gonna fix dinner for you all tonight, so . . ."

"What are you making?" Aïsha asks, revealing that she *can* hear even with the earbuds in.

"A hot Niçoise salad," Tristan says. "Any objections?"

Aïsha shrugs.

"A hot salad?" Cliff asks, his tone dubious.

"It's not really a salad. As long as you're OK with tuna it'll be fine," Tristan says.

"I like tuna," Luke volunteers.

"Yes," Hannah confirms. "We all like tuna. That sounds lovely." She catches Jill rolling her eyes. "What?" she asks.

Jill just smiles and shakes her head. "Sounds lovely," she repeats, and Hannah isn't sure if she's agreeing with her or somehow mocking her.

Just as Tristan has left the table, a stranger appears from the rear of the house. Hannah jumps when she sees him and Jill sits up very straight and flicks her hair back. Cliff sees Jill do this and moves his chair so that he can study the man. He is tall and muscular with closely cropped hair, olive skin and thick, dark stubble. He's wearing muddy dungarees (with no shirt underneath) and mustard builder's boots.

"Bonsoir," he says. "Vous deviez arriver demain, non ?"

At the foreign sounds, Aïsha and Luke turn wide-eyed to

15

their parents in faith that they will somehow understand. The three adults glance at each other.

"Pardon ?" Hannah says, one of only ten French words in her vocabulary.

"Vous deviez arriver demain," the man says, again. "Mais ce n'est pas grave. Je l'ai mis à remplir." He nods at the table, and adds, "Bon appétit."

"Bon appétit," Hannah repeats. She knows, at least, what that means.

The guy frowns at her as if her words have confused him, then nods, says, "Merci !" and returns the way he came.

"Who was *that*?" Cliff asks.

"How should I know?" Hannah says. "I didn't understand a word."

"He's hot," Jill says. "We should have called Tristan."

"Really? Do you think he's gay?" Hannah asks.

"No! Tris' speaks French, silly," Jill replies, laughing.

"Oh. Of course. Luke, go watch where he goes. Discreetly."

Luke stands uncertainly. "What, like spy on him?"

"Yes. You can be our secret agent," Hannah says, smiling and giving him a little push.

"I wonder what he wanted," Cliff says.

"As far as I'm concerned, he can have *anything* he wants," Jill says lasciviously, and Aïsha, for the first time today, smiles – a smile that quickly morphs into a blush. She lowers her head and stares at the screen of her phone.

"Yeah, I guess he was quite pretty," Hannah agrees. "If you like a bit of rough."

"You know I do," Jill says.

Cliff watches this exchange and feels a pique of jealousy. Because, of course, he never looked like that, not even in his youth. And he has always wondered what it would feel like, how easy life would be, if one did. He wonders what it must be like to walk into any room and see desire on the faces of all of the women (and a few of the men). Because you can go to college and get first-class degrees, you can build a business and be an expert in investments and tax schedules worldwide, you can provide generously for your family and your ageing parents, and be well off enough to help any member of the extended family that might happen to need it . . . But the women will always want the guy with the muscles, the guy with the stubble, the guy with dirty dungarees and the buttocks. And quite honestly he would have swapped all of his achievements to look like that if he had had the choice. He shuffles in his seat, and then takes a hefty swig of wine.

"He climbed over the fence," Luke declares when he returns.

Hannah glances at the height of the fence. "Really?" she asks.

Luke nods. "There's a low bit around the back. With a big brick on the ground. He climbed over there and went off down the track."

"A neighbour maybe?" Hannah suggests.

"The owner perhaps?" Jill ventures.

"Gardener more like," Cliff says.

"There's a hosepipe filling the pool up," Luke says. "And the dead bird is gone too, so I reckon he's the pool guy."

"Well, *Goodbye Old Guy*, and *Hello Pool Guy*," Jill says, and Hannah rolls her eyes.

"What *did* happen with whatsisname?" Hannah asks and Cliff, despite his best efforts, rubs an eyebrow as if to presage the headache the conversation will give him.

Jill sighs deeply. "Saïd?" she says. "Well . . ."

FOUR

Jill

I love Jill. Of course I do – she's my sister. When you have a single sibling there's really no other choice. But is she annoying? Of course she is.

I'm perfectly aware how irritating poor Cliff finds her, and I empathise entirely. But she's my sister. She comes with the terrain. And Cliff, thank God, understands this.

I'm pretty much immune to it all, myself. My little sister's capricious nature has been washing over me since age two, after all.

Jill is selfish and contradictory, hypocritical and sometimes arrogant. She changes her beliefs so often that you'd need an encyclopaedia of spiritual movements to keep up (if you wanted to – I don't.) And she gets through men so fast that it's *impossible* to keep up. I sometimes wonder if she's addicted to men, or if she hates them. It's a surprisingly fine line.

But Jill has another side too, of course. And as her sister, I suppose that I just try to concentrate more on that.

As is often the case, so much of Jill's brittle exterior is bravado. I've seen her cry over every breakup. I know that there have been times when, if it were not for her daughter, she might have killed herself through sheer loneliness. And I know that, just as I am always there for her, she would, if push came to shove, always be there for me. And let's face it, there aren't that many people in a life that you can say that about.

Luke loves her – kids will always gravitate towards adults with the most relaxed parenting techniques.

I worry about her smoking dope in front of the kids, and I worry about her talking about rave-parties and sex in front of them. But in a way, I'm also glad that Luke sees – through Jill – this side of life too. There's a big, bad, exciting world out there, and I wouldn't want Luke to grow up thinking, like so many mollycoddled kids, that life ends where *EastEnders* begins.

I suppose, if I'm being honest, that I'm grateful for the excitement – albeit second hand – that Jill brings to my own life, too. I complain and tut, and purse my lips, but I love to hear about Jill's adventures, her trips to ashrams, her parties on 'e', and her forays into sadomasochism. It's like having your own personal Madonna.

Am I jealous of Jill? Certainly. Would I swap any part of my life for any part of hers? Never.

I know, too, that, obtusely, Jill is jealous of me. She craves love and stability and reassurance, but, being incapable of acting in a manner that might bring those things to the table, she will always crave them.

We have never fallen out for more than a day or so, both because I'm very easy-going (Jill calls me Little Miss Sunshine behind my back) but also because ours being one of only three stable relationships in her life – her daughter, Tristan, and myself – Jill simply can't do without me.

Tristan isn't the easiest person to get on with either. He is so similar to Jill in so many ways that the slightest argument between them generally reaches epic proportions within minutes. When they do fall out – and it happens frequently

– Jill is not only heartbroken, but, I think, *scared*. She is too competitive to get on with other women, and too predatory to get on with men. Thus gay Tristan is pretty much her only hope. So for all of these reasons (and because he supplies her with drugs) she will compromise in any way, will jump through any philosophical hoop to make up with him.

If only she applied the same determination to her romantic entanglements she would, I think, have a much happier life. But then, perhaps, I of all people understand that if she did, it wouldn't be such an exciting one either.

FIVE

Tristan appears, three plates of food balanced on his right arm, just as Jill is finishing her whinge-fest about Saïd.

"Saïd again?" he asks as he moves precisely around the table. "I'm glad I missed that one."

"Hey, she asked, OK?" Jill says.

"I did," Hannah admits. "He doesn't sound like a very nice character. Did you meet him?"

"Sure," Tristan says, placing her plate before her and giving it a quarter turn, presumably for aesthetic effect. "He was nice enough to me. Which from an observant Muslim is as much as any gay man can ask."

"This looks amazing," Hannah says. "Luke, go fetch Aïsha, will you?" But Aïsha appears at that exact moment.

"Oh, there you are. Come and sit down," Jill tells her daughter, tapping the seat beside her.

Instead, or probably in reaction to this, Aïsha chooses to take Tristan's seat at the table instead. Jill simply reaches over and swaps Tristan's wine-glass with Aïsha's Coke.

"I'm always amazed when I see you do that," Jill says as Tristan returns with the second batch of plates on one arm.

"Once a waiter, always a waiter," he says, placing the dishes before them with renewed flourish. "It's pretty easy once you learn how."

"So is this a dish you serve at your restaurant?" Cliff asks, slicing into the tuna steak and noting the raw red colour of the interior. He likes his tuna *cooked* personally, but you'd have to be a braver man than Cliff to criticise Tristan's handiwork.

"Yes," Tristan says. "Yes, this is on the lunchtime menu at Rez." He glances at Cliff, who attempts but fails to manifest an expression of blank contentment.

"That's how it's eaten," he tells Cliff, nodding at the tuna. "It's blue-fin, the same as they use in sushi. The same as they use *raw* in sushi."

"Dad hates sushi, don't you?" Luke says.

"No," Cliff says. "Not at all. I don't *hate* it."

"Aren't blue-fin almost extinct or something?" Jill asks. "I think I saw a programme."

"No. This is Atlantic blue-fin, not southern," Tristan tells her, slicing into his own and forking a mouthful. "Southern blue-fin is hundreds of pounds a kilo. You'd *never* cook it."

Cliff forks some vegetables, and to avoid eating the fish – just yet – he asks, "So this is what, spinach?"

"Yep. All the other ingredients are the same as a Niçoise salad," Tristan tells him. "Only cooked."

"*Mine's* not cooked," Luke says, and everyone else at the table is secretly grateful for his innocence. "There's blood oozing out of it," he continues.

"It's supposed to be like that," Hannah tells him, even though she's having the same drama. "Just eat up, otherwise it won't be a hot Niçoise salad at all."

"It'll be a cold one, won't it," Luke says.

Tristan puts down his fork, sits back in his chair, and then sips his wine. He looks around the table. He looks bemused.

Everyone freezes.

Tristan slips into a grin, laughs, says, "OK!" and jumps

back up. Before anyone can even ask why, he is whizzing around the table whisking people's plates from before them.

"Tris!" Jill protests, but it's too late. Her plate is already in the kitchen.

When he returns for the second three dishes, Tristan says, "Your faces! Unbearable! I shall cook the fuckers to death. And you had better eat them."

Once he has gone, Hannah glances at Jill who raises one eyebrow, then at Cliff who winks at her.

"The pool isn't filling very quick," Luke says whilst they wait. "Will it be full by tomorrow?"

"Quickly," Hannah corrects him. "It isn't filling very quick-*lee*."

"No, it won't be full by tomorrow," Cliff, who the question was directed at, replies.

Jill tuts. "Of course it will," she says.

Cliff shrugs. "I think you're underestimating the amount of water needed to fill a pool like that," he tells her. "It holds thousands of gallons."

"And you, the power of positive thought," Jill says. "If we all believe it will, then it will. Belief becomes reality. Don't be so negative."

Cliff pinches the bridge of his nose as he considers whether to discuss the likely effects of positive thought on the flow-rate from a tap. Or not. Luckily he is saved by the return of Tristan, who plonks, far less elegantly this time, his plate in front of him. "Thanks, Tristan," he says. "I know it's wrong of me, but I've always struggled a bit with raw fish."

"You didn't spit in them, did you?" Jill asks, feigning real concern.

"*Jill*," Aïsha protests.

"It's OK," Tristan explains. "It's an 'in' joke. And no, I didn't."

"'Tris' reckons you should never send food back. The chefs spit on it," Jill says.

"Not always," Tristan laughs. "It's not unknown. But I don't. And didn't."

"This is gorgeous now," Cliff says, honestly. "Thanks." He frowns at the thought that the phrase would have been better without the word *now* but it's too late.

"It *was* a bit on the raw side," Tristan offers. "It's how I like it, but well, I can't expect everyone to have exactly the same tastes as me. Can I, Cliff?"

Cliff notices that Tristan is staring at him, specifically, as he says this last sentence. He looks down at his plate, pierces the poached egg with his fork, and watches as the yellow of the yolk floods out over the surrounding area. He hates it when Tristan does that cute stuff.

After dinner they sit around the cosy glow of the oil lamps and sip glasses of Cognac.

Aïsha and Luke are in the hammock together battling each other on the Nintendo.

"They're doing well," Hannah points out. "It's a good sign."

"Don't worry," Jill tells her. "It won't last."

"What happened to the power of positive thought?" Cliff asks.

"Oh you know what they're like," Jill says. "They always argue. It's because he's Libra and Aïsha's Aries. They're fundamentally incompatible."

Tristan produces a tobacco tin from his jacket pocket and starts to roll a joint.

Hannah tops up her Cognac and then says, addressing her sister, "You know I never say anything about you smoking around them."

"Oh, here we go," Jill says.

"But when you told me about the teddy bear."

Tristan snorts, blowing tobacco over the table. "Look what you made me do," he says.

"It's not funny," Hannah says. "I'm sorry, but it isn't."

"What's this about?" Tristan asks, grinning.

"I told Hannah about how we smuggled our half a kilo of dope through customs in Aï's old teddy bear," Jill says.

"Oh," Tristan says, grinning broadly. "*That.*"

Cliff runs his tongue across his teeth and represses a frown. The exaggerated quantity has, for him at least, given the game away.

"I can't believe that you all think this is funny," Hannah says, a wave of indignation rising within her. "It's totally irresponsible. She could have ended up in prison. You all could have."

"Better her than me," Jill says with a shrug.

Hannah, wide-eyed, turns to Cliff for support. He reaches over and lays his hand upon hers, but she snatches it away, angry at his expression, a smirk.

"They're winding you up," he tells her quietly.

Hannah looks from one lamp-lit face to another, her mood quivering on a knife-edge between anger and embarrassment. "Is that true?" she asks.

"Not at all," Jill says, sounding aggressive now. "How else were we supposed to get it here?"

But Tristan, like Cliff, can sense that Hannah is on the verge of a serious upset. He glances at Jill and wonders if she doesn't realise this, or simply doesn't care. "Actually I picked it up from a mate in Lyon," he tells Hannah. "We spent last night at my friend Pierre's place."

"Oh," Hannah says. "Well . . ."

"And it wasn't half a kilo. It was this," he says, holding up a small brown lump the size of a toffee. "They don't even arrest you for this anymore. They don't even fine you."

Hannah doubts this, but she isn't sure enough to argue the point. She shakes her head and squints at Jill. "You're horrible to me," she says, half joking, half not. "You always were."

Jill shrugs. "You're so gullible, it's irresistible," she laughs. "As if Aï' would bring a teddy bear!"

SIX

Luke – in a deckchair – has fallen asleep, so Cliff carries him to his room. It takes half an hour before Hannah realises that Cliff isn't coming back either, that the *fell asleep with Luke* thing, which they both use to escape, when they need to, has happened.

Aïsha is off somewhere doing her thing, and all three remaining adults are tipsy on wine and then Cognac and now wine again. Tristan and Jill, in addition, are stoned.

The conversation is taking on the random nature it always does when marijuana is thrown into the mix. Avenues are explored then abandoned simply because two out of the three people here can't remember what they were talking about.

Hannah remembers, but she doesn't mind. She won't go to bed yet. She's enjoying sitting outside in this balmy Mediterranean evening, frogs croaking somewhere to the right, a thousand stars silent above their heads, clouds of exhaled smoke drifting above them.

"So are you seeing anyone at the moment?" she asks Tristan.

Jill finds this funny and snorts. Red wine drips from her nose.

Tristan, after a short delay, starts to laugh as well, and Hannah can't work out whether he's laughing at the wine dripping from Jill's nose or her question.

"What?" she asks, amused, but confused, by their reaction. "What did I say?"

Jill blows her nose on a napkin and says, "God, that hurts. Do not snort wine. Jesus!"

"It's not you, Hannah," Tristan says. "It's just, well, as they say on Facebook, *it's complicated.*"

"I don't use Facebook," Hannah says. "Sorry."

"He's seeing three guys at once," Jill tells her. "It is *just* the three, right?"

Tristan nods. "It's not as bad as it sounds," he tells Hannah.

"It *is*," Jill laughs.

"OK, it is then," Tristan says. "But it's not as *frenetic* as it sounds then. Wolfgang – he's the main one . . ."

"The *main* one!" Jill repeats, sniggering.

"Well, he *is*!" Tristan says. "But he lives in Berlin. So I only see him about once a month."

"Right," Hannah says, nodding knowingly.

"And Pete and Matt live in Staffordshire, so . . ."

"Both of them?"

"They're a couple," Tristan explains. "So . . ."

"Of course," Hannah says as if this is the most natural thing in the world. Which she doesn't think it is, of course. But she isn't shocked either.

OK, maybe she *is* shocked a bit, but she isn't *surprised* that she's shocked. Tristan's love life has always been devilishly complicated, which is precisely why she asked him the question. It's another world, really, nothing to do with her world, but interesting all the same. She enjoys these windows into other worlds the same way she enjoys a good novel.

"Hannah thinks *I'm* a slag," Jill says, then, pointing one finger at Tristan, "but *you*, are *sommat* else."

Hannah smiles at her sister. "I have *never* said such a thing," she says.

"You've thought it."

"I haven't."

Jill shrugs. "I don't care anyway."

"So don't any of you get jealous?" Hannah asks, turning back to Tristan. "I would have thought jealousy would be the main worry."

"What? Generally? Or in bed?" Tristan asks.

"Either. Both," Hannah says.

"Wolfie doesn't know about the other two," Jill says. "Tristan hasn't told him."

"No," Tristan admits. "No, well, there would be no point, would there."

"I see," Hannah says, nodding and thinking about this. "And the couple? Presumably they're immune to jealousy issues."

"Yeah, pretty much," Tristan says, lighting a fresh joint. "I mean, in bed, it gets dodgy sometimes. Obviously. You have to make an effort to make sure no one gets left out."

"But someone always *is* left out," Jill says. "That's my experience, anyway."

Hannah turns and narrows her eyes at her little sister in a comical fashion.

"I *told* you already," Jill says. "When I was with Barry."

"Oh, the swingers' club."

"Yeah."

"I didn't know you actually . . . you know . . ."

Hannah is interrupted by Tristan coughing, exhaling smoke and waving the joint randomly in Jill's direction as he does so.

"What?" she asks, taking it from his grasp.

"S–" Tristan splutters, and Hannah realises that he is, in fact, laughing – doubled up with laughter in fact. "S– Sw– swingers."

29

Jill, starting to laugh as well, asks again, "What, Tris'?"

Hannah tries to force a smile. She can sense that it's an unconvincing smile, and this realisation makes her feel unexpectedly old, unexpectedly out of it, like a parent trying to ingratiate herself to her kid's friends.

"S . . . Swingers!" Tristan gurgles, tears in his eyes now. "It's just . . . It's just such a weird word for it. God."

"Swingers!" Jill repeats. She is laughing as well now.

Hannah shakes her head and pushes her chair back. "Right," she says. "That's enough for me."

"Oh don't go, Han'," Jill says. "We weren't laughing at you."

"No," Tristan agrees, struggling to contain himself. "I didn't mean. It's not you. It's just, sometimes, you suddenly realise how funny a word is, right? And swing—" He cracks up laughing again.

Hannah smiles demurely, circles the table, kisses her sister on the back of the head, runs a hand over Tristan's shoulders as she passes him, and says, "I know. But it's almost one. I'm shattered. Good night, kids."

It isn't true though. She isn't tired at all.

It's just that with dope, as apparently with threesomes, unless you participate, you at some point realise that you are just sitting on the sidelines.

Hannah checks on Luke. He's snuggled up with his head squashed into a teddy-bear. He looks beautiful and angelic still. Hannah ineffectually repositions the quilt around him and wonders how much longer this can last. How long do they have before he becomes like Aïsha?

In their bedroom, Cliff is asleep, snoring lightly. She undresses and eases herself into the bed gently so as not to wake him. There have been times in the past when she has done the exact opposite in the very hope of waking him. But it's been a few years if the truth be told.

She slides one hand down beneath the covers and caresses her inner thigh gently. It's not a sexual caress, but it isn't quite asexual either. From outside she can hear fresh peals of laughter.

She tries to imagine what it must be like alternating between three different lovers. She supposes that she could have done that. She supposes that she could have made different choices and been the kind of girl who had three different lovers. Or could she? Perhaps that stuff is pre-destined.

She wonders if they all kiss differently, if they all have different identifiable smells, different dick sizes, different shaped bums. She wonders if Tristan prefers making love to one of them over the others.

She wonders who, out of Tristan, Pete and, Mike? Was it Mike? Or Matt? – she wonders who does what to whom. She wonders if they all sleep together in the same bed afterwards, like some Mediaeval family snuggled together for warmth. That would feel nice, she reckons. Arms and legs everywhere. Lovely in winter. Maybe unbearably hot in summer.

She wonders if they snuggle up, or curl away, wonders who sleeps in the middle, or whether they take it in turns, or draw straws.

As she hovers on the edge of sleep she wonders if they have a big bed, a king-sized bed, or a round bed, or a bed the size of a room, or a bed the size of the moon . . .

And then suddenly it is morning, and Luke is standing in the doorway, saying, "Mum? Mum? Are you awake? Mum?"

SEVEN

Luke

To want your child to remain innocent whilst toughening up enough to survive *This Life* is entirely contradictory, but, as far as I can tell, an almost universal parental desire.

It's a widely held belief that the reasons we parents mollycoddle our children are fundamentally selfish. But it's not true. It's not because we want them to stay infants, as playthings for ourselves – it's because they're so happy rollicking around in the Garden of Eden, we can't bear for it to end. As adults, we know that life, once the apple of knowledge is bitten into, becomes so much more complicated, so much more fraught.

There's something so simplistic, almost autistic, about Luke's outlook still, about his lack of philosophical angst. It's a wonderful thing to behold.

Perhaps this comes from Cliff. He certainly doesn't seem too worried about the big questions of our time: ecology, politics, the planet . . . Nor does he seem overly concerned about the big questions of our lives: where do we come from, why are we here, what is the point . . . Perhaps it's a fundamental difference between men and women.

Tristan doesn't seem overly angst-ridden either as he hops from bed to bed. Like Cliff, his solutions to unhappiness all involve action verbs: buying something, going places, shagging more . . . We women spend so much time in our heads, passively thinking, worrying, hoping.

So perhaps Luke, like his father, will continue to leap out of bed of a morning, full of beans, will continue to fall asleep the second his head hits the pillow. I certainly pray (there's another passive verb) that he'll be happy, contented.

That maternal bond, of hope and fear, of love and terror is aching in intensity – it knows no equal. It's a cliché, perhaps, but there is nothing I wouldn't give for Luke to be happy, nothing I wouldn't sacrifice to keep him safe.

Is that normal? Do all mothers feel the same? I have no idea, though I would guess so. Perhaps my bond with Luke is a bit stronger than "normal" because of what he represented in my own life.

My first pregnancy failed in the third month. She (it was a girl) would have been born in the midst of so much misery that, even at the time, it seemed a logical if heartbreaking outcome.

If she had lived, would I look at her today as I look at Luke? Or would I have forever seen her as the reason my life got stuck? I'm really not sure.

At the time I thought that it was my desire to break free, my resentment, specifically, at being held back, that had killed her.

By the time Luke came along I understood that there was nothing else to run to anyway, nowhere better to go.

Like a mirage at the end of a hot day, James had faded, leaving only Cliff and myself and a child-sized gap in our lives. So Luke felt like a second chance. Another chance at motherhood. Another chance for my marriage. Another chance to forget everything that had happened.

EIGHT

The pool hasn't filled up. This is the important news flash for which Luke has woken her.

Hannah blinks to remove the sleep from her eyes and finally manages to focus on her son, standing in the doorway.

"It's only up to here," he says, pointing just below his knee.

"It's filling though, is it?" Hannah asks.

"Yes, it's *filling*. But I can't swim in it."

"It's a good job we're here for two weeks then, isn't it," Hannah says, becoming aware only now that the bed beside her is cold, that Cliff is already up.

"I wanted to swim today," Luke says. "Dad says it's gonna be really hot."

"Well, you'll just have to wait," Hannah says. "Now go outside and play with Aïsha and let me wake up properly."

By the time she has dozed off, woken up a second time, and dragged herself out to the patio, everyone is in the midst of breakfast. The sky is pure unadulterated blue, the light blinding, and already heat is radiating from the terracotta floor tiles.

"Hey, sleepy head," Cliff says, smiling at her from across the table.

"What time is it?" Hannah asks, sitting down and reaching for the carton of orange juice. "I feel like I have been drugged or something."

"I slipped some Rohypnol into your wine last night," Tristan says.

"Um?" Hannah replies in a tone that expresses that though she doesn't understand what he has said, she *has* understood that it was a throwaway line of no importance and requires no further explanation.

"Tristan's taking us swimming," Luke says.

Hannah sips her juice and nods at Tristan. "Really? That's nice of you," she tells him. She turns to Aïsha. "Are you going too?"

Aïsha nods, shrugs and rolls her eyes simultaneously. Heaven forbid that someone might catch her looking enthusiastic.

"It's just that the pool's still empty," Tristan explains, "So I thought . . ."

"It'll take days," Cliff says. "I told you."

"I'm saying nothing," Jill says, and Hannah sees Cliff shoot a tiny glare at her. She could work out what that's about if she concentrated upon it. She knows it's within her grasp to remember, but she chooses not to.

"We can all go if you want," Tristan says. "It's only about an hour to the coast."

Hannah vaguely raises one hand. "No," she says. "No, it'll be a few days before I'll be willing to get in a car again."

"That's what I said," Cliff agrees.

Hannah glances at Jill, busy picking the dried fruit out of her bowl of muesli – she says it contains sulphites or something – and wonders if she's going with them or staying. But she doesn't ask her yet, because how she phrases that question could influence Jill's decision. So does she want Jill to go and leave her here alone with Cliff, or doesn't she?

It might be nice. It happens so rarely these days. They would

35

probably end up having sex. In fact they would definitely end up having sex. And therein lies the problem. Because it wouldn't be *two-bodies-passionately-drawn-together* sex or even *hey-babe-fancy-a-quicky* sex. It would be *this-is-what-we-do*; it would be *this-is-what-we-do-when-we-find-ourselves-alone* sex.

It's not that Hannah dislikes sex with Cliff. It varies on a scale between feeling mundane but OK to (occasionally) really rather nice. It's just the predictability of everything that suffocates her, that inevitable unfolding of where it will happen and when it will happen and how it will happen. If Jill leaves with the others, Cliff will stand and round the table. He will nuzzle her hair, and then nuzzle her neck. And then he will slide one hand across her shoulder, down over her breast, and reach for her hand. He will say, "Come," and she'll smile and stand and follow him to the bedroom. Every move has been choreographed over the years. Nothing is left to chance. There are no surprises.

Jill, who Hannah now realises she has been staring at, says, "Well, I'm with you guys. I'm not moving a muscle today," and Cliff catches Hannah's eye and shrugs.

Even now, Hannah can't decide if she feels disappointed or relieved.

Once the Jeep has gone, yesterday's techno picking up exactly where it left off, the two sisters clear the breakfast table.

Jill makes an effort to contribute, but in that special way of hers which is more of a hindrance than a help. Jill's ability to perform even the most mundane tasks in the least efficient way possible never ceases to astound Hannah. She often wonders how Jill has managed to raise her daughter at all. But manage, she has.

When Hannah has finished removing the unstable tower of dishes that Jill has piled up in the sink, she starts to empty and re-stack the dishwasher as Jill washes and dries, very slowly, a single mug.

"The culture gap was just too vast to be bridged, really," Jill is saying – Saïd again. "They expect you to do everything, Muslims. Shopping, cleaning. He liked his dinner to be on the table when he got in, d'you know what I'm saying? It was crazy."

Hannah knows she's a bit old-school, but she doesn't consider that crazy at all. Cliff, after all, is right now ensconced in his crime novel while the women present clear the breakfast table. Hannah doesn't consider that macho. She considers it fair. Cliff's long days at the practice pay, after all, for all of this for all of them.

"He was working, though, wasn't he?" she asks.

"Yeah. I told you. At Stansted."

"Yes. Really long hours you said." Hannah doesn't really know why she bothers to scatter pointers this way. Jill has never seemed able to spot them.

"Yeah. It was a drag," Jill says. "Sometimes he didn't get home till ten."

"I think I'd want my dinner ready if I got home from work at ten."

"All the same. I mean, we're not in the fifties anymore, are we? Just because he's the breadwinner doesn't give him the right to meals on wheels and sex on demand."

"You've never been one to complain about sex on demand," Hannah says, straightening from the dishwasher and smiling at her sister, who, she sees, is still drying the same mug in slow, circular movements.

"Well, no," Jill says. "That was the upside really. He was *very* pushy in bed."

"Pushy?"

"Yeah, you know. Do this, do that. Suck this. Roll over. And lord knows I like a man who knows what he wants in the bedroom."

And *there*, Hannah thinks, is Jill's problem. She *likes* pushy men. She needs to feel that the man in her life is running the show, is attracted, in a nutshell, to arrogant bastards. They *excite* her. Of course she splits up with them, every time, for exactly the same reasons. It's a tiny psychological conundrum, an insoluble riddle so simple you could describe it in its entirety on the back of a postcard. But it's sufficient to wreak havoc throughout Jill's life.

Back in the conversation, Jill is still talking. ". . . he actually bought me a dog collar. Can you imagine? He used to put it on me and then I knew we were gonna have a really good session. I mean, I wasn't complaining. I like a bit of kink, as you know. But it's pretty revealing, you've got to admit. It's pretty revealing about how the guy sees women."

"But you liked it," Hannah says, throwing her sister another pointless pointer.

"Yes. Well, yes and no," Jill says.

Hannah turns back to the sink so that Jill doesn't see her roll her eyes.

NINE

They are trying to read. Theoretically, all three adults are trying to read, only Jill can't concentrate, which means, of course, that no one can concentrate.

"The guy in this book reminds me too much of Saïd," she says. She's reading – theoretically – *Wuthering Heights*. All roads, it seems, no matter how unlikely, lead to Saïd. From past experience Cliff, listening despite himself, would place money on the fact that they'll get back together.

"Have you read it?" Jill asks.

"Of course," Hannah says. "Years ago though. Heathcliff is the archetypal bastard."

"At the beginning of May," Jill says, "we went to Margate for a weekend. Saïd found this really good hotel deal, so we just went for it. It was a four-star hotel and everything, but really cheap. I thought it was a great idea until we got there. What a dump! Margate that is, not the hotel. Do you know the shops in the high street were boarded up there? I mean talk about recession. Anyway . . ."

Hannah closes her book. She does this gently so that Jill won't think (or rather realise) that the gesture is a reproach for her blathering. She sits and listens as each of the standard elements of a Jill story are revealed: the disappointing surroundings, the determination to have a good time despite it all, a soupçon of rude service wittily put down, an evening of alcohol, rough (but good) sex, and finally, of course, The Argument.

"We didn't speak to each other the whole way home," Jill says, concluding her story.

It was rather a good story actually. They generally are. But Hannah wants to read. "No, well," she says, faking a yawn. "I'm still sleepy. I might go have another snooze."

Cliff peers over the top of his novel and winks at her, and Hannah, realising that Jill must be driving poor Cliff insane already, raises one eyebrow conspiratorially.

No sooner has Hannah lain down and re-opened her book than Cliff enters the bedroom, locking the door behind him.

Hannah realises that he has misinterpreted her complicit eyebrow wiggle and thinks, *Oh well, we might as well get it over with.* She chides herself immediately for the thought, unsure even as to why she is so uncharitable. In truth, she acknowledges, she wants this. In truth, she needs this.

Sex has always been complicated for her. In fact, pleasure, in general, has always been something slightly alien to her. She has always felt a requirement to accept it under duress rather than throw herself into it. She really doesn't know where that comes from.

"Lord, your sister can talk," Cliff says, shucking his shorts and shirt.

"She can," Hannah agrees, wriggling out of her dress without standing. Cliff yanks off his underpants as she removes her bra. There was a time, at the beginning, when they found undressing embarrassing. For almost a decade, she undressed in the dark or in the bathroom, then sprinted beneath the covers. This easy familiarity is so much easier, yet so much less exciting.

"So are we reading, or . . ." Cliff says, now naked and crawling up the bed towards her, tiger-style.

" 'Or . . .' I reckon, don't you?" Hannah says.

The sex follows the dots and squiggles they have laid down over the years – he kisses her like this, she slides a hand there and pulls him in . . . and though predictable, Hannah decides that it's none the worse for that. No one complains that the *Four Seasons* sounds the same every time, do they? Things don't have to be original and unique to be satisfying. They just have to be faithfully performed.

When it's over, they fall into a surprisingly deep slumber and wake two hours later, sweaty and hungry and groggy from too much sleep.

"Half three," Cliff says, answering an unspoken question.

"Wow."

"I'm starving," Cliff says. "I wonder when Master Chef gets back."

"I'll make a sandwich," Hannah says. "We have cheese, and ham. Smoked salmon . . . Gosh, I'm hungry too."

"Is that allowed?" Cliff asks, sitting on the side of the bed and rubbing his face in his hands.

"What, is anyone except Tristan allowed to prepare food?" Hannah asks, laughter in her voice.

"I guess we don't have to tell him," Cliff says. "But if you use up some vital ingredient he'll go crazy."

"He will not," Hannah says.

"Anyway, they're back," Cliff tells her, cocking one ear.

Hannah holds her breath and hears the slamming of doors and Luke's bouncing voice. "They are," she agrees. "God, I feel so woozy!"

"It's the heat," Cliff says. "We're not used to it. Maybe we need to drink more. Water I mean."

By the time they have showered and reached the patio, Tristan is seated, gutting fish. Aïsha is taking photographs of the removed fish innards.

"Ew, you're brave," Hannah comments.

Tristan shrugs.

"We bought fish from the fisherman," Luke tells them. He is, for no apparent reason, wearing a diving mask.

"What's with the mask?" Hannah asks.

"Tris' bought it," he explains.

"He was chatting up all the fishermen," Aïsha says. "It was awful. Embarrassing."

"Not *all* of them," Tristan says.

"Just the hunky one," Luke says, and both Hannah and Cliff bristle at some subconscious discomfort.

"You don't even know what hunky means," Tristan laughs. "But, yeah, he was. He was gorgeous. I was powerless to resist."

"I saw fish in the sea," Luke says, thankfully moving on. "Like, this big," he says, holding his hands apart to demonstrate an unfeasibly large fish.

"Did you see any fish, Aï?" Hannah asks.

She shakes her head.

"Missy forgot her cossie," Tristan explains. "We tried to buy one but she didn't like any of them."

"They only had these lame Paris Hilton things," Aïsha says,

and Hannah thinks she can read between those particular lines.

"You could have swum in shorts and a T-shirt," she tells her. "Like the Australians do."

Aïsha shrugs – her standard response – but then she belies her indifference by asking, "Do they really?"

Hannah nods. "I saw it on TV. The sun's really strong there so they get lots of skin cancers and stuff."

"It's the hole in the ozone layer," Jill says. "From aerosols."

"So they swim in T-shirts to protect themselves from the sun," Hannah continues. "They have a TV campaign. Slip, slop and slap or something."

Egged on by the fact that Aïsha looks, for once, genuinely interested, Hannah explains. "I think it stands for *slip on a T-shirt, slop on some sun-cream, and slap on a sun-hat*. Something like that anyway."

Aïsha wrinkles her nose. "But they *swim* like that?" she asks.

"They do," Hannah says with a serious nod. "They think it's cool."

"I'm gonna check on the pool," Luke says, standing.

"So tell me about the spunky fisherman," Jill says.

Aïsha groans and heads off after Luke.

Tristan looks up from his gutting. "He was beautiful," he says. "He looked like Jean-Marc Barr in *The Big Blue*. D'you ever see that?"

Jill shakes her head. Hannah shrugs.

"I did, I think," Cliff says, surprising them all. "French film, right?"

Tristan raises his eyebrows and nods to show that he's impressed. "Well, he looked like the diver guy from that."

43

"The younger one, presumably," Cliff says.

"Yeah, not Jean Reno," Tristan laughs. "Though he's hot too. If you're into older guys. But no, this one was all muscles and five o'clock stubble. I was in heaven."

Cliff catches Hannah staring at him, staring though him. "It was on Film 4," he tells her. "You went to bed to read, so I watched it. It's about competition divers."

"There's a guy like that here," Jill says. "Something to do with this place. He came by yesterday to fill the pool when you were cooking. He'd be right up your street. He'd be right up *my* street."

"We have a hot pool guy and you didn't come tell me!" Tristan protests.

"Sorry," Cliff says and then, suddenly embarrassed yet unsure why, he dips his head and stares at his book.

TEN

Tristan

Tristan came to us through Jill. They met in Ibiza as I recall, during one of the summers when Aïsha and Luke were over at our place. (In theory the kids spend alternate summers at Jill's, but as this rule is suspended any time Jill meets someone new or anytime Jill splits up with someone, they're more often than not at ours . . .)

I honestly didn't expect her friendship with Tristan to last so long. As I explained, Jill doesn't really do stable relationships, whether they be friends or romances. And Tristan Wilde (his real name is Brian Smith or something – he changed it) seemed highly strung enough that I assumed he wouldn't put up with Jill for long. But eight years on he's still here, and we've more or less got used to him. He's a pretty good friend to her, and I'm grateful for that. It takes some of the pressure off me at least.

I felt pretty uncomfortable around him at first, it has to be said. Of course I have known gay guys before, but I've never been privy to quite so much detail about their personal lives. Tristan is a chronic over-sharer and it's hard not to be shocked by some of what he gets up to. But you get used to being shocked by people. You get to appreciate it even. Difference is good. Difference is interesting. That's what Tristan taught me.

He has some great qualities as well. He's a brilliant chef

(Rez, his first restaurant, has Michelin stars) and he loves to cook even when he's on holiday, which suits me just fine. He's always bouncy, always 'on' and even when he isn't – because Tristan clearly has his share of heartache, perhaps *more* than his share – he has a unique ability to turn disaster into amusing fiction. If you see him regularly you can witness him telling the same story over and over, and each time it becomes a little funnier, a little more ridiculous, and a little less painful.

As I say, the over-sharing made me nervous at the beginning, especially because he does it in front of the kids. Of course I didn't *actually* think that Tristan talking about his boyfriends would make Luke into a gay, but, well, as a mother, you wonder, don't you. You have to wonder if it's healthy.

Tristan must never find this out – I'd be mortified – but I asked the psychologist at the first school where I worked what he thought about it.

He said, with reassuring certainty, that there was nothing to worry about, that if Luke is going to be heterosexual then he'll be heterosexual, and that if he's going to be a homosexual, he'll be one, whatever goes on around him. He said that the only effect having a gay 'uncle' would be likely to have would be to make Luke feel comfortable around gay men no matter which way he turns out.

I had a drunken conversation with Tristan once about Luke, too. He asked me how I would feel if Luke turned out gay (his own father threw him out) and I said, quite honestly, that I'd be OK about it. I'd be worried that he'd be lonely of course, but then plenty of heterosexuals manage that. I'd be worried about Aids, and I suppose I'd be disappointed not to have grandchildren too. So it's hardly my ideal. But I'd be OK about it. And I remember I asked Tristan how I would know if

Luke was going to be gay, and what I should do, what I should say. Tristan made me laugh so much. He said, "Honey, he likes insects, football, video games and guns. If you catch him playing with your jewellery then call me, but until that day, relax." And the very next time I looked at Luke I realised that I knew already. I realised that I don't have anything to worry about. Or not on that score, at least.

ELEVEN

After a lunch of tomato and buffalo mozzarella salad (the tomatoes actually taste like tomatoes here) followed by the fish, snapper, *en papillotte* with asparagus and wild mushroom risotto – a lunch that lasts so long it merges into dinner – Cliff proposes that they go for a walk, and Tristan suggests a bar he has spotted as an ideal destination.

As the sun sinks lower, throwing ever-longer shadows across the garden, they lock up the house and start, en masse, to crunch their way along the lane.

Each property is set within an acre or so of land, so they walk for five minutes chatting quietly, and then pause to peer over a gate or through a hedge, commenting, "*Nice pool,*" or, "*Grass could do with a cut,*" or, "*Someone's a hoarder.*"

"Most of these look empty," Cliff says.

"Holiday homes, I guess," Hannah says, taking his arm.

"But it's July," Cliff says. "Shouldn't people be *in* their holiday homes?"

"It's weird," Tristan agrees. "I thought that as well."

Hannah watches Luke and Aïsha walking in front. Luke's gait is still boyish and sprightly. Aïsha has picked up a stick and is whacking the plants at the side of the road mercilessly as she walks.

"Must be amazing to live somewhere like this," Jill says. "I mean somewhere where it's hot all summer long. It must be heavenly to wake up in the morning and just *know* it's gonna be sunny."

"Maybe you should move," Hannah says. "I wouldn't mind visiting."

"I would," Jill says. "If I met a bloke who lived somewhere like this, I'd move in a second."

"You'd never put up with the French," Tristan says.

"Really?" Hannah asks, a little shocked. "They can't be that different, can they? Surely people are people wherever you go."

"Tris' is just being racist," Jill says.

"Not racist," Tristan says. "Xenophobic. Anyway, I did my training in Paris. I think I know what I'm talking about."

Aïsha turns around. She looks vaguely panicked at the tenure of the conversation. "Jill, we are *so* not moving to France," she says.

"Wouldn't you like that, sweetie?" Jill asks, her tone mocking.

"No," Aïsha tells her. "It's well boring."

Once Aïsha has returned her attention to whacking the bushes, Hannah murmurs, "Well, that told you."

Jill sighs. "That's what they're like at that age. You'll see soon enough. Everything's boring, or . . ."

"Or?"

"Aïsha? What's that word you use for anything that's rubbish? She uses it all the time, only I can't remember."

Aïsha looks back at them and shrugs. "Gay?" she says.

"Hum, not too keen on that one," Tristan says.

"It doesn't mean *gay*," Aïsha tells him. "It just means lame."

"Lame! That's the one," Jill says. "Yep, everything's boring or lame. Once in a blue moon something is awesome, but it really is once in a blue moon."

"It's all very American," Hannah says. "Lame. Awesome . . ."

"Still not keen on the whole gay equals rubbish analogy," Tristan says.

"She doesn't mean anything by it," Jill says.

"I know," Tristan says, "but all the same . . ."

The bar, when they reach it, is tiny. It comprises a single room (Formica and strip-lights) and a small roadside terrace covered with a vine-woven trellis.

There are three clients in the bar, without exception ageing alcoholics with pickled eyes and red noses. As there is no sign of a barman or owner, they return to the terrace and brush leaves from the seats.

"This is nice," Hannah says looking around.

Jill snorts.

"What?" Hannah asks, determined to deal with this head-on this time.

"Well," Jill says. "This is nice . . ."

"It *is*," Hannah tells her. "I *love* places like this. Look at that." She nods at a painted advert, a badly faded wall-sized mural advertising Ricard. "It's so . . . It's just so French."

"Can we go and explore?" Luke asks.

"Of course," Cliff tells him. "Just don't get lost. Do you want a drink?"

Luke looks puzzled. "Do they have Coke in France?"

Everyone grins. Luke shrugs and looks embarrassed.

"They do," Hannah tells him, gently. "They have Coke pretty much everywhere in fact."

"Coke then," Luke says, doubtfully.

"Actually, there's a French drink if you want something different," Tristan suggests.

Luke looks doubtful.

50

"It tastes like Sprite."

"Sprite's OK," Luke says. "But I prefer Coke."

"The thing about the French version is that it's quite fun to ask for," Tristan tells him.

Luke frowns.

"It's called Pschitt!" Tristan explains.

"Shit?"

"Pschitt! With a P. P-S-C-H-I-T-T. It's supposed to be the sound you get when you open the bottle. *Pschitt!* See?"

Luke wrinkles his nose. "I think I'll just have Coke," he says.

Tristan shrugs. "I always quite enjoyed saying, 'I'll have a Pschitt!' myself."

"Tristan!" Hannah protests.

"Hey!" Tristan says. "I didn't invent the stuff. It's been around for years."

Luke smirks. "Maybe I will have a Pshitt," he says, reddening with restrained giggles. He looks at Hannah. "Can I?"

Hannah grins and nods. "But you have to ask for it yourself. I'm not saying it."

"Aï'?" Cliff asks.

"Coke," she replies, pulling a face.

"You're sure you don't want a Pschitt as well?" he asks.

"Totally," she says. "Sounds gross."

"Vous voulez quelque chose ?" A voice, behind them. They all turn to see the barman. He's a good-looking guy in his twenties with a vaguely old-fashioned-looking mop of hair drifting over one eye and an open shirt revealing a hairless chest and a gold crucifix.

"Sorry, but . . . Vous parlez anglais ?" Hannah asks him.

"I speak French," Tristan volunteers, then, "Je parle français."

51

"Is OK," the barman tells them. "I can speak English. A little."

"Great. So it's a beer for me," Cliff says.

"I'll have a Pastis," Tristan says.

"A glass of dry white wine," Hannah says.

"Me too."

"And . . . what was it you wanted, Luke?" Tristan prompts.

Luke looks about to burst with excitement at the idea of being able to order his drink. He looks at his mother, barely able to believe that he's allowed to say it.

"Go on then," Hannah prompts, smiling broadly.

"Can I have a Pschitt please?" Luke asks.

The barman nods. "Deux vins blancs, une biere, un pastis, et un Pschitt, c'est ça ?"

"Oui," Tristan confirms.

"You liked that, didn't you?" Hannah laughs, once the barman has gone.

Luke nods. "I think I'm going to have a Pschitt every time," he says.

"Well, you haven't tasted it yet."

Luke shrugs, says, "Pshitt," once more, then runs off, closely followed by Aïsha.

"Well, I like the barman, anyway!" Tristan comments.

"I was waiting for that," Jill laughs.

"Definitely dances my side of the fence, that one," Tristan says.

"You reckon?" Jill asks. "I can't tell with the Frenchies. They *all* look a bit gay to me."

"How can you tell?" Cliff asks, genuinely intrigued.

Tristan shrugs. "Gaydar," he says.

The barman returns with a tray of drinks, a dish of olives, another of peanuts, and a third with tiny squares of pizza.

"I love the way they do that," Hannah says. "I love the way you get a mini meal with your drinks."

"It's nice," Cliff agrees, taking a square of pizza. "Do they always do that in France?"

"No," Tristan says. "No it's more of an Italian thing. But we're not so far from the border here, so . . ."

"So are you liking France?" Hannah asks, patting Cliff's hand on the table. He hadn't been keen on the idea of this holiday. He said he couldn't see any reason to change from the usual place in Dorset.

"It's OK so far," he says, then, forcing a smile, "Yes, it's fine actually."

Luke reappears at the table. "We found a ping-pong table," he says. "We found a ball in the bushes too, but there's no bats."

"They probably keep them behind the bar," Tristan says.

Luke turns his bottle around so that he can read the label. "Pschitt!" he says. He points it at Hannah.

"Yes, I saw," she laughs. "So, go on. Taste it."

Luke sips at his drink.

"Well?" she prompts.

"It's lemonade," Luke says.

"Yes, pretty much," Tristan says. "Do you like it?"

Luke shrugs. "It's OK," he says. He bumps his dad with his hip.

"What?" Cliff asks.

"Can you find out?" he says.

"What about?"

"About the bats for the ping-pong."

Cliff laughs. "I don't even know what the word for ping-pong is in French."

"It's ping-pong," Tristan tells him, looking up from his phone. "It's le ping-pong."

Cliff nods in his direction. "There you go, Luke. Tris' will sort it for you," he says.

"Tris?" Luke prompts doubtfully.

"I'll do better than that," Tristan says. "Just let me finish . . ." He types something on his phone, then slips it into his pocket. "There," he says. "Now, what did you want?"

"Bats," Luke says. "For the ping-pong."

Tristan presses his fingers to his forehead in a faux-mystic manner, rolls his eyes and says, "There. I just ordered them. Telepathically."

Luke raises an eyebrow, then slides into a seat and sips noisily at his Pschitt.

Everyone is watching Tristan. He strokes his chin. "Patience," he says.

Luke tuts. "Can't you just ask them?" he says. "Please, Tris'."

Aïsha returns from the other side of the building, kicking gravel as she zigzags towards them, then slides into a chair and swigs at her drink. "Well?" she asks, looking around at the adults, and frowning.

"Tris' is doing magic," Luke says.

"Right," Aïsha says. "Of course he is."

The door to the bar opens and the young barman appears, grinning broadly and carrying bats and a pack of balls. "C'est ceci que vous voulez ?" he asks.

"Oui," Tristan says. "Oui, c'est parfait, merci."

The barman proffers the bats and Luke seizes them, says, "Thanks, Tris'," and apparently both untroubled and unimpressed by the magic, runs back to where the ping-pong table is.

Once Aïsha has followed on, Cliff asks, "So?"

"So what?"

"So how did you do it?" Jill asks.

Tristan sips his drink and smiles smugly. "If you can guess I'll buy you a drink," he says.

"You texted him," Jill says.

"Hum. But I don't have his number."

"You texted that number," Cliff says, nodding at the sign above the door.

Tristan shakes his head. "It's a landline," he says. "You can't text a landline."

"You phoned them," Hannah offers.

Tristan pouts and shakes his head. "You saw me. I didn't move. And I didn't phone them."

"You did a mime when we were looking the other way?"

"I reckon the barman just saw the kids around the table," Cliff says.

"Nope," Tristan says, then in false French accent, "*Zats not eeet.*"

"It's definitely something to do with the phone," Jill says. "You were fiddling with your phone."

"Warmer."

"So you did send him a message?" she says.

"Yes. But how?"

They sit in silence for a few seconds, then Jill says, "Oh, I know. He's on Grindr, isn't he. I bet he's on Grindr."

"Clever girl."

Neither Cliff nor Hannah know what being "on Grindr" means, so Tristan passes his phone around so that they can see. The display shows rows of little thumbnail photos of men in the area, and shows how far they are from this spot. The top one is a reasonably clear photo of the barman. It says, "- 10m."

"That means that he's less than ten metres away," Tristan explains.

When the phone gets to Cliff, he stares at the screen and frowns.

"You look worried, Cliff," Tristan says.

"No," Cliff replies. "I just don't . . . I mean . . . How does it know?"

"Where people are?" Tristan says. "By GPS."

"Sure, but how does it know that they're *gay*?" Cliff asks. "Or aren't these guys necessarily gay?"

"They are," Tristan says. "But the phone doesn't know. It just shows other people who are running Grindr. And seeing as it's a gay hook-up app, it's a pretty safe bet."

Cliff nods, but continues to study the screen. "Some of these are just black squares," he says.

"They haven't put photos up," Tristan explains. "They don't want anyone to know who they are."

"Doesn't that kind of defeat the purpose?" Cliff asks.

Tristan nods. "A bit. Probably married guys cheating on their wives. But they'd send a photo if I asked. Well, they'd probably send a photo of *something* . . ."

"I see," Cliff says, handing back the phone. "Technology! Amazing really."

"There's a straight version too," Jill says.

"There is," Tristan agrees. "It's called Blendr."

"Brenda?!" Hannah asks, pulling a face.

Tristan laughs. "Not Brenda. Blendr."

"Oh. I thought it sounded a bit silly. Then again, so does Blendr."

"And that's for what, guys who want to meet girls?" Cliff asks.

Tristan nods.

"Don't tell him any more," Hannah says. "You'll give him ideas."

"I don't think it ever really caught on," Tristan says. "A friend tells me there are loads of guys and no women on it."

"Hum," Jill says, sipping her wine. "Now that's giving *me* ideas."

It's just after midnight by the time they leave the bar.

Luke is tired and, Hannah guesses, on the verge of becoming fractious. With Aïsha it's harder to tell. Fractious is pretty much her average state of being these days.

"I wish we'd brought the car," Aïsha says.

"We all wish that," her mother agrees.

"Next time you can forego alcohol and *you-know-what* and drive us all then," Cliff suggests.

"I rather like it," Hannah says. "It's a lovely evening, and it's not that far. But I wouldn't want to be Tristan walking home alone."

All the adults are a bit drunk, but Tristan, who has stayed behind to talk to the barman, is particularly so.

"What makes you think he'll be walking home alone?" Jill asks, amusement in her voice.

"Yes, I suppose that barman chappy might give him a lift," Cliff says, pretending to miss Jill's point.

"It's a lovely clear night," Hannah says as they enter another pool of yellow light beneath a street lamp. A cloud of insects is frenetically buzzing around and banging into the glass cylinder as they hurl themselves at the brightness.

"Look," Jill says, pointing at the sky, her finger describing a figure of eight. "Is that a bird, or a bat?"

They all pause to stare into the blackness but can see nothing. Then as they start to move again the animal – very clearly a bat – swoops back into the light.

"Yuck," Aïsha says. "I hope it's not a vampire bat."

"It's not," Hannah says. "They don't even live here, do they, Cliff?"

"No," Cliff agrees, even though he hasn't the foggiest idea where vampire bats live. But he felt the way Hannah gripped his hand when the bat appeared, so he knows that she's trying to reassure the others. Not passing on their own irrational fears to the children is something they agree on. "No, that's just a normal bat. They're attracted to the light because they eat the insects," he says.

As they move farther away from the village the gaps between the street lamps get wider. The trees and bushes make strange, unnerving shapes against the blackness of the sky. At times they can barely see the ground beneath their feet.

"It's creepy out here," Aïsha says, running to catch up with the others and taking, unusually, her mother's hand.

"It is a bit," Hannah agrees as Luke squashes himself between her and Cliff. "But I'm sure there's nothing to be afraid of. It's just that there's no moon tonight."

"If Tris' is going to have a holiday fling with that barman, I hope the pool guy comes back," Jill says, off, as so often, on her own train of thought. "I don't want to end up being the raspberry of the holiday."

"Gooseberry," Hannah corrects, suppressing a smile.

"Yeah, sorry. Gooseberry. That's what I meant," Jill says.

Luke licks the back of his hand and makes a farting noise by blowing against it, one of his specialities. "*That's* a raspberry," he says.

"Yes," Hannah says. "Thanks for that, Luke."

"It's really dark up there," Aïsha says, nodding forwards and sounding vaguely excited but also genuinely distressed.

They all peer out at the blackness ahead. "It's because there's a bend," Hannah says. "I remember it. There was the green gate with the noisy frogs and then a bend."

"How can that make it darker?" Aïsha asks, her tone dismissive.

"No, Hannah's right," Cliff says. "It's because you can't see the next street lamp, that's all. It's around the corner. We should have brought the torch."

"Have we got one?"

"Sure. There's one in the boot of the car."

As they leave the final edge of the pool of light and head towards the void, Luke pulls his phone out and switches it on. It only casts the vaguest beam of bluish light a few feet in front of him, but it's better than nothing.

"Good idea, Luke," Cliff says, and both he and Aïsha do likewise. But even with the light from three phones, the lane ahead is pitch black.

"The corner must be here somewhere," Hannah says.

"Yes, I think that's it," Cliff says pointing at what he thinks might be the grey curve of the tarmac.

As they reach the blackest section of the bend the next streetlight comes into view, a pin-point of light in the distance. Hannah pauses and pulls Cliff and Luke to a halt with her.

"Look at the stars," she says. "Gosh, I've never seen so many stars."

They crane their necks and look at the sky, and as their eyes adjust, small stars appear between the bright ones, and then even smaller ones between those.

"Aeroplane," Cliff says, pointing at a flashing light to the east.

"There's two," Luke says.

"Yes, I can see two," Hannah agrees.

"Gosh that's the Milky Way, isn't it?" Cliff says. "I don't think I've ever seen that before. Not in real life."

"What is?" Luke asks, and Cliff crouches down behind him so that he can point and explain. "See those swirly clouds," he says. "That's millions of tiny stars. That's the Milky Way."

"I wish we had a telescope," Luke says.

"Yes, that would be good," Cliff agrees.

"Can we get one?"

"No, I think they're a bit expensive. And I don't think there are a lot of telescope shops around here."

"There are so many stars," Jill says. "It makes you feel quite alone in the middle of it all."

"It's cold here," Aïsha says. "Can we go?"

Hannah shivers and realises that this is true, but also that Aïsha sounds scared. "There's a river or something," she tells her. "It's damp here, that's why."

"I don't like it," Aïsha says, her tone more urgent now. "Can we go?"

"Sure," Hannah says.

"There's nothing to be scared of though," Cliff tells her. "It's just nature." A mere second after he has spoken these words, an unseen creature in the darkness, not ten metres away, grunts loudly.

Luke makes a short sharp, "Uh!" sound and Aïsha shrieks. The shock of each person jumping is transmitted, through held hands, to their neighbours, somehow amplifying the fear.

They start, as a group, to walk quickly towards the distant street lamp, but when the creature, farther behind them now, grunts again, first Aïsha and then Luke break free, sprinting ahead, squealing. Soon they are laughing hysterically.

At the next oasis of light everyone regroups. "What the fuck was that?" Jill asks.

"It was a monster," Luke says, and Hannah can see from the children's excited faces that this is already the best thing that has happened on the holiday so far.

"I think it was a pig," Cliff says. "A wild pig maybe."

"It sounded like a pig," Hannah agrees, her own heart still racing. "But here? Do you think?"

"Do pigs bite?" Luke asks. "Can they jump up and rip your throat out?"

Aïsha pulls a stick from the undergrowth, presumably to defend herself with, and Luke follows suit.

"No," Cliff says, thinking that he would quite like a stick himself, but that it might look a bit wimpy. "No, pigs don't bite, do they, Hannah?"

"Of course not," Hannah agrees, even though she has absolutely no idea.

"What if there are more?" Jill asks.

"What if there's a pack of them?" Luke asks. "What if they surround us, like wolves?"

"*Luke*," Aïsha wines.

"Yes, stop it, Luke. You'll give yourself nightmares," Hannah says. "They don't like noise. Wild animals never like noise. So just talk loudly or sing a song or something and you'll be fine."

"Wooh wooh wooh!" Luke shouts, brandishing his stick.

"You don't have to wake up the whole neighbourhood," Cliff admonishes.

He shrugs and starts to sing his favourite song from *The Lion King* instead – *I just can't wait to be king*.

"Don't sing *that*, Luke, that's lame," Aïsha says. But as they head into the next patch of darkness even she joins in.

When half a mile down the road the street lamps become more regular and they all start to relax, Hannah moves to Jill's side. "She can sing!" she murmurs. "Aïsha can sing."

"I know," Jill says. "It's amazing, isn't it?"

"It is. She's got a great voice."

"Luke can't," Jill says, and Hannah laughs.

"No! No, he gets that from his mother, unfortunately," she says.

TWELVE

The next morning Hannah is first up – even Luke is having a lie-in.

She quietly makes herself a cup of coffee and sits nursing it as she watches the shortening shadows of the olive trees.

She feels a little tired still, and vaguely hung-over too, but contented also. She likes the calm before the day begins, this sensation that everyone she loves is sleeping nearby. It's so much easier to love them when they're asleep, after all.

When she has finished her coffee she wanders around the garden, looping the house and listening to the morning sounds of Provence: the buzz of insects around the lavender, snoring from Tristan's shutters (a smile), a distant moped buzzing up a hill, water falling from the hosepipe into the now half-filled pool.

When she reaches the front of the house she sees an extra car parked behind Tristan's Jeep, a turquoise Twingo. Its two-tone paintwork shimmers in the morning light. *So Tristan got more than a lift home*, she thinks.

The house continues to sleep, dark and heavy, so, careful not to disturb anyone (for her own benefit, not theirs) she fixes herself some toast and another cup of coffee, and takes them, along with her novel, back to the patio. She reads for a whole hour, uninterrupted – a rarity.

"Morning!"

Hannah jumps and turns to see Jill hanging from the doorway. She's wearing men's pyjamas.

"Is everyone else still in bed?" Jill asks.

Hannah nods. She doesn't want to speak yet. Her head is still stuck in her novel, and she likes it there.

"I think I'll go back to bed for a bit then," Jill says. "I just got up for a glass of water."

Hannah nods again, winks at her sister and flutters her fingers in a goodbye wave.

Another hour passes by before Cliff appears in the same doorway. "How long have you been up?" he asks.

"Since eight," Hannah says quietly. She stretches and stifles a yawn and realises that the day is hotting up – that she's sweating.

"Couldn't sleep?"

Hannah shrugs. "Just reading," she tells him, now reluctantly closing her book.

Cliff's booming voice could wake the dead, and, sure enough, within a minute first Luke then Aïsha appear, requiring breakfast. They are closely followed by Jill and Tristan.

Hannah is the only person who isn't surprised when the barman appears behind him, his floppy hair now a dishevelled bed-head wonder.

"You all know Jean-Jacques," Tristan says by way of intro-duction. "Now, I'm gonna make pancakes if anyone wants them."

"I'll help," Luke says, jumping up and following Tristan into the house.

The easy morning chat that had prevailed up to that point vanishes the second Jean-Jacques takes a seat at the table.

Hannah looks at him and forces a smile. She nods at him in a friendly way and he smiles weakly.

"So," Hannah says.

Jean-Jacques clears his throat.

"So Tristan got you to drive him home last night?" she says.

Jean-Jacques nods.

Aïsha gets her iPhone out and puts her earbuds in. Hannah wishes she could do the same.

"He's lucky," Hannah says.

"Thank you," Jean-Jacques says, averting his gaze and blushing deeply.

"I meant . . . I just meant that the road was very dark," Hannah explains, flushing with heat herself. She catches Jill's eye and gives her an exaggerated stare and a vague shrug – a plea for help.

"There were wild beasts," Jill says. "On the road. We were scared."

Jean-Jacques frowns. "Beast?" he says.

"Yes, animals," Jill says, miming a four-legged creature on the table-top with one hand.

"Ah. Un daim? Un sanglier ?" Jean-Jacques asks.

Everyone stares at him blankly. They have no idea what he is saying.

"It's a nice bar," Cliff says. "It must be nice working there."

Jean-Jacques shrugs. "C'est tranquille," he says. "It's just a job for summer."

"Of course," Cliff says. "So what do you do the rest of the time?"

"Station de ski," Jean-Jacques says, then, "Ski station. I am teaching the snowboard."

"Snowboard? Cool," Aïsha says, almost immediately looking surprised at her own utterance.

Luke, thankfully, appears with the first plate of pancakes. Everyone is grateful for the distraction.

"That was quick," Hannah says.

"Tris' made the gloopy stuff yesterday," Luke says. "More coming!"

Once everyone is served, Tristan returns with his own plate and sits. "So what have you people been talking about?" he asks.

"Oh this and that," Hannah tells him. "Jean-Paul here is a snowboard instructor."

"Jean-Jacques," Jean-Jacques corrects her.

"Sorry, of course," Hannah says. "Sorry."

"Is there much call for that? Here, I mean?" Tristan asks, looking around the garden as if in search of snow.

"The ski stations is two hour away," Jean-Jacques says. "Is OK."

"I see," Hannah says. "How amazing."

A silence falls over the table again. Cutlery clinks against plates. People chew on pancake.

"So where do you go out around here?" Jill asks.

"Pardon ?"

"I mean, it must be a bit boring being gay in a tiny place like this," Jill says. She sees that Tristan is bristling, but whatever the problem is, it's too late now. "So I just wondered where you go when you want to have some fun."

Jean-Jacques furrows his brow, then swallows and turns his attention to his plate. His hair falls forward, almost completely hiding his face.

"Jean-Jacques here isn't gay," Tristan says, his tone a strange mixture of crisp over-emphasis and amusement.

66

"Oh, sorry," Jill says. "Sorry, I . . . I just assumed."

"Yeas," Tristan says, sounding quite camp now. "Yeas, so did I. But no! So you see. Life still has fresh surprises to throw at us."

Jean-Jacques pushes his plate – which still contains half a pancake – away from him and stands. "So, I 'ave to go," he says. "Sorry. But many things today. Thank you for your hospitalité."

As he leaves, awkwardly, he knocks his chair over, stoops to pick it up, and then, combing his hair with his fingers, vanishes from view.

"What on earth was all that about?" Jill asks once they hear the car driving away.

"Don't ask," Tristan says. "Really. Don't ask."

"No," Jill whines. "Tell me."

Hannah shoots Tristan a warning glance, then seeing that it's a lost cause, turns to Luke.

"Why don't you go off and play for a bit?" she suggests. "You too, Aïsha."

Aïsha pulls a face. Luke mimics her expression and says, "Play? What at?"

"The pool is full enough to swim in I think," Hannah says.

"Really? Is it?" Luke is already standing, already trying to remember where the diving mask is. He had forgotten there was a pool.

"It's over half-full," Hannah tells him. "But don't dive in yet. You don't want to hit your head on the bottom."

"Help me blow up the air beds?" Luke asks Aïsha, and she forks a final mouthful of pancake, stands and, feigning reluctance, follows him.

"So?" Jill prompts, once they have gone.

Tristan pulls a face. "Oh God," he says. "Well . . ."

Cliff stands. "I'll clear the breakfast things," he says, gathering some cups together.

"I can do it in a bit," Hannah offers.

"It's fine," Cliff tells her. "You three have a natter." He always feels a little uncomfortable with these intimate conversations. He never quite seems to be able to strike the correct balance between showing polite interest and sounding as if he's showing too much interest in something that he believes should ultimately remain private.

"Is he really not gay?" Jill asks.

Tristan laughs. "He drives a Twingo," he says. "What do you think?"

Aïsha, who has for some reason returned, asks, "Is a Twingo really gay or something?"

Tristan laughs. "Let me see: a little car with rounded edges in two-tone turquoise-slash-purple no doubt selected personally by Victoria Beckham."

Aïsha shrugs. She looks confused. "OK . . . What about a Jeep then?" she asks.

"A Jeep's far, far worse," Tristan replies. "Especially if it's red."

"I thought you were helping Luke," Hannah reminds her.

"We can't find the pump," Aïsha says. "And I'm not blowing them up. It makes me dizzy."

"It's in the car," Cliff, who is still lingering, says. "Come. I'll get it for you. It's still in the boot."

"So yes, of course he's gay," Tristan says as they head off. "But he can't admit it yet. Not even in bed. Classic Catholic angst."

"He is quite young I suppose," Hannah says.

68

"Yes, how old is he anyway?" Jill asks.

"Twenty-three I think," Tristan answers.

"Yum," Jill says. "Lucky you."

Hannah frowns at her sister. "Really?" she asks.

"Uh-huh! They're up all the time at that age. You only have to say the word sex and they're ready for action."

"I'm afraid I can't even imagine it," Hannah says after a couple of seconds of trying to do just that. "As far as I'm concerned, if they're young enough to be your offspring then they're too young. That's my theory anyway. No offence, Tristan, it's just me, I guess."

"No offence taken, you're probably right as it happens," he says. "Youth is much overrated."

"Really?" Jill sounds disappointed.

"Totally frigid. Didn't move a muscle."

"Not even . . . you know . . . that muscle?"

Tristan laughs. "That," he says, "isn't a muscle. But yes, that worked. It's just that nothing else did. He got a hard-on, but spent the whole time on his back like this." Tristan links his hands behind his head to demonstrate. "Handy if you need an ironing board, but he really doesn't win any prizes as the world's greatest lover."

"Gosh," Hannah says, thinking about how much she moves when she makes love with Cliff. She doesn't fold her hands behind her head, but all the same . . . She would have to admit that she puts less effort into it these days than she once did. Perhaps she needs to watch that.

"He told me he was straight too," Tristan continues. "Once he had come he asked if I wanted him to leave, and I said, no, he could stay. And he said, 'OK, but I'm not gay. Just so you know.' Can you believe that?"

69

"Lord," Jill says. "What did you say?"

"I just said, 'Non, chéri, bien sûr.'"

"Meaning?"

"Meaning, 'No dear. Of course you aren't.'"

"The pool guy's back," Cliff says, returning from the car and sliding back into his seat. Then, visibly remembering that he had been in the process of clearing the table, he stands to continue where he left off.

Jill sits up straight, suddenly alert. "He's here? What, round there?" she asks, gesturing towards the other side of the house.

"Yes. He's putting chemicals in the pool. It looks quite complicated."

Hannah has to strain to look up at Cliff, now standing behind her with a pile of plates. "Chemicals?" she asks. 'Chemicals' sounds worrying.

"Chlorine and stuff, I guess," Cliff says. "To keep the water safe."

"Of course."

Jill stands and flicks back her hair.

Hannah laughs. "Where are you going?" she asks. "You don't even speak French."

"I do," Tristan says, smiling and starting to stand as well.

"I'm going for a swim," Jill says. "I'm allowed, aren't I? I just hope I can find my bikini, otherwise I may have to skinny-dip."

Tristan follows Jill inside the house and Cliff catches Hannah's eye – a moment of complicity.

They can hear Tristan and Jill arguing light-heartedly inside the house and then, less than a minute later, they burst from the interior in their swimming costumes, laughing and jostling for position like teenagers.

"Stay back!" Jill is saying as she whacks at Tristan. "Stay back I tell you! You've had yours." They sprint across the lawn and then vanish from view.

"Do they make you feel terribly old?" Cliff asks.

Hannah nods and snorts. "A bit," she says. "You'd certainly never guess that she's only two years younger, would you?" She pushes her chair back. "But I think I need to see this. Are you coming?"

"No," Cliff says. "No, I'll clear this stuff away."

By the time Hannah has found her shoes and rounded the house, Jill is lounging along one edge of the filling pool and Tristan is using the foot-pump to inflate Luke's air-bed, rather absurdly pulling in his perfectly toned stomach.

"God, you're pale, Jill," Hannah says. "I don't think I've ever seen you so white."

"I know," Jill says. "I stopped going to the tanning place. Pale-and-wan is the new brown-and-sexy or something."

"Well, be careful you don't burn."

The pool guy, in the same dungarees as yesterday, is holding a test tube of pink liquid up against a colour chart and saying something in French.

"He says it's fine to swim in, but he'll have to come back tomorrow to add more acid or something," Tristan translates.

"Très bien," Jill says smoothly. She sits up and stretches so that her toe just touches the surface of the water. "It's freezing," she says. "I mean, like, Arctic freezing. Can you ask him how long it takes to warm up?"

Tristan translates Jill's question to French and the man replies, pointing at a duct in the pool wall as he does so.

"He says he can't switch the heater thingy on until the water

71

reaches that tube," Tristan says. "But after that it will be ready in forty-eight hours."

"So it's heated then. That's good," Hannah says.

"Apparently so."

"Do you speak any English?" Jill asks the man, squashing herself back against the pool edge in order to enter his line of vision.

"Ma copine veut savoir si vous parlez anglais," Tristan translates when he shrugs.

"Alors, pas de tout !" the man replies.

"Sorry dear," Tristan says smugly. "He says not one word. Sucks to be you, huh?"

Jill licks her lips. "We'll see," she says.

"Stop, Tris, you'll pop it," Luke says, tapping Tristan's leg with one hand to grab his attention.

Tristan glances down to see that the air-bed is more than amply inflated. He crouches down to disconnect the pump and plug the filler valve. "There you go. Now yours, Ai' – bring it over."

The pool guy starts to collect his various tubes and boxes of kit together, placing them in a bucket, and then straightens and takes the handle of this in one hand and the huge container of chlorine in the other.

Hannah watches Jill surveilling his departure. She looks, Hannah thinks, like a lioness about to pounce.

"Au revoir," he says vaguely, to all of them. "À demain."

As he turns away, Jill sits upright, hesitant. And then, a decision taken, she jumps to her feet and runs across the grass to catch up with him. Joining him halfway across the lawn, she puts one hand next to his on the handle of the bucket and says, "Let me help you with that."

The guy pauses, looking alarmed, as if perhaps he suspects that she's trying to steal his bucket. But then he smiles, looks bashful, lowers his head, and continues to walk, linked now, to Jill, via the bucket.

As they vanish from view behind the house, he starts to talk to her in French.

Hannah stares wide-eyed at the mid-distance where they no longer stand, then refocuses on Tristan and shakes her head.

"Unbelievable," Tristan, who has momentarily ceased foot-pumping says. He grins broadly. "Absolutely un-be-lie-va-ble."

Hannah nods. "My little sister, eh?" she says. "Never ceases to amaze, that one."

She turns to glance at Aïsha to see how she's reacting to this, but she has her headphones on and is tapping her hand in time with the music. She seems totally oblivious.

Hannah turns to leave. "Call me when the pool's warm," she says.

Cliff takes Stieg Larsson to the hammock with him but immediately falls asleep, the novel spread across his chest.

Hannah offers to help Tristan prepare lunch, and Tristan, ever the chef, tasks Hannah with salad-washing duties whilst he fries potatoes and beats eggs for a Spanish tortilla.

From behind the house, Hannah can hear the shrieks of Luke and Aïsha splashing around in the pool. A sound of summer – a sound of childhood momentarily restored. She smiles to herself, is pleased with herself, even, for having insisted on this destination. "Don't you ever get fed up with cooking?" she asks Tristan after a moment's silence.

"I don't cook so much these days," he replies. "Since we

73

opened the fourth restaurant in Hoxton, I spend more time just managing the business really. Choosing menus, replacing staff, accounts . . . It's pretty hectic."

"Of course," Hannah says.

"So I quite like it really."

"Yes. Yes, I suppose so."

"And anyway, this is hardly what I'd call cooking," Tristan adds.

Hannah pulls a face at this. A mixed salad, fresh salsa, homemade vinaigrette and a twelve-egg Spanish tortilla is about as challenging as her cooking ever gets.

"Jill's back," Tristan says, and Hannah looks up from the sink and sees that this is so.

Jill, beyond the open kitchen window, turns to face them, then pushing chairs out of her way makes her way towards them. Finally she leans on the windowsill, peering in at them and looking despondent.

"That was quick," Hannah says.

"Even for you," Tristan adds cheekily.

"Excruciating," Jill declares. "Why didn't you just stop me?"

Tristan lays down his egg beater and crosses to join Hannah at the sink. Hannah can smell his aftershave – a warm vanilla-honey smell. She wonders if it would be impolite to ask him what it is so that she can buy it for Cliff. "What happened?" he asks.

"I followed him down the track. He was rabbiting away in French. Of course it might as well be Chinese for all the good it did me."

"And?"

"Their place is about a hundred yards away behind those big trees. It's not much more than a shack. A big shed really."

"They?" Hannah asks.

"Well, he lives with his mother, doesn't he? I think he lives there anyway. She certainly does. She's about a hundred. No teeth." Jill pulls her lips down and mimes having no teeth just in case there was some doubt.

"His mother!" Tristan says. He claps his hands. "Love it!"

"So I ended up with them both rabbiting on at me in French. It was just . . . it was embarrassing really. And all a bit Hitchcock, to be honest."

"But did you get a bit of slap and tickle?" Tristan asks.

"Nothing. Not even a kiss. Well, I got to kiss the old dear. Which was lovely, of course. She made us coffee, that Turkish stuff where they boil it for hours and then serve you the dregs."

"Nice."

"I still have the bits caught in my teeth. The cups were dirty too," Jill pulls a face. "Honestly, it was awful."

"And then?"

"And then . . . Wonder Boy climbed into his little Fiat rust bucket and drove off. To do someone else's pool I think. He took the stuff with him anyway."

Hannah breaks into a broad grin. "He left you with the mother? How funny."

"He left me with the mother," Jill confirms. "I still didn't know what she was banging on about. In the end, I just waved at her and left. She was still yakking as I walked away."

"It could only happen to you, Jill," Tristan says, returning to the stove.

Aïsha appears behind Jill. She's wearing shorts and a black T-shirt. Water is pooling around her feet. "What could only happen to you?" she asks.

"You're soaked!" Jill says, turning to appraise her daughter and reaching out to take the hem of the T-shirt between finger and thumb. "Why are your clothes soaked? You'll catch your death!"

"We're swimming," Aïsha says. "The water's freezing but if you stay on the lilo and don't move, it's all right. You just drift around."

"Why are you wearing this when you have a perfectly good swimming costume?" Jill asks.

Aïsha shrugs. "This is fine," she says. "But can you get me a towel? I want to go to the loo and I'm dripping."

"It's not fine," Jill says. "I'll get you a towel but . . ."

Hannah hands a towel through the window.

"Oh, thanks, Han'," she says, passing it on to her daughter. "Here. Dry yourself off and then go and put your bikini on."

"I don't know where it is," Aïsha says.

"It's in your suitcase. Where else would it be?"

Hannah leans across the sink and reaches through the window to gently touch Jill's shoulder. "Jill," she says, quietly.

"Hang on," Jill says, gesturing behind her. "Aïsha. Aïsha!" she shouts as her daughter disappears inside the house.

"Jill!" Hannah says again.

Jill glances back at her. "Hang on, Han'," she says. "Just let me deal with this and . . ."

"She doesn't want to wear the bikini," Hannah says forcefully but quiet enough that Aïsha won't hear her.

"I don't care what she wants," Jill says. "She chose it. She can wear it. I'm not made of money."

"She's embarrassed, Jill," Hannah says.

Jill freezes. She pulls a face. "Embarrassed? How can she be embarrassed? She chose it."

"She's embarrassed about her body. Give her a break."

Jill wrinkles her nose. "She's got nothing to be embarrassed about. I mean she's packing a few extra pounds, but it's just puppy fat. That will go soon enough."

Hannah sighs deeply. "You don't get it, do you, Jill? Just stop and think. Remember when you were thirteen."

Jill pauses. "I don't remember last night, babe, let alone when I was thirteen."

"I remember," Hannah says. "I remember you putting masking tape around your boobs because you didn't want to tell Mum you needed a bra."

"You didn't!" Tristan exclaims, looking up from his frying pan.

"Just . . . cook, Tris'," Jill says, making a little shooing gesture, then to Hannah, "OK," she says. "Point taken."

"She's getting breasts," Hannah whispers. "It's a shock."

"Yes, yes, I get it," Jill says. She shakes her head. "God, am I a terrible mother do you think?"

Hannah shakes her head. "No," she says. "No, you're fine. You're just a bit too close to be able to see sometimes. We all are."

Jill nods, then she laughs. "I'll tell you what," she says. "It didn't half hurt when you pulled off the tape. I remember that."

After lunch, Hannah, persuaded by Luke, lowers herself onto one of the air-beds. Initially the icy water lapping over the edges makes this excruciating, but, as Aïsha explained, by lying totally still the pain ceases. The water already around her warms up, and the cold water of the pool remains at bay.

As the bed drifts in a seemingly random fashion she watches a single cloud in the blue sky skirting away to the east, now circling above her as the bed spins. She senses invisible waves of air moving across her body. She wonders if this is what a water-bed feels like, and decides that she must ask Jill. She's pretty sure that Jill must have come across a water-bed at some point. Or Tristan. Tristan might even have one at home. She can hear a bird tweeting somewhere, and the rustle of the wind in the leaves and then . . .

Hannah gasps in shock and sits up, causing more icy water to flood around her waist. A fresh jet of spray hits her face and she rolls for protection from the bed and into the pool, gasping at the temperature shock as her sun-baked body is enveloped by the water.

"Luke!" she shrieks, now finding her feet and wading as fast as she can towards the ladder.

Luke, her assailant with a hosepipe, is radiant with glee. "Yes!" he declares, still pointing the jet at her back.

"You cheeky little bugger!" Hannah shouts. "I was asleep. I was fast-a-bloody-sleep and having a lovely dream." She climbs the ladder and starts to run around the pool towards her son, who drops the hosepipe and flees, giggling maniacally.

Hannah chases him barefoot around the back of the house and on towards the patio, in truth enjoying the chase. She feels for the first time as if she's on holiday. She feels young and exhilarated and awake. It's only in these fleeting moments of wakefulness that she realises that she spends most of her life asleep.

Catching sight of Jill climbing back over the fence at the rear of the garden, and making a mental note to question her later, she runs on. "You wait until I catch you, boy," she shouts.

Luke, looking behind him to check on her progress, runs

straight into Cliff, who unsure as to whether Hannah's pursuit is in anger or jest, grabs Luke by the waist.

"Let me go!" he shouts, writhing and kicking at Cliff's shins.

"Hey!" Cliff says, holding him at arm's length and laughing.

"Hold onto him," Hannah says. "The cheeky monkey squirted me!"

By the time she reaches them she is out of breath. "I was fast asleep and he squirted me with the hosepipe!" she explains, trying but failing to grab Luke's flailing feet.

Aïsha, drawn by the noise, has now joined them. She grabs one of Luke's feet, and Hannah manages to seize the remaining one.

"That's not fair," Luke whines, now hesitating between throwing a genuine temper tantrum and allowing this to remain something he calls fun.

"Well nor is squirting your mother with a hosepipe when she's asleep," Hannah laughs, as the three of them manhandle him back to the pool.

"We're gonna throw you in," Aïsha chants, and Hannah, always hypersensitive to Luke's moods, notes that he caves in, sees that he has decided to go along with this, and knows that she doesn't therefore have to cave in herself.

"One, Two, Three!" Cliff shouts and they drop him, ever so gently, into the pool.

"I'll get you back," Luke says, now surfaced and hanging onto the side of an air-bed, apparently oblivious to the cold.

"I think you already did, Luke," Hannah says. "Thanks," she says, smiling at Aïsha and Cliff as they walk back to the house.

"Any time," Aïsha says, restraining a smile.

"Actually, it's good he woke you," Cliff tells Hannah. "You've gone a bit pink."

"God, have I?" she says, touching her arm and sensing the heat of her skin. "I forgot to put any cream on."

"You're not burnt, but I think you've had enough," Cliff tells her.

That evening, Tristan leaves them to their own devices. He has "stuff to do", he declares mysteriously.

Hannah knows, from the fact that Jill doesn't question him, that he must have told her where he is going, but as the Jeep crunches out of the driveway, she denies this. "I've really no idea," she says. "He's probably just bored. You know how high-maintenance he is. He's probably gone off to find a club or something."

"You'd go with him if that was it," Hannah points out.

Jill shrugs. "Maybe it's not the kind of club I'm allowed in," she says.

Hannah looks around, and seeing that both Aïsha and Luke are absent, she asks, "Anyway, where were you earlier on?"

Jill frowns.

"I saw you climbing back over the fence."

"Oh, that," Jill says. "There's a track going down the hill. A hiking trail. I went to see where it goes. There's a little river down there. I'll show you later if you want."

"Right," Hannah says, somehow unconvinced despite Jill's Oscar-worthy performance.

"So the chef's taken the night off, huh?" Cliff is looking out at them through the kitchen window.

"He has," Hannah says.

"So are we staying here or going out for dinner?" he asks. "Because if we're staying I'm opening this." He brandishes a bottle of white wine to demonstrate what this refers to. "But if I have to drive, I'll hold off."

"If we're staying, it's just pasta with pesto sauce," Hannah says. "But if you'd rather go find a pizzeria that's fine with me."

"I'm OK with pasta," Cliff says. "Jill?"

"Sure. Pasta's fine."

"I thought we might take them to the water park tomorrow," Cliff says quietly, confidentially. "Luke's been on and on about it. It's near Antibes, so if we stay in tonight, we could have lunch out tomorrow and then take them to the water-slide place."

Hannah nods. "Sure," she says. "That sounds good." She turns to Jill. "Do you think Aïsha will be up for it or is that too babyish for her now?"

"Um . . . no, she'll be fine. She won't be enthusiastic, but she'll be fine. She'll enjoy it once she gets there. Just don't say anything about how much fun it will be. Over-expectation freaks her out."

"Good. So that's settled then," Hannah says. "Pasta it is. I'll go cook."

"I'll come, too," Jill says.

"To the water park?"

"No. Not my scene. I meant I'll help you cook."

Hannah shakes her head. "I'm boiling pasta and pouring on the sauce," she says. "I'll be fine."

Hannah sleeps badly that night. For some reason the pasta and white wine keep repeating on her. Cliff, as ever, snores soundly at her side.

Shortly after she finally does manage to fall asleep, she is awakened by the sound of Tristan's Jeep returning. The alarm clock reads 03:08.

What seems like a few seconds later, she is awakened by another sound, this time the crunch of feet on gravel. She checks the clock again and is surprised to see that it is almost five.

She silently climbs from the bed and crosses to the window. Frogs are croaking loudly somewhere in the distance; cicadas are clicketing lazily. As she peers through the slats of the shutters she sees someone start to move again, heading now towards the rear of the house. With only the tiniest hint of moonlight it's impossible to see who it is, but judging from his sure-footed plod, she's pretty sure that it's the pool guy. She wonders if he has been visiting someone. Surely he wouldn't be checking on the pool at five a.m., would he?

As she climbs back into bed, she wonders who he has been visiting. As sleep takes over again she wonders if, had she left their shutters open, the pool guy would have visited her. That would have been a shock for Cliff. She laughs at the thought in her sleep.

THIRTEEN

The drive to Antibes takes just over an hour. Luke spends the journey pointlessly naming everything he sees, as if an Esso petrol station or a McDonald's becomes a point of interest simply for being situated in France. Aïsha, for her part, is listening to music on her phone. Hannah knows, from experience, that not only is it not likely to be something they would all want to listen to – she favours a genre called glammetal, awful – but that even a suggestion that they might want to try would be an embarrassment for poor Aïsha.

"Someone was creeping around in the garden last night," she tells Cliff once they are safely installed on an unchallenging stretch of main road.

"Really?" he says. "I didn't hear anything."

"Of course you didn't. You were fast asleep," Hannah says.

"Was it Tristan coming back?"

"No, this was later. About five a.m."

"The gardener maybe?"

"That's what I thought, but what would he be doing nosing around at dawn?"

"Maybe he's just an early bird," Cliff says. "Maybe he came over to switch the pool filter on or something. But next time, wake me up if you're worried."

Hannah smiles to herself at this suggestion. She has, on

occasion, attempted this in the past. Cliff invariably groans and rolls over without even a pause in the rhythm of his snoring.

They find Antibes without drama – heading to the coast is simply a case of following the signposts. They leave the Mégane in a big sea-front car park and head into the tiny streets of the old town. The day is already heating up and Hannah can sense that the kids won't tolerate wandering around for long. They are already onto the next thing, already anticipating the water slides.

Hannah and Cliff walk through the shady streets peering into shop windows, sniffing at kitsch lavender cushions and listening to the sounds of water falling from fountains whilst Luke and Aïsha drag their feet ten yards behind them, talking constantly about what features may or may not reside in the park.

Hannah would love to be able to explain to her son that though the water slide may represent a ten on his personal preference chart, a walk through a beautiful, sunlit, foreign town whilst licking a velvety Italian ice-cream should be at least a nine. She would love to be able to convey the concept that the present is all that you ever have in life, and that these moments of magic are too precious to be ignored because you're too busy thinking about the next thing. But there are no words, of course, to express this to an eleven-year-old.

"Just enjoy your ice-cream and shut up about the park for a minute, can't you?" is as close as she gets. If she can't fix Luke's present, she can at least try to stop him wrecking hers.

"He's OK," Cliff says, rubbing her shoulder. "He's just excited."

And Hannah knows that he's right. She's just suffering from lack of sleep.

When they reach the edge of the historic town centre, they sit and have an outrageously expensive round of Cokes, then climb up onto the ramparts and circle the town in the other direction.

"The sea is so blue!" Hannah says.

"Well, of *course* it's blue," Luke says.

"Don't be rude, Luke," Hannah reproaches him. "It's not always *that* blue. It's not always azure blue." These flashes of cheekiness scare her a little. They warn her that she needs to prepare herself for a time when Luke will become like Aïsha. It's happening already; these bursts of insolence are creeping in. For the moment, it's only an occasional burst, but she suspects that soon enough it will become a twenty-four-seven feature of their lives.

On the harbour wall, Cliff takes their photo standing inside a huge iron sculpture of a head made out of a latticework of apparently random words, and then the parents cave in to the kids' demands and rather than choosing a nice relaxing restaurant somewhere, they buy sandwiches that can be eaten en route to the water park. "It wouldn't be any fun anyway," Cliff points out. "Not with these two champing at the bit."

This turns out to be a wise decision, because when they reach the location Tristan put into Cliff's GPS, they find not a water park but a vast bill-board advertisement for a water park in a place called Fréjus. The GPS informs them that though the route to Fréjus does begin in the direction the yellow arrow on the signpost indicates, it is, in reality, an entirely different town an hour and a half's drive away.

"So we drive to Fréjus, I guess," Hannah says.

"There's no turning back now," Cliff agrees. "We'd never hear the end of it if we did. Let's just hope that it's worth it."

The sun is dipping behind the olive trees by the time they get back to the Villa.

Hannah finds Tristan and Jill drinking rosé and smoking on the patio. They look up lazily to greet the returned travellers.

"Wow! Someone's caught the sun," Jill says.

"I know," Hannah replies. "I kept smothering myself in that factor fifty stuff, but after yesterday's fry-up . . ."

Tristan glances at Jill. He raises an eyebrow and Hannah pauses, thinking that he's silently prompting Jill to say something, something they have previously discussed – an agreed announcement perhaps.

After an almost-imperceptible head-shake on Jill's part, Tristan turns back to Hannah. "So how was it?" he asks. "Fun?"

Hannah glances behind her to check that she's still alone – the others are emptying the car – before whispering, "Awful. A million screaming children. And loads of chavvy adults barging their way into the queues. Those two *loved* it though."

"I didn't know they had chavs in France," Jill says.

"Nor did I," Hannah says, "until we got to Aquasplash."

"Poor you," Jill says. "Was Aïsha OK?"

"Honestly, Jill, she had such a good time. She was like a little girl all over again. It was a joy to see."

Aïsha, Luke and Cliff appear laden with towels and bags and booty, which they dump on a free chair.

"Good?" Tristan asks again.

"Awesome," Luke says. "Look!" He rounds the table and thrusts a fridge magnet under Tristan's nose. It contains a photo of him and Aïsha on an inflatable tyre in white-water rapids.

"They have a machine that makes these," Luke says, waving the magnet. "It was ten euros."

"Wow, that does look like fun," Tristan says.

"Show me?" Jill holds out her hand and then studying the photo, continues, "Gosh, yes. That does look good."

"Mum went down it too," Luke says, "but she fell off and hurt her ear."

"It's true," Hannah says, nodding shamefully. "It kept bouncing off the sides and eventually it threw me off completely. I thought the whole thing was pretty dangerous to be honest."

"Do we have a photo of that?" Tristan asks.

Hannah shakes her head. "It's automatic so it took a photo of my rubber ring, but I was drowning some way behind."

"And there were those tubes you slide down," Luke says. "And a thing like a helter-skelter but with water in it. And there were these ropes that you hold on to and they pull you really fast across the pool."

"Wow," Jill says. "All of that, huh?" She reaches out to touch her daughter's arm. "And you. Did you have fun?"

Aïsha shrugs. "It was OK I suppose," she says.

A wave of anger rises up in Hannah. She could almost slap Aïsha for that. They have driven a hundred miles today. They have spent almost two hundred euros. And Aïsha spent the four hours in the water park grinning like a five-year-old on Christmas morning. Her response is disingenuous to say the least. She opens her mouth to say something, but then catches Jill's eye, and Jill winks. Jill gets it, which means that it doesn't really matter. So Hannah just licks her lips and exhales instead.

"The pool here is full now," Tristan says. "The heater is on too. It's almost bearable. I reckon it'll be nice and warm by tomorrow."

Luke and Aïsha head immediately to the pool and in less than a minute can be heard splashing and shrieking again.

"She had such a good time," Hannah says. "I don't know why she can't just say so."

Cliff returns from the kitchen with two extra glasses. He sits down and slops wine into both of them. "A really good time," he confirms. "They both did. But it wasn't at all where you said it was, Tris'."

Tristan frowns. "What d'you mean? We drove past it. It's just outside Antibes."

Cliff and Hannah shake their heads in unison.

"You drove past the *sign*," Cliff explains. "It's actually just an advertisement. The park is in Fréjus – an hour up the motorway."

"God, sorry," Tristan says. "I was driving, you know? I was in traffic, so I didn't read the small print."

"It's fine," Hannah says. "The extra drive was just a bit of a surprise, that's all."

Everyone reaches for their glasses at the same time and a silence falls over the table. Hannah suspects that she's picking up a vibe. Tristan seems still to keep glancing at Jill. He looks nervous. They both do.

"So what have you two been up to?" Hannah asks, determined to pierce this particular mystery.

"Nothing," Tristan says, a little too quickly.

"Nothing," Jill repeats, and there it is again: that nervous glance between them.

"It was just a normal lazy day, wasn't it, Jill?" Tristan says.

"Yep," Jill says.

Jill never says 'Yep'.

"We just lazed around," she adds. "Nothing really happened."

"Right," Hannah says. She doesn't believe them one bit.

FOURTEEN

After dinner – a goat's cheese and artichoke salad which Tristan prepared earlier, served with fresh crispy chunks of baguette – Hannah leaves everyone at the table and starts to tidy the kitchen. Tristan is a good cook, but a messy one. But she doesn't mind; something in the atmosphere outside has been unsettling her, and she'd rather just escape it to be honest. She's too tired to spend the evening trying to decode something if no one wants to tell her.

She is stacking the dishwasher – specifically scraping the contents of Aïsha and Luke's plates into the bin – when Jill enters the room.

She crosses to the window, tosses a, "Sorry, mosquitos," to those beyond it, and closes both sides firmly. She then returns to the kitchen door and closes that too.

"I knew there was something going on," Hannah says, straightening.

"I need a word," Jill says, looking nervously beyond the window to check that everyone has remained seated.

"That sounds ominous," Hannah says. "You haven't had a row with . . ."

The kitchen door bursts open and Aïsha peers in. "Can I make some toast?" she asks.

"No," Jill says, uncharacteristically. "No you can't."

"But I'm still h—"

"You should have eaten your salad."

"It was rank," Aïsha says.

"It wasn't *rank*. It was absolutely gorgeous. As you would have found out if you had tried it instead of wrinkling your nose and pushing it around the plate."

"*Jill*," Aïsha wines. "I'm starving."

"Tristan went to a lot of trouble to make that, so, you know, just wait a bit. If you're still hungry later then I'll let you make some toast, but doing it right after dinner is just plain rude."

"Luke says he's hungry too," Aïsha says. "Anyway, it was Tristan who told me to come and make toast in the first place. Can I? Can I?"

"Oh for Christ's sake," Jill spits, grabbing Aïsha's arm and yanking her into the kitchen. "Just do what you want. You always do anyway."

She then pushes Aïsha – who looks as if she might cry – towards the toaster, and grabs Hannah's arm and pulls her *out* of the kitchen before starting to bustle her down the hallway towards the bedrooms.

"Jill," Hannah protests. "Whatever is the mat—"

Jill pushes Hannah into the blue room and then closes and locks the bedroom door behind her. She then crosses and closes the bedroom window as well – the shutters are already closed.

"Jill, you're scaring me now," Hannah says, drying her wet hands on the back of her jeans.

"Come," Jill says more softly now, sitting side-saddle on the bed and holding out both hands.

Hannah twists her mouth sideways but places her fingers in Jill's hands and sits.

"There was a phone call while you were out," Jill says.

91

"A phone call."

"Yes."

"Oh God!" Hannah says. "It's not Mister Mittens, is it?" Mister Mittens is Luke's cat. A neighbour is feeding him while they're away. Luke loves Mister Mittens more than life itself.

"No," Jill says, smiling briefly at this. "No, it's not Mister Mittens."

"Thank God for that," Hannah says. "But what then?"

"It's . . . Look . . . It was James," Jill says. "James phoned."

Hannah looks at her blankly. She doesn't know anyone called James. Or rather she doesn't know anyone *alive* called James. She wracks her brain, but no, the only James she ever knew belongs to the past, belonged, in fact, to a different century. "James?" she repeats.

"James," Jill says, nodding as if encouraging her to guess a quiz question.

Hannah mentally lists Jill's boyfriends in case she has missed one. Then she starts on Tristan's many partners. "I'm sorry, Jill," she says. "I don't know who you mean."

"God!" Jill exclaims, glancing at the ceiling for inspiration. "James!" she says again, with added panache, as if this might somehow help. "Cliff's brother."

Hannah freezes. She holds her breath and stares into her sister's eyes. She can see the reflection of the lampshade in them, two little orange squares stretched across the spherical surface of her eyes. She can sense the blood draining from her face. She shakes her head. "But that's impossible," she says. "James is dead. You know he is."

Jill grips her hands tightly and peers into her eyes. "Only he isn't, Han'," she says. "That's what I'm trying to tell you. He phoned this afternoon to get the address. He's on his way here."

92

Hannah sighs and frowns deeply, then slowly she shakes her head. "No," she says, matter-of-factly.

Jill nods, visually contradicting her.

"God, I get it. You're high, aren't you," Hannah says, starting to breathe again as the absurdity of Jill's proposition sinks in.

"I knew this was going to be hard for you," Jill says.

"Jill!" Hannah says, her voice shrill now. "It's not *hard* for me. James *died*. He had a bike accident in India years ago. You know that, I know that, we all know that."

"Only he didn't," Jill says, struggling, but failing to keep hold of Hannah's hands as she pulls them away. "I spoke to him, today."

"This is ridiculous," Hannah says. "Why are you doing this? Why are you lying to me?"

"Hannah . . ."

"Even if he were alive – which we both know he isn't – he couldn't possibly know we're down here. Is this supposed to be funny? Are you so stoned that you think this is funny?"

"He went to the house. To *your* house. Marjorie told him."

"Marjorie."

"Your neighbour."

"You see! Lies!" Hannah laughs sourly. "Marjorie doesn't even have the address. What on earth has got into you?"

"I *know*," Jill says. "That's why he *phoned*. To get the address. Marjorie gave him the number here – you must have left it with her – and he phoned and I gave him the address."

Hannah stands. "This is rubbish, Jill," she says. "I don't know what you think you're playing at, but this is bullshit. And I'm not playing."

"Hannah?" Jill says. She is still seated on the bed. "*Hannah!*"

she shouts as Hannah fumbles with the lock and then bursts from the bedroom.

Hannah collides with Cliff, who is at that second stepping out of the bathroom. "Oh!" he says, in shock, then, registering her expression he asks, "What's wrong? Whatever's happened?"

Hannah opens her mouth to reply, but nothing comes out. Cliff glances past her and sees Jill standing in the doorway. "Jill?"

Hannah shakes her head. "She's lost it, Cliff," she says. "This time, she has really lost it."

Jill is advancing nervously towards them. "Han'," she says. "Wait. Let me . . ."

"Just . . . just keep her away from me, Cliff," Hannah says. "I can't be doing with it."

Hannah pushes past Cliff and strides to the front door, out past Tristan and the kids – all gaping – then rounds the house and leans back against the wall. It's still hot from the sun, almost too hot to bear.

She stares at the shimmering water of the pool and she tries to catch her breath. Moths, attracted by the underwater lights, are fluttering against the surface of the water.

"Will you please just tell me what is going on?" – Cliff's voice. He's walking towards her looking almost angry. "Jill won't tell me."

"You shouldn't get involved in this," Hannah says. "It would just . . . it would be . . . You wouldn't . . . God. Look, there's no need for you to get involved. Just leave me alone and . . ."

"I think there's every reason for me to get involved," Cliff says. "Look at you. You're shaking. Jill's upset. You're freaking Luke out. What just happened here, Hannah?"

"It's her," Hannah says, nodding vaguely into the distance. "She's high on drugs or something."

"And this is news, because . . . ?" Cliff says.

Hannah shrugs. She wonders if she can tell Cliff what Jill has said. She tries to calculate how much hurt that might cause him. She tries to work out if there's any way to *avoid* telling him.

"Look, one minute we're having dinner and everything's fine, and the next . . ." Cliff is saying.

"I'm sorry," Hannah says. "But I suppose you'll have to know. Jill claims that James phoned."

"James," Cliff says flatly.

"Yes. She's been trying to tell me that James phoned. Here. While we were out. She reckons he's been miraculously raised from the dead and he's on his way here."

"My brother James?" Cliff says.

"Yes."

"And he's coming *here*?" Cliff exclaims, his eyes widening. "Why would he be coming here?"

Hannah shrugs. "That's what my crazy doped-up sister . . ." Her voice fades. Cliff's response has belatedly struck her. "Cliff?" she asks.

Cliff stares back at her. He looks anxious. He looks like a rabbit in the headlights.

"Oh, *Cliff*! Oh God, no."

"I . . ." Cliff says.

"You . . . you know, don't you?" Hannah says.

"I . . ." he says again.

"Jesus Christ!" Hannah says, feeling faint now. "He isn't dead at all, is he?"

"I . . . I'm sorry," Cliff says, reaching out to touch her arm.

Hannah uses her right hand to push him away, and her left to cover her mouth. "Oh, Cliff," she says. "Oh, how could you?"

Cliff only approaches Hannah one more time that evening. She is lying in the hammock with a blanket, staring at the night sky. He approaches and says, "Hannah, we need to . . ."

"Stay away from me, Cliff!" she says. It came out too loudly, and the whole household probably heard. But she doesn't care. It will keep them away.

And she needs them to stay away. She needs the time and space to remember, time and space to rewrite the narrative of fifteen years of married life.

FIFTEEN

James

James meant nothing to me to start with. He was Cliff's younger brother. That was it. It was the fifteenth of June, and it was raining.

I was three months pregnant, a pregnancy that was neither planned, nor a shock, nor even much of a surprise: though we hadn't been trying to have a child, we hadn't been trying very hard not to have one either. We both wanted kids. It was fine.

It had been raining for days, endlessly, relentlessly. It was so dark outside that I had the lights on. I remember thinking that if one more person said, "I hope it clears up by next Saturday," I would scream. No one wants to get married in the rain. Well, maybe someone somewhere in Africa does, but we certainly didn't.

Everything was ready. We're both good organisers and we were back then too. There was no real stress to focus on other than the weather, which I suppose is why everyone kept banging on about it. Neither Cliff nor I were religious so it was to be a simple registry office service, and neither were we flamboyant, so the reception we had booked was a simple catered affair in a country pub. We had been living together for two years by then anyway and Cliff's mother, our only remaining parent, had died the year before – there was no point making a fuss.

Was I disappointed already by the lack of lustre? Perhaps, a little.

There had been a time, just a few years earlier, when I had wobbled on a knife-edge between gothic flamboyancy and being ordinary. It really could have gone either way.

At the beginning of my fling with Ben I had fantasised about marrying him, and that fantasy had involved Blur playing a concert at our wedding (Ben claimed to know Graham Coxon, the guitarist, though I never saw any proof of that while I was dating him), and inevitably a Harley Davidson to whisk us away to our honeymoon (Ben was a biker).

It's not that this image matched who I was any more than the cliché of becoming a Surrey housewife did; it's just that I was young – I was still a blank canvas ready to take whatever life wanted to throw at me.

When Ben's ego turned out to be impossible to live with, Cliff's calm middle-England approach seemed like the obvious alternative.

So it was raining. Hard. Cliff was upstairs painting a bedroom in neutral green (we didn't know what sex the baby was yet) and I was watching the TV and listening out for James' arrival. He had just finished a degree course in Edinburgh and was driving down with a carload of stuff. I had spent half the week clearing enough storage space in our shed so that James could stack his things there whilst he went travelling. I had fixed up the spare room for him as well. As I say, we were both good organisers.

I had met James only once before, in a London pub. He had been drunk and loud, and I had been bored – it was my turn to drive. We said hello, gave him his birthday gift – a camera, I think – and James vanished to the bar for a round of drinks. He took so long that by the time he came back I had convinced Cliff to leave. It didn't take much – they had never been close.

So I had met James already and I had found him unremarkable; there was no sense of expectation that Saturday in June. I was more concerned about what was on the television. A bomb had gone off in the centre of Manchester. A big one.

Cliff appeared in the doorway.

"You've got paint on your nose," I told him.

He dabbed at it with a finger. "Oh yeah," he said, then, "Still no sign of Wonder Boy then?"

I shook my head, then nodded at the images of carnage on the television screen. "They say hundreds of people have been injured. And at least two deaths."

"The IRA?"

"They don't know yet."

"But it probably is."

"Yes, that's what they think. There's no reason James would stop off in Manchester is there?"

Cliff shook his head. "No. His car's full of stuff. He'll drive straight down. I suppose I might as well go start the skirting boards then."

"OK," I said, waving at him mockingly and turning back to the television. I didn't feel guilty. I had spent three days sanding the buggers down and had been officially exempted from painting because the fumes made me retch.

A car pulled up outside, and I tore my eyes away from the screen to check that it wasn't James. It was one of those big four-by-fours – everyone seemed to be getting them back then. A woman and kids got out – they all had matching umbrellas. Funny the things you remember. I wondered if they would move on before James arrived. It would make it easier to carry his stuff in if he could park outside, I reckoned. But that's as much thought as I gave it. He was just Cliff's younger brother, after all.

John Major came on the television talking about terrorism and I think I turned the sound off. I had never liked John Major. There was always something about his sweaty top lip that made me feel a bit queasy.

By two o'clock there were four people dead in Manchester and James still hadn't arrived. We needed bread for lunch, so I shouted up to Cliff that I was nipping out.

"Get white spirit if they have any," he said.

I opened my own umbrella and headed up to the Spar, where I bought bread and some extra cheddar (they didn't have any DIY materials) before heading home. 'The Day Before You Came' was playing in the shop, and I had it stuck in my head as I walked home. A premonition almost.

When I got to our house a faded orange Volvo estate had replaced the four-by-four. The windows were all steamed up.

As I reached the car, the passenger window opened and James' face appeared, peering up at me. "Can you tell me which house number twenty-two is?" he asked.

"James!" I said.

"Hannah! God, sorry!" James laughed. "Get in!"

"Get in?"

"Yes." He leaned across and part-opened the door.

"Don't be silly," I said, opening it just wide enough to look inside. "Come indoors."

"I will," James said. "But get in first. I want to ask you something."

I folded the umbrella and climbed into the car. The rain was drumming so hard on the roof you had to talk loudly just to make yourself heard. "Why are you sitting out here?" I asked, turning myself as far in the seat as I could.

"I only just parked," he told me. His eyes were the most astounding blue, the exact same blue as his T-shirt. In the dark interior of the pub where I had met him previously, I hadn't noticed. Cliff's are green.

"I just wanted to check with you," he said, "you know, honestly."

"Yes?"

"Are you OK about all of this? About me staying? About me leaving all this shit at your place?" He gestured over his shoulder, and I glanced behind at the mixture of boxes and bin-bags and tatty furnishings.

"Of course," I said. "You must have spoken to Cliff about it."

James smiled at me, and as he did so, he reached across and touched, ever so lightly, my shoulder. I was fully clothed; I was wearing a mac – there was nothing intimate about the gesture. "Oh, you know what Cliff's like," he said. "He always says the right thing, always *does* the right thing. But you never know what he's really thinking, do you?"

"No," I said. It was so true. And it was something I had realised subconsciously but had never really thought about until now.

Because it seemed disingenuous somehow to gang up on him I simply said, "Yes, anyway, as far as I know he's absolutely fine about it. We've been looking forward to you coming all week."

"Have you?" James asked. He was peering into my eyes, a strange air of concern upon his brow, as if it were suddenly terribly important that this were true.

"Yes," I said, unexpectedly flustered. "Now let's get inside. It's crazy sitting out here."

"Sure," James said. "You go in. I'll be there in a second."

When I got indoors, I hung up my mac. I stared at the wall for a second, then snapped myself out of it and shouted up to Cliff, "James is here, he's just parking."

"I'll be down in a minute," Cliff called back. "I just have to finish this stretch."

I went into the lounge and crossed my arms and watched the Volvo and waited for James to reappear. And I wondered why my heart was pounding so.

SIXTEEN

London – 19th June 1996

Dear H.

Just a note to wish you the best on your wedding day.

As you know(!) I'm unable to be there, but I hope it is wonderful and that everything turns out just the way you want and all your wishes come true.

I'm so sorry about the precipitous departure, but, needs must . . .

For my part, I have postponed my departure for Thailand. I have been feeling pretty shaken up since I left last Tuesday, and there would simply be no point traveling when I feel this miserable.

Plus, I keep hoping you'll appear outside my door (my address is above) though of course, I know that you won't (will you?).

I can't seem to get you out of my mind, but I expect that's because I don't yet want to.

Anyway, I hope you are happy, and that Cliff is well. I hope above all that he realises just what a lucky bloke he is. Forgive me for everything.

J.

SEVENTEEN

"Are you OK?"

Hannah rolls her head to see Jill crouching at her side. She barely remembers moving from the hammock to the sofa.

She stares at her sister, only now realising that she has been asleep, that she had finally fallen asleep.

"I've been worried about you," Jill says. "Are you OK?"

'OK.' The two letters sound alien and strange, the way any word can if you think about it long enough. OK. Is she OK?

She doesn't know what time it is, but it's barely light, and she has barely slept. She has lain awake half the night thinking about the same things over and over and over again. That James isn't dead. That her husband has been lying to her for fifteen years. That she perhaps didn't have to choose the life she chose at all. That she didn't actually choose this life either, that it just happened, because it seemed, because of the lie, that there was no choice. But James isn't dead. James is alive. James is on his way here.

"Hannah," Jill says. "How are you feeling?"

She feels excited. Which is absurd, ridiculous even. Would it be shameful to admit that? "I'm fine," she says. "I'm just tired. And shocked."

"I've hardly slept," Jill says. "I've been so worried I did the wrong thing."

Hannah frowns as she tries to drag herself from her own

thoughts enough to be able to converse with her sister. "Why, what did you do?" she asks.

Jill looks confused. "Well, I was the one who gave him the address," she says. "I told him to come."

"You told him to come?"

"No . . . No, I didn't *tell* him to come. But I didn't tell him he couldn't come either, did I?" Jill says.

Hannah nods. Given the scope of the drama in which they are all embroiled, giving James the address is pretty insignificant in the scheme of things.

"He just seemed so nice," Jill says, taking Hannah's silence as reproach and trying to justify herself. "He sounded really rounded and friendly. He has a really lovely voice. But then I always think Aussie accents sound lovely."

Hannah moves to a sitting position and runs a hand across her face. "God. You're an outrage, Jill," she says.

Jill stands and then moves to sit next to her sister. "Oh, that came out wrong," she says as she slides one arm around Hannah's shoulders. "I thought you'd want to see him, too."

"Too?" Hannah repeats.

"I thought you'd want to see him," Jill says. "That's why I gave him the address. I mean, he asked for it. So I had to choose. And he sounded nice."

"Yes," Hannah says. "You said."

"But imagine if I hadn't. Imagine if I hadn't and he never phoned again," Jill says. "I didn't think about the effect it would have on Cliff, I admit. But I knew you'd want to see him again. You do, don't you?"

Hannah flops her head onto her sister's shoulder. She knows the way Jill's mind works, and she is almost certain that Jill didn't think about her at all. A nice-sounding guy phoned and offered to add extra spice to Jill's holiday. That's the only thought that Jill will have had. But there's enough drama in this situation without falling out with her sister on top of everything else.

"So did Cliff think he was dead?" Jill asks. "That's what I can't work out. Or was that a—"

"A lie," Hannah says. "Yes, it was a big, bold, fifteen-year lie."

"God," Jill says. "But why would he do that?"

"Jealousy, I think," Hannah says. "I guess he thought I hadn't forgotten James."

"But you hadn't, had you?"

"No," Hannah admits. "No, I never forgot James. When is he coming? When's he arriving?"

Hannah feels Jill shrug beside her. "He didn't say," she says. "In a couple of days, I think. That's what it sounded like. He said he was going to look at flights and cars and things."

"So it's not definite?"

"I think it was. He sounded pretty sure."

Hannah nods, sits up straight again and tries to force one complete breath of air into her lungs. They feel as if they are compressed, as if she has a weight compressing her chest that won't let her breathe. "Don't tell Tristan or Aïsha, will you?" she asks.

Jill doesn't answer, so Hannah turns to look at her.

"Tris' already knows," Jill says. "He was here when James called, so . . ."

"I know," Hannah says, blinking slowly. "That's fine. I mean just don't tell him the back story. That stuff is private."

Jill licks her lips.

"Oh, Jill!" Hannah says.

"I'm sorry," Jill says. Her sister suddenly reminds her of their mother. When disappointed she had exactly the same expression. "I was stoned, Han'," she says. "You know what I'm like when I'm stoned. I can't keep anything secret."

Hannah shrugs Jill's arm from her shoulder. "You're . . . Honestly . . . You're impossible."

"Look, I'm sorry," Jill says.

"Sure," Hannah says. "Anyway, just, you know . . . don't tell Aïsha. I don't want her filling Luke with a load of confused ideas, OK?"

"OK," Jill says.

Hannah dozes on until the rest of the house starts to awaken, then folds and stores the blanket. She doesn't want Luke to realise that she has slept here.

Breakfast is negotiated through forced smiles – a sterling rendition of normality. But once everyone has eaten, Cliff says, "Can you kids clear the breakfast stuff away? Hannah and I want to go for a stroll together."

"Do we?" Hannah asks.

"Yes," Cliff says flatly. "Yes, we do."

Jill nods encouragingly at her, and reckoning that she is too tired to judge what is best, Hannah capitulates.

Once she has showered and changed her clothes, she goes in search of Cliff, finally finding him sitting in the car listening to classical music. "You can play that in the house you know," she says, as she opens the door.

"I know," Cliff replies. "I just needed the space."

Once they have closed the gate behind them Cliff reaches for Hannah's hand.

She snatches it away, unable to believe that he is able to

misread her mood so severely. "I don't think so, Cliff," is all she says.

They walk for a few minutes in silence, each lost in their own thoughts.

"It's a lot less scary by day," Cliff eventually comments.

"Yes. Look. Why are we out here?" Hannah asks, her tone terse. The last thing she feels like is a summer stroll. "If you have something to say to me, please just get on and say it."

"I'm sorry," Cliff says.

"It's fine, but just, you know, whatever you want to say . . ."

"No. I meant, that's what I wanted to say," Cliff says. "I'm sorry."

"Oh, right."

They walk on for another minute before Cliff says, "So are we OK then?"

Hannah exhales sharply, a barely contained snort of derision. "You're joking, right?" she says.

"I . . . I don't really know what else to say."

"You lied to me for fifteen years," Hannah spits. "Or have I got that wrong?"

"Well, yes. I mean no. No, you haven't."

"So, sorry doesn't really cover it, does it?"

"No," Cliff says. "No, I suppose not."

Hannah stops walking and turns to face her husband. "How could you, Cliff?" she says. "How could you? He's your brother. Can't you see how . . . disturbed . . . that is?" Disturbed isn't really the right word, but she can't think of a better one.

Cliff shrugs. "I thought it was better," he says.

"Better? To pretend that your brother is dead?"

"I thought it was better for *us*," Cliff says. He drops his regard to the ground and kicks at a stone. "I thought it was better for you, for me, for Luke."

Hannah gasps. "Don't you dare try to make this about Luke," she says. "Luke wasn't even born when this started. This is *me* you're talking to. I remember. I remember everything. It was years before Luke was born."

"I'm not . . . I wasn't . . . I just get confused with the dates," Cliff stammers. "Really I do."

"The letter arrived the summer we got back from Scotland," Hannah says. "Which was . . . God!" A wave of shock washes over her. Because beyond the lie itself are the constituent acts of deceit. Layer upon layer of lies required to maintain that first fictional creation. "That letter . . ." she says. "The letter about James' accident. You wrote it yourself. It was a fake."

Cliff chews at the inside of his mouth, then swallows and nods dolefully. "I'm sorry, Hannah," he says. "I didn't know what else to do."

A car, one of those new Beetles, rounds the corner heading towards them, and they are forced to separate momentarily to let it pass. At the last minute, Hannah glances in to see who the driver is. Her heart flutters strangely when she sees that it is not James (would she even recognise him now?) but a woman.

The car past, they begin to walk again.

"I know you're angry," Cliff says, "but . . ."

"Angry?" Hannah laughs derisively.

"But I'm not the only one who . . . I mean, it's not all . . ." Cliff coughs. "Look, what I'm saying is that this isn't only about me," he finally manages.

"But to say he was *dead*," Hannah says.

"I didn't think we'd ever get over it. That was the thing.

I didn't think we would ever be able to forget what had happened. Not unless you could forget about James."

"So you killed him," Hannah says.

"I didn't actually . . ."

"Well, clearly not! On paper, I mean. You killed him on paper."

"I knew he wasn't coming back anyway. So . . ."

"How?" Hannah asks. "How could you possibly know that?"

Cliff licks his lips, opens his mouth to speak, but then closes it again and turns away.

"Oh Jesus," Hannah says, pulling a pained expression. "He's been in contact then? Of course he has."

"Yes, he wrote," Cliff admits. "Just a postcard. To say that he was taking Australian nationality."

"Australian?" Hannah says, her mind's eye attempting to fill in all the missing years with the collage of random images she has seen of Australia. "Of course, Jill said that, yes."

"Jill said what?"

"That he has an accent, an Australian accent."

They reach the bend in the road which was so terrifying in the dark last night. "There is a street lamp," Cliff says pointing. "It must just not work."

"Yes," Hannah says. "Yes, there is. They need to fix it."

When they reach the apex of the bend, it seems obvious to both of them that this is the right point to turn back, so without having to discuss it, they do so.

Cliff's mind is occupied performing a cost–benefit analysis, wondering how many of these dissimulations he should now own up to. He's wondering if James will help him out, whether he can get to him first and ask him to keep at least part of this story under wraps. He hardly has any reason to. He owes Cliff nothing. But perhaps he'll do it for them. Perhaps he'll do it for Hannah.

Hannah is realising that, in his own twisted way, Cliff is right. That James' "death" did mark the point when she gave up imagining parallel lives, did mark the point when she gave in, did, indeed, mark the moment in time when she abandoned herself to a certain kind of happiness – a rather ordinary, passion-less contentment, but a certain kind of happiness all the same.

"Australia," she says again, that single word somehow encapsulating the one thing that she had always sensed. That James' life would be exciting.

"I loved you. I *still* love you, Hannah," Cliff says. "And I didn't want to lose you. You do understand that, don't you? You do get why I had to . . . ?"

Rather absurdly, a song pops into Hannah's head. It's 'If you love somebody, set them free'.

"I couldn't let James just steal you from me," Cliff says.

"Yes," she says. "Yes, I see your logic." It's the best she can manage.

Lunch passes in an ambiance of uneasy truce. Hannah's and Cliff's acting isn't fooling anyone, of course, but they have had arguments before and they know how to do this – no one gets to be married for thirteen years without getting good at playing happy families in front of the kids.

So though everyone, including Luke, can tell that something's not right, everyone is reassured that they're at least behaving in a known, if incomprehensible, manner.

By the time they have finished lunch – prawn and jerusalem

artichoke salad with rice-and-tuna-stuffed peppers – the pool, now in full sunshine, has reached twenty-six degrees. As the day is the hottest yet, the pool becomes the centre of attention, pulling not only Luke and Aïsha from the front of the house, but Tristan and Jill too. This leaves enough room for Hannah and Cliff to perfectly avoid each other.

Hannah nabs the hammock before the table has even been cleared. It's the one place in the garden where – unless you're prepared to share the hammock itself, which she isn't – no one is likely to disturb you.

Cliff is on the far side of the porch pretending to read his novel. He can't concentrate. His eyes keep skimming the page, and after a few failed attempts at starting a new chapter he gives in and does the same thing as Hannah. He remembers the past.

EIGHTEEN

James II

I didn't speak much over lunch. I made cheddar sandwiches and mugs of tea and watched my paint-splattered husband struggle to be civil to his brother. I watched the two men interact and tried to work out what it was about James that annoyed Cliff so. And what it was about him that I found so appealing.

He was very quick-witted. That is the first thing that anyone would have noticed about James. He was daft and silly but fast enough to run semantic circles around most people, including Cliff.

That's not to say that Cliff is, or was, stupid – far from it. But intelligence takes many forms, and Cliff simply never had the fast-footed sarcasm that James so excelled at. In a bear-baiting kind of way it was pretty entertaining to watch.

Because there appeared to be a lull in the rain, and because we were all a little stir-crazy – Cliff and I from being trapped indoors, and James due to the drive from Edinburgh – we decided to go for a walk. Cliff drove us to Puttenham and we walked to Hog's Back. It was cool and misty, but lovely to be outside again.

The rain didn't start again until we were on the ridge, at the farthest point from the car.

As Cliff was wearing his walking anorak, he was the only

person with a hood. And so it was that James and I were forced to huddle underneath my umbrella.

The drizzle soon turned to rain proper, and so as Cliff strode ahead – he had generously volunteered to bring the car as close as possible – James and I sheltered ourselves beneath a tree and then, as the rain intensified, underneath my umbrella, beneath the tree. When it became clear that the rain wasn't going to fade, that it was, in fact, getting worse, we relaunched ourselves into the downpour.

In the interests of reducing our exposure at the edges of the umbrella, James and I linked arms, and then as the downpour intensified we started to run, and James started to laugh.

I remember intentionally splashing through a puddle – we were so wet it didn't seem to make much difference – and as we ran, James turned to glance at me. His face was shiny from the rain, but lit up with mirth – glowing with joy. It was fun; I couldn't help but laugh too, and it struck me that it had been a while since I had laughed like that. I was only twenty-three but already it had been a while since I had felt that light-footed, that carefree. And that was the first time I wanted to kiss him, the first time that desire had crossed my mind.

By the time we got home, reason had prevailed, and I was steering well clear. I didn't know quite what these feelings were, but I sensed that they were dangerous. And so I stayed as far from James as I could, busying myself with as many unlikely tasks as possible to avoid having to share the sofa with him. Cliff, as ever, had taken the armchair.

On Sunday I launched myself, with exceptional enthusiasm, at the task of producing a full Sunday roast. The idea was to be busy. The idea was, again, to stay out of James' way.

Cliff decided to apply a second coat of gloss paint upstairs, and James volunteered to help me peel the potatoes for lunch so we ended up in the kitchen together. I was hyper aware the whole time, of his body there beside me, of his arm occasionally brushing against me as we worked at the sink. And though I tried to be stern and unamused, I couldn't help it. James knew how to make me laugh, and he took relish in doing so.

I can't remember the exact conversations, but I remember he regaled me with funny, self-deprecating stories of student life. I had been a student too, of course, but I had been living at home. I had been living at home with Jill – who was already a handful – and our sick father: my college years had been far from effervescent.

James, on the other hand, had spent four years in a shared house in Edinburgh. He had taken drugs and gone to rave parties and had protested against the poll tax. There really was no comparison. Even then I could see how exciting he was, how much *more* exciting he was. James was like my ex-boyfriend Ben, only without the crazed ego. It was a combination I hadn't known could exist.

"You two are having fun." It was Cliff, standing in the doorway. His tone was condescending, and like naughty schoolchildren who had been caught out, we did our best to wipe the smirks from our faces.

Once Cliff had finished washing his brushes and left the kitchen we looked at each other. James pulled a face and said, in a silly, stern, mocking voice, "You two seem to be having fun," and we both cracked up laughing all over again. Cooking Sunday lunch had never been so much fun.

NINETEEN

Bombay – 10th December 1999

Dear H.

I'm sorry I haven't written for so long. I mentioned you yesterday to my new friend and confidant Suga. He thought me literally wicked for not writing, so here we are: I'm writing.

How are you? How is your kid? What did you have, a boy or a girl?

I have been living in this weird country for nearly two years now. I think I was wanting to lose myself somewhere. India seemed perfect. It is full of lost hippies, lost businessmen, just about every European you meet seems somehow lost here.

I am living in a very strange little cottage which used to be the guard house to a rich Englishman's estate way back. Now it is an out of place, draughty cottage surrounded by half finished concrete hi-rises.

I am working as a satellite dish installer. Whoever would have thought it? In India!

This is an amazing country, so many people, so many extremes. The streets are teeming with the poor and the rich. The strange thing in India is that the poor are mostly happy whilst the rich seem mostly unhappy – a strange state of affairs. Suga, my very close friend here, who is part-time teacher, part-time philosopher, considers this to be perfectly normal. In fact he doesn't believe my view that in England the rich are happier than the poor. I wonder if it is true after all.

Bombay is a very shocking place. Even after all this time, I see at least one sight a day which takes my breath away. The colours, the people, the mix of religions and cultures, the smells and the tastes, it's really quite indescribable.

I work most days, installing these satellite dishes on schools and community centres and banks so that all of the categories of people who go to these places can see images, beamed in from space, of other parts of the world which mean nothing to them.

In the evenings Suga and I sit beneath the stars and play chess, and sometimes as we play he tells me about some philosophy or religion he's been reading about. Last night it was Taoism, which apparently comes from China. The only thing I understood about it was that it was unexplainable, like India perhaps.

Sometimes, now, as I talk to Suga, as I tell him about my adventures they seem like different lives, unrelated to each other. I think, am I the same person who grew up with Cliff in Reading? Do you really exist or did I just read about you in a book somewhere? I sometimes wonder.

God I wish you were here to see all this.
HAPPY CHRISTMAS!
J.

TWENTY

That night Hannah returns to the bedroom. She waits until she thinks Cliff is asleep before she does this, and Cliff obliges by fabricating vague snoring noises. Though he has never heard himself sleep he's surprisingly accurate – accurate enough, in fact, to fool Hannah.

Hannah herself lies awake again. She can't sleep either. She needs to sleep but her mind won't stop churning. She can't stop wondering when James will come, *if* James will come, what will happen if he does, how she will feel seeing him again. It's utterly ridiculous to be this upset, this obsessive, this *excited* about someone she last saw when she was twenty-three. Isn't it?

She glances at the clock. It's almost half-past one and still sleep evades her. She's not sure she can cope with another sleepless night. She's a wreck as it is. She should have asked Jill for a sleeping pill. Jill always has sleeping pills.

Hannah slides silently from the bed and creeps through the sleeping house to the bathroom. She rummages in Jill's wash-bag and finds a pack of Introvate – which she knows are birth control pills – and a blister pack of Triazolam, which for some reason sounds like a sleeping tablet. But she isn't sure, and she doesn't know the dosage, so she decides to wake Jill. She'll forgive her, just this once.

Her hand barely caresses the handle to Jill's room before

she snatches it back. Beyond the door she can hear voices. She stands there a moment in silence. It doesn't sound so much like conversation in fact. It sounds more like two people making out.

In shock, she heads back to the kitchen where, with a fatalistic shrug, she downs one of the pills with a glass of water.

She sits at the small kitchen table until she starts to feel drowsy – that special kind of heavy-headedness washing over her in waves – and then reassured that it was, indeed, a sleeping pill, she makes her way back to bed.

She is just drifting off when a voice says, "He wouldn't have been any good for you, you know." The voice sounds like Cliff, but at the same time not-like-Cliff. Hannah wonders if she is dreaming.

"No?" she asks, unsure if she is talking to Cliff or her own subconscious or perhaps some angel of truth.

"James was always all sparkle and no substance," the voice says.

Hannah forces her drugged head to turn so that she can look at Cliff. He has his back turned to her. His breath sounds slow and steady. There is nothing to demonstrate that he is awake.

It's gone ten by the time Hannah wakes up from her drug-induced slumber, and it's gone eleven by the time she manages to roll from the bed.

There is no one on the patio, so she pours a cold cup of coffee from the pot (breakfast things still strewn across the table, wasps buzzing around the empty orange-juice carton) and then walks, intrigued by the silence, to the corner of the house.

Tristan and Jill are sunbathing on towels next to the pool. Cliff is reading in a pink deckchair she has never seen before with his back to her and Luke is draped sideways over an air-bed with his head underwater. Were it not for the hollow rasp of his breathing through the snorkel, one could think that he had drowned.

"Where's Aïsha?" Hannah asks, and Luke surfaces with a splash, Tristan looks up at her, Jill props herself up on her elbows, and Cliff leans around the side of his deckchair and slips off his sunglasses. It's as if a pause button has been released.

"Morning, drug thief," Jill says.

"Sorry, Jill. I just really needed to sleep. You know how it is sometimes."

"Yes, I guessed," Jill says. "I found the packet in the kitchen. Did you take a whole one? They're really strong, those are."

Hannah nods. "Yes," she says. "I noticed. You don't mind, do you?"

Jill blinks, pushes her lips out, and shakes her head.

"Can I make you some breakfast?" Cliff asks.

"No," Hannah says. "No, I'm fine. So where *is* Aïsha?"

"She went down to the river," Jill says.

"On her own?"

Jill shrugs. "Apparently so."

"And is that OK?" Hannah asks.

Jill shrugs again. "Apparently so," she says. "She is thirteen, Han'."

At the sound of a car coming along the track, everyone pauses. Hannah, the only person in a position to see, turns to watch as a yellow postal van comes into view beyond the gate.

"Just the post," she says, realising as she returns her attention to the others, that she sounded disappointed.

"S'il vous plaît?"

Hannah looks back to see the post-lady leaning over the gate waving a letter. "Tris', can you come talk to her?" she asks. "I can't . . . you know . . . speak the lingo."

"Sure," Tristan says, jumping up.

Hannah returns to the patio, where she swipes at wasps and picks at the breakfast leftovers. The shock of James' potential visit is in danger of ruining her whole holiday, she realises. It's in the process, in fact, of ruining *everybody's* holiday. She needs to get a grip. "*If he comes, he'll come,*" she murmurs. "*If he doesn't, he doesn't.*"

She looks up to see Tristan standing on the far side of the table, waving an envelope, and realises, with embarrassment, that he has heard her talking to herself. She nods at the letter, a mimed question mark.

"Recorded delivery. I signed for it," Tristan says.

Hannah sits up straight. Maybe James has written. She didn't even think of that possibility. "Is it from . . . ? I mean, who's it for?" she asks.

"A Monsieur Hoff," Tristan says.

"Oh. That's the owner," Hannah says, slumping back into her chair.

"That's what I thought; I'll just . . ." Tristan steps inside the doorway and then returns. "I just left it on the table next to the phone," he says with a shrug.

Hannah nods.

"Are you OK?" he asks, sliding into a seat opposite her.

Hannah laughs sourly.

"I'll take that as a 'no' then."

Hannah gestures vaguely with her open hand. "Look, I'm fine, Tris'," she says. "I just need to pull myself together."

"You must try to have a good holiday all the same," Tristan says. "I know it's difficult, but . . ."

What do you know? Hannah thinks, and as if to answer that thought, Tristan continues, "Jill told me, you know . . . a bit about what happened."

Hannah takes a deep breath and blinks slowly. "Yes, I know she did," she says.

"I had a thing a bit like that once," Tristan says.

"A thing?"

Tristan glances over his shoulder to check that they are alone before continuing, "A guy I was in love with. From way back," he says. "Tom. He became a real obsession. I bumped into him in the gym. In Bath of all places. It was such a shock."

Hannah nods. Her brain is a little sozzled still from the drug. She can't for the life of her work out what this has to do with her and James.

"I had really, you know, idealised him over the years," Tristan continues. "But he was pretty ordinary when it came to it. It was quite a disappointment."

Hannah frowns. "I don't really . . ." she says.

"I guess I just mean, you know, don't get your hopes up," Tristan says. "He may not be as much as you remember. It may not be such a big deal after all."

Hannah laughs unconvincingly. "I don't know what Jill told you," she says, "but I was never in love with James."

"Oh," says Tristan. "Oh, sorry . . . I must have got the wrong end of the stick."

"It's OK," Hannah says. "Now, if you'll excuse me, I really need to shower if I'm ever going to wake up properly."

She collects fresh clothes from the bedroom and takes a long, hot shower. The water pressure in the villa is amazing and by the time she has finished, the bathroom is full of steam and she feels as if she has taken a sauna – she feels revitalised. She feels ready to pick up the holiday where she left off.

She opens the tiny bathroom window to let out the steam and as she does so she hears a snatch of conversation between Luke and Aïsha who are walking around the back of the house.

". . . being so weird?" Luke is saying.

"It's 'cos of that James bloke," Aïsha replies.

"I know," Luke says, "but so what?"

"Everyone thought he was dead," Aïsha says, "only he ain't. And he's, like, your mum's old boyfriend. And he's your uncle. I s'pose he might even be your dad."

Trailer trash, Hannah thinks. She makes us sound like trailer trash. She clasps one hand over her mouth and stands on tip-toe to better hear Luke's reply.

Thankfully, Luke just laughs. "Don't be stupid," he says. "Dad's my dad. So are we going to the river then?"

Once she has dressed, Hannah heads back outside and returns to the corner of the house. With the exception of Luke – who is presumably at the river with Aïsha – the configuration is exactly as before.

Hannah waves to get Jill's attention, but it is Tristan who spots her and sits up, so she points at Jill beside him and beckons.

"Jill," Tristan says quietly, nudging his neighbour gently.

Jill lifts her sunglasses and sits up. "Yes?" she says, causing Cliff to turn and peer back at her as well.

"Is everything OK?" Cliff asks.

"Fine," Hannah says. "I just need Jill for a minute."

Jill yawns, stretches and then stands. "Oh dear," she asks jokingly as she crosses the lawn. "What have I done now?"

Once they have reached the patio, Hannah leans back against the wall of the house. "It's about Aïsha," she says.

"It's a tiny river," Jill says, misunderstanding the reason that Hannah has summoned her. "It's about three feet deep. They're perfectly safe."

"Oh. Good," Hannah says. "Look, I need to know what you've told Aïsha."

"Oh," Jill says, pulling a face. "Why, what has she said?"

"Nothing to me. But I overheard her talking to Luke. She was telling him that James is my old boyfriend."

"Oh God," Jill says. "God, I'm sorry, Han', I told her not to say anything. I specifically said . . ."

"You shouldn't have told her, Jill," Hannah says. Her voice sounds a little more edgy than she intends it to be, a little more quivery. She clears her throat before continuing. "I specifically asked you not to say anything."

Jill sighs and gently grasps her sister's elbow. "I already had. When he phoned. That's the thing. So I just told her to keep her mouth shut. I didn't think . . ."

"She told Luke that James might be his father as well," Hannah says. "I mean, honestly!"

"No! Really?"

"That didn't come from you, did it?"

Jill shakes her head sharply. "Of course not," she says. "He isn't though, is he?"

Hannah cups her hands across her nose, closes her eyes and murmurs, "Oh God!" before continuing, "Of course he isn't! How could he be? For Christ's sake."

Jill shrugs. "I don't know," she says. "Stranger things have happened."

"Luke was born two years after James . . . after James *supposedly* died," Hannah says.

"Right," Jill says. "Of course. Sorry. So what? Shall I have another word with her?"

Hannah shakes her head slowly. "I don't know," she says. "I mean, I don't want Luke thinking that James is my ex, but . . ."

"Even though he kind of is," Jill says.

Hannah rolls her eyes skywards. "For God's sake, Jill. It's bad enough as it is, without everyone embroidering the situation."

"But you two did . . . you know . . . Didn't you?"

"No. We didn't. We didn't do anything. I just . . . I just had a crush on the guy I suppose. That's all it was. That's all that happened."

"Oh, I assumed, you know . . . What with all the fuss and everything."

Hannah sighs deeply.

"Hey, it's not my fault if you don't tell me anything," Jill says, relaxing her grip on Hannah's elbow and gently stroking her arm instead.

"There wasn't anything *to* tell," Hannah says. "Anyway, isn't there something *you* want to tell *me*?"

Jill shrugs, all innocence.

"I came to your room last night," Hannah says. "You had someone in there with you."

"Oh," Jill says. "That."

"Yes, that."

"It was just Pascal."

"Pascal."

"Yes."

"Pascal being . . . ? The pool guy?"

Jill licks her lips and attempts to restrain a smirk. She nods and flashes the whites of her eyes at her sister. "He is such a good shag, Han', you have no idea."

"That's outrageous," Hannah says.

"Why?" Jill laughs. "I'm single. I'm on holiday. What's so outrageous about it?"

"But . . ." Hannah shrugs. "I don't know. You can't even talk to each other, can you?"

Jill snorts – a genuine out-loud laugh. "You're so funny, Hannah," she says.

"Why? Why am I funny?"

"Well, I don't *want* to *talk* to him."

"Jill! Jesus!"

Jill looks so pleased with herself, Hannah becomes confused about whether she herself should feel angry or amused. "Anyway, how did you even *book* your midnight rendezvous? Was it when you were over there? When you had coffee with his mother?"

"We pointed at the clock," Jill says, as if this is evident. "And his mother wasn't *really* there. You realised that, right?"

Hannah looks confused. "Well, no; no, I didn't."

"The mother was a decoy. I just didn't want to announce it front of everyone," Jill says. "Even I like to keep some mystery."

"You didn't want to announce what?"

"Well, that I'd had a quick shag against the wall of the shed," Jill says. "It doesn't sound very classy, does it? Even I know that. I do have some standards, Han'."

"Of course you do. The highest standards."

"So again. Do you want me to talk to Aïsha about the James business or not?"

Hannah tips her head back and rubs the back of her head against the cool stone of the wall. "No," she says. "No, I don't think so. Luke seemed to just laugh it off. I'd rather let sleeping dogs lie. And anyway, there's nothing really to tell. But if he says anything . . ."

"Sure," Jill says. "If he says anything, I'll let you know."

TWENTY-ONE

James III

On the Monday, Cliff had to work. I was still trying to avoid James, not out of any logical thought process, but from an instinctive feeling that he was dangerous. I was pregnant with Cliff's child after all. Perhaps the mother in me felt threatened, perhaps even the baby did.

To avoid James, I told him that I had shopping to do, errands to run. I needed some food from Waitrose, and I had to pick up Cliff's suit from Moss Brothers and my dress from the seamstress. It was a plain little white dress but expensive and hand-made for the simple reason that I hadn't been able to find anything straight-forward enough for my tastes anywhere else.

The rain had stopped and James declared himself in need of exercise, so my escape plan failed miserably. We would end up spending most of the day side-by-side.

On the way into town we stopped at Costa and had toasted tea-cakes and mugs of frothy cappuccino. I remember that because James aped around by putting a blob of froth on his nose and going up to the counter to ask for sugar. He wanted to see if the barista would tell him about his nose – she didn't say a word.

In Waitrose he continued his one-man show by hiding behind the bread-shelf I was looking at and hanging onto the other side of the loaf I selected. It will all sound a bit childish now, I suppose, but it wasn't. It was charming and funny. We were still so young I suppose.

And then we went to the dress shop . . .

The assistant assumed that he was my fiancé and James played along magnificently. When I stepped out of the changing rooms, James clapped his hands and said, "Wow! Stunning," and I sensed from his regard that it was true, and felt good about myself.

The woman smiled at me and nodded her approval, then said to James, "You shouldn't really be seeing this, you know. People say it's bad luck."

"We don't believe in luck, do we, Han'?" James said. "We're going to make our own luck."

I felt myself blushing. Because I had momentarily wished that it were true. I had momentarily imagined that it was funny, grinning, blue-eyed James that I was going to marry in less than a week and not Cliff. As I changed back into my jeans, I felt disgusted at myself for even having had the thought.

After the dress shop, James convinced me to go for lunch in a pub we were passing. It was late and I was hungry and my nerves were all jangled from trying the dress on – in short, I felt in need of a drink.

Lunch was nothing special really. I had a not-very-nice burger and James had fish and chips. I downed two glasses of white and James two pints of beer. But the alcohol helped me relax. It stilled my racing heart.

The sun finally came out while we were inside. The rays shone through the dirty pub window and lit up the back of James' head. He looked freaky really, like some Christian icon. He was talking constantly, being funny still. And then he suddenly changed tack and asked me what it was I loved about Cliff.

I told him I was exhausted thinking about Cliff and the wedding and that I'd rather hear more of his stories. But that wasn't true. It was simply that I couldn't, when put on the spot, think *what* it was I loved about Cliff. Or rather it was that the things that I would have listed, that Cliff was level-headed, and good-humoured, and reliable, suddenly didn't sound like love at all. I kept thinking of a song lyric – the Smiths perhaps – that asked how you would know what love looked like if you had never seen it. And I remember thinking, that the more important point was, how would you know what love *wasn't* if you had never seen it. My definitions of what love was and wasn't seemed suddenly to be shifting, and I wasn't sure how I felt about that. I wasn't sure how I felt about that at all.

James was eating chips and rabbiting on about something or other in that animated manner of his and I saw that he had a spot of mayonnaise on the corner of his mouth.

Without thinking, I reached out and smudged it away, and then I flinched, knowing instantly that some taboo had been breached by my doing so.

In a fluster of false excuses about the food defrosting at our feet – food which had been forgotten until that point – I stood and clumsily knocked over James' empty glass and announced that we had to leave; that we had to leave right now.

We walked home in near silence. I was carrying the dress and a carrier bag, and James was carrying Cliff's suit and the second bag of shopping. It crossed my mind that James and Cliff were about the same size and I wondered what he would look like in the suit. The silence between us became quite uncomfortable. I think we were both aware that something had happened.

When we got inside, I went straight to the freezer. I could tell from the soggy packaging that things were melting. As I turned from stacking the freezer, I bumped into James – he was standing right behind me. He was just inches away, with an expectant look on his face.

I laughed falsely, and said, "What on earth are you . . . ?" And that's when he kissed me.

TWENTY-TWO

Brisbane – 15th December 2001

Dear Hannah,

So I finally managed to get my shit together and drag myself from India. I made it to Australia. The other side of the world. If I go any farther, I'll be coming back.

This is an amazing place, so English and yet so different.

It is summer here, Christmas will be mid-summer, imagine! The houses are English, the people are English, and yet they're not. They're tougher and more friendly, more solid, like country people in England maybe. When you leave the city, amazing animals are everywhere, kangaroos and parrots and crocodiles. It really is like living in a kid's pop-up book.

I am boarding in a hotel on the edges of Brisbane, a friendly, clean, basic place over a pub. (They call all the pubs hotels here.) I am working for an outfit installing electric fences in the outback. It is not technically breathtaking, and it's not that well paid either, but my money ran out, so ...

I want to tell you about Australia, but I can't work out what to tell, it is such a strange place, so much is different and so much the same.

I still haven't found anyone to replace you. I look at this country and I wish you were here to see it with me. Is that crazy after all these years?

I'm still not sure I will be happy here, though, but perhaps one never really ever is. Perhaps they all just pretend.

I hope you are all well, I wonder if you get my letters? A reply would be cool, just to let me know that you're OK.

And HAPPY CHRISTMAS!

All my love as always. J.

TWENTY-THREE

After a second night on Triazolam, Hannah wakes up feeling floaty and relaxed. The whole James thing has taken on a surreal, dreamlike quality. She is even starting to doubt that he will come at all.

When, after breakfast, further interrogation of her sister regarding the exact nature of her conversation with James provides nothing further of substance, nothing but further reasons to doubt, she decides, unilaterally, that he *isn't* coming. She's surprised at herself that this leap of faith is not only possible, but relatively easy.

Re-centred in the here and now for the first time in two days, Hannah notices that Luke and Aïsha are becoming bored and argumentative. Tristan, too, is spending more time tapping messages into his phone than interacting with anyone else.

It's at the moment Hannah suggests that they drive somewhere for dinner that she realises why no one has suggested leaving the villa for the last two days. No one wants to be elsewhere if and when James should finally arrive. No one wants to miss the action.

But her suggestion is seized upon by Luke and Aïsha – who immediately specify that the restaurant must serve pizza – and from that point there is no going back.

Just after four, as they are leaving, Cliff offers to stay behind so that everyone can fit into Tristan's Jeep.

Hannah is having none of it. There is no way she is letting Cliff head James off at the pass. "Just get in the car," she says with a sharpness that surprises even her. Cliff, bless him, buckles.

Hannah, Luke and Aïsha climb into Tristan's Jeep whilst Cliff and Jill follow on in the Mégane. Hannah glances back occasionally and sees that they are engrossed in a very serious-looking conversation. She wonders what they're talking about.

When Tristan hits the open road and accelerates, the present momentarily overwhelms her. She had forgotten that she was in France. She's in France and it's hot, and they're out of the house, and the sensations of driving with the top down and her hair whipping crazily around her head are ecstatic. She's tapping her hand to Tristan's crazy electronic music and the kids, in the rear seats, are grinning again. She's overcome by a surprise wave of the joy of now, so powerful it moves her to tears. She's tired, she rationalises. She's tired and drugged – no wonder she's emotional.

She glances across at Tristan, and he smiles back briefly before his expression changes to concern. "It's too windy for you," he shouts. "Your eyes are watering. Do you want the top up?"

"No," Hannah says, smiling back at him and reaching out to touch his shoulder. "No, it's fine. It's better than fine. It's brilliant, Tris'. I love it."

They end up in a beautiful little pizzeria in a hilltop town called Cabris. The tables are covered with red and white checked tablecloths, and the cutlery glimmers with the light from the oil lamps placed on each table.

Luke and Aïsha leave the table almost the second the pizzas

135

are served, returning only occasionally for another mouthful before running off again to explore the tiny streets.

Hannah cuts into her calzone and watches as raw egg-white oozes out. "Ooh. Look. This egg's not cooked," she says. "D'you think that's OK, Tris?"

Tristan shrugs. "It's impossible to fully cook the egg inside a calzone," he says. "If you send it back they'll just cremate it."

"But it's OK to eat?"

"Sure," he says. "Why wouldn't it be?"

Hannah nods and starts to cut into the other end of the calzone. "Look how all the French kids just sit there," she says, looking around the terrace. There are three French families eating here tonight, and their kids, ranging from about five to fifteen, are without exception sitting elegantly, engaged in polite conversation with the adults.

"Oh, they're fine," Cliff says, meaning Luke and Aïsha. "They've just been cooped up a bit. It'll do them good to run around."

"Anyway," Jill says. "You wouldn't want Luke to behave like that, would you?"

Hannah discovers that by tipping each slice of calzone sideways the raw egg simply runs off. "Maybe," she says, forking a mouthful.

Jill scans the terrace again and then pulls a face. "They look like they've been drugged to me," she says. "They look like they've been given tranquillisers."

Hannah and Tristan laugh. "It's true," Tristan says.

"They do," Hannah agrees.

"Maybe there's a special kid's pizza with Valium. You should have asked."

"I'd rather Aïsha grows up stroppy and rebellious," Jill says.

"I'd far rather she grabbed life by the balls than became some placid L'Oréal queen."

Hannah nods. "I suppose," she says. And there it is again, she thinks. How best to live a life? Respectably? Politely? Or as a stroppy rebel?

"Talking of which, I need to be back at midnight by the way," Jill says. "We will be back by midnight, won't we?"

"I would think so, but why?" Cliff asks. "You gonna turn into a pumpkin?"

Hannah glances at Tristan and she can tell from his restrained smile that Jill has told him and that he approves.

"Jill has a regular midnight visitor," Hannah explains.

"Really?" Cliff asks. "Who?"

TWENTY-FOUR

James IV

His lips grazed mine, and, at first, I kept my mouth firmly shut. But even then, even like that, that kiss felt like no kiss I had ever had. And yes, I know how ridiculous that sounds, but it happens to be true.

I had only ever had sex with Ben before Cliff, remember. And I had only kissed a handful of boys before Ben.

So though I had known good kissers and bad kissers (Cliff was actually one of the better ones) I had never experienced such heart-stopping desire. I *wanted* James. The second our lips touched, I felt as if I had been drugged, as if I had been injected and heroin or something was suddenly rushing through my veins. It was as much as I could do to remain standing. I had never experienced that before, and if you've never experienced something before, how could you possibly know what you're missing?

I slowly started to open my lips (I was melting, my defences were vanishing) but then a noise, the slamming of a car door, jerked me back to the here and now of who I was and where I was and, above all, who James was. My heart beating crazily, I pushed him away and ducked under his outstretched arm and ran to the front door, grabbing my coat as I passed it in the hallway. I don't think he even attempted to follow, but I don't know. I didn't look back.

I walked to the park and wandered around until I came to a bench. I sat and stared at the still wet grass and felt numb. I watched as the sun dipped in the sky, finally disappearing behind a purple bank of cloud.

I waited until I knew that Cliff would be home before I returned to the house. I half expected that James would be missing, that he would, in shame, have vanished.

Cliff was drinking a can of beer and watching the news. "Hi love. Where have you been?" he asked, in an unsuspicious tone.

James, from the sofa, was eyeing me warily.

"I went to see Shelley," I lied, realising as I did so that it was the first time I had ever lied to Cliff.

"Ah, I said you'd gone shopping," James said. "I thought that's what you said, sorry."

"I intended to, but you know what I'm like when I get together with Shelley," I said. "I'll have to go tomorrow now."

"I'm pretty hungry," Cliff said. "I know it's early, but . . . Do you want me to get a takeaway? I can go and get fish and chips if you want."

"No, it's fine," I replied, remembering the dob of mayonnaise on James' lip. "I have stuff for tea. I'll get it going."

I had just dropped the spaghetti into the pan when James entered the kitchen. "I'm sorry about before," he said. He was standing too close to me for comfort. He had his arms folded. He looked uncomfortable.

"It's fine," I said, "Just, you know . . ." I made a shooing gesture, and he took a step further back.

"The thing is, Hannah," he said.

I was stirring the bolognese sauce around the pan, and then squishing the spaghetti into the boiling water. Only once it was submerged did I look up. "Yes?" I asked.

James glanced behind him and then said, "The thing is, I think I'm falling . . ."

I stepped forward and placed my fingertips on his lips, effectively silencing him. "For fuck's sake, James," I whispered, glancing towards the lounge.

"But I need to . . ." he said.

I tutted sharply and yanked him out of the back door.

"You just can't do this, James," I said once we were outside. "It's not fair."

"But I'm in love with you," he said. "You know I am."

"I don't know anything," I said, but then he slipped one arm behind me and kissed me, and I felt myself melt against him all over again.

We kissed for a few seconds before I turned my head sideways. I rested it on his shoulder. "God, James," I said quietly. "You're just so . . ."

I had been about to say, "*sexy*", but it suddenly struck me as the sort of thing Jill might say. It sounded slutty.

"You're amazing, Hannah," he said, and he kissed me again, and I let it happen – it was wonderful, and the last of my defences collapsed and I allowed myself to fall into him. His tongue slipped into my mouth and I shivered and wanted more of him, all of him. I wanted every bit of him deep inside me, I wanted, somehow, to merge with him. *Oh God*, I thought, simply.

And then, as if from nowhere, the absurdity of the whole situation hit me again and I started to laugh.

James pulled away. He looked hurt. "What?" he asked.

"Well!" I said. "Can't you see how ridiculous this is?"

"I don't see why."

"I'm *pregnant*," I said. "I'm getting married on Saturday. To your *brother*."

"But what if you didn't," he said, his eyes looking a little crazed. "What if you came away with me instead."

"Away?"

"Yes, travelling. To India, and Thailand. We'd have such a great time you and me. I know we would."

"You're crazy, James," I said. "You know that, right?"

James shrugged and broke into a broad smile, and I looked into his eyes, and just for a second, I glimpsed that, despite everything, this madness was a possibility, and I started to grin stupidly too.

"This sauce is burning!" It was Cliff, calling from the kitchen.

I broke from James' grasp and ran back inside to snatch the spatula that Cliff was ineffectually using to stir the still-burning sauce. I pulled the pan from the heat. "Sorry about that," I said. ". . . got distracted. Don't worry. I have another jar."

"I just smelt it burning," Cliff said. "What were you doing out in the g—"

At that instant, James stepped back through the door. He smiled at Cliff, and there was something aggressive, something challenging about his stance.

"Oh," Cliff said. "Right." And then he turned and left the kitchen. "Let me know when dinner's ready," he said, flatly.

James watched him walk to the lounge and then whispered, "Hannah, I . . ."

I turned to face him, furious now. I raised the palm of my

hand. "Stop!" I hissed. "Just stop it." And then I added, quite loudly, "Please get out from under my feet, James. Please just go and watch television or something." And that's what he did.

Everything seemed normal enough that evening. I think we were all pretty good at playing normal, even back then. I served dinner, and we watched some TV, and then I went to bed followed, after half an hour, by Cliff.

I couldn't sleep for ages. I stared at the ceiling and calculated possible lives. I tried to imagine getting up the next morning and announcing that I wouldn't be marrying Cliff, that I was leaving with James. I imagined announcing nothing at all, simply eloping with James in the old-fashioned way – the way they did in films. I pictured going downstairs and telling James that he should leave, expelling him from the house so that Cliff and I could get married in peace. But all of the options seemed as unlikely as parallel universes. I couldn't imagine myself doing any of them.

So I stared at the ceiling and listened to Cliff snoring and wondered, as if there were a script to all of this, as if there were no such thing as free will, what would happen next.

And in a way, I was right. There *were* no choices to be made.

Because what happened next was that I finally fell asleep. And by the time I woke up in the morning James had gone.

TWENTY-FIVE

Brisbane – 3rd July 2003

Dear H.

I am writing to tell you that I'm gonna get hitched.

Her name is Judy, and she is an amazingly strong woman – the daughter of farmers – very lively, very organised. She keeps my life in good order, keeps us busy and well kept. I sometimes wonder if my heart isn't still a bit broken, and Judy does too. She calls me the ice-man, but swears she will melt me. Please wish her luck.

We met over a year ago and have decided that it's time (now she's pregnant!) that I made an honest woman of her.

I haven't sent you an invitation, as it's not a practical proposition for you to attend, but the date of the wedding is 2nd August, so if you don't hate me too much you could toast us on that date.

Deepest apologies for any hurt I ever caused you two.

Much love, J.

PS: The above is our new address. I have enclosed a photo so that you can see how we live over here. Through the big window you can just see the amazing Glasshouse Mountains. It was summer though, when the photograph was taken, it's winter now, and a cold, windy one at that.

TWENTY-SIX

"Where's your mum?" Hannah asks.

They are seated on the patio awaiting Cliff's return. He and Luke have bravely ventured into Frenchy-land in search of fresh bread and croissants.

Aïsha shrugs. "The door's locked," she says. "She locks it when she wants a lie-in."

At the sight of the Mégane returning, Hannah heads indoors to fetch the coffee. She crosses paths with Tristan coming out of the bathroom, a towel wrapped around him, his hair still wet.

"Morning," she says, and he nods, and returns the greeting before turning and heading towards his room. Hannah, despite herself, steals a glance at his muscular back as he walks away.

She then carries the pot of coffee outside before walking around the back of the house to peer through Jill's shutters. Sensing that they aren't locked, she pulls on them gently and looks into the room – into the empty room.

Back at the table, Tristan, now in shorts and a T-shirt, is taking a seat.

The croissants – still warm – are a buttery marvel, and combined with the thick dark coffee they make a perfect, if not particularly healthy, breakfast.

"Are we doing something today?" Luke asks.

The adults glance at each other. "I suppose we could go

somewhere this afternoon," Cliff says. "We could maybe go to Cannes or something."

"What's in Cannes?" Luke says.

"It's a seaside town. Beach, shops, cafés . . ." Hannah says. "Why, are you bored?"

"A bit," Luke admits.

Aïsha, who has been jabbing at the screen of her phone, sighs and slaps it down on the table.

"Careful, Aï"," Tristan says. "You'll break it."

"It doesn't work anyway," she says.

"Internet?" Tristan asks. "Or the whole thing?"

"Facebook."

Tristan holds his hand out. "Show me," he says.

Aïsha stares at him. She looks alarmed.

"I'm not gonna look at your stuff," Tristan says. "I just want to check the settings for you."

"Promise?" Aïsha asks, dragging her phone towards her, and then rounding the table to Tristan's side.

"I promise," Tristan says. As he starts to fiddle with the phone he mumbles, "Now, it might be your network settings . . . and those are in here . . ."

"I didn't do anything," Aïsha says. "I was on Facebook talking to Jess and then it stopped."

"How is Jess?" Hannah asks. Jess is Aïsha's best friend.

"She's OK," Aïsha says. "Her mum's pregnant again."

"Ah!" Tristan says. "Eureka! You've reached the limit, haven't you."

"What's eureka?" Aïsha asks. She doesn't know what Tristan is talking about.

"There's a fifty-euro limit," Tristan explains. "That's what this text you got says."

145

"What's fifty euros?" Jill has reappeared, standing in the doorway.

"Oh, you're back," Hannah says, smiling falsely at her sister. "Sorry, I mean 'up' of course. You're *up*!"

"Yes," Jill says, shooting her a knowing glance, and then, returning her attention to Aïsha, "So what's this about fifty euros?"

"She's reached the data limit," Tristan says. "There's an EU limit. Fifty euros. After that it stops working unless you phone them and get the limit removed."

"I only used Facebook," Aïsha says defensively.

Jill takes her seat at the table. "Croissants," she says. "Yum."

"Me and Dad got them," Luke explains. "Those square ones have chocolate in them. The man was French and we didn't know what he was saying and Dad made me pay."

Jill takes a bite and then speaking through a mouthful of croissant, says, "Ooh, these are good. So have you really spent fifty euros on Facebook? That's crazy. We've only been here four days."

Hannah sits and stares at her sister, ever a mystery. Jill never has a penny, and yet when her daughter spends fifty euros on Facebook, she only sounds vaguely surprised, and certainly not angry.

"Can we phone them?" Aïsha asks. "Can we phone them and do the thing so it works again?"

Jill laughs. "No, we can't," she says, and Hannah thinks, *Well, thanks be for small mercies.*

Aïsha frowns at Tristan. "So when will it work again?" she asks.

"When you get home," he says, handing the phone back.

"You're joking me," Aïsha says.

Tristan shakes his head. "Sorry, babe."

"Does yours still work?" she asks.

He nods. "Mine's for work though. I need my emails. So I have to pay for it."

"I *need* my Facebook," Aïsha says.

"It'll do you good to have a break," Hannah says. "You're on there all the time."

Aïsha shakes her head in disgust. "That's so lame," she says, turning and walking away from the table. "I hate France," she adds – her parting shot.

"Fifty euros!" Jill says, once she has gone.

"How much is fifty euros?" Luke asks, sipping his orange juice. "In pounds I mean."

"About forty," Cliff tells him.

"Wow. I'd be in trouble for that, wouldn't I?" Luke says.

"You would," Hannah agrees.

"I better not switch it on then," Luke says.

"No," Cliff says. "No, you had better not."

"Facebook's boring anyway," Luke says, and all the adults smile, because they understand that Luke doesn't think Facebook is boring at all; Luke just knows that it's a cool thing to say to the oldies.

Breakfast over, Hannah manages, for the first time in days, to read her novel. James is still occupying half of her mind and occasionally – whenever a car comes along the lane – all of it. But the rest of the time she is managing to abstract herself from thoughts of James as one might manage to ignore the rhythm of a washing machine.

When Jill appears at her side and asks, "Han', d'you know where the kids are?" she realises that she has been lost in her book for the last five chapters.

"Um?" she says. "Um, no. I thought they were with you at the pool."

"My guess is that they're down at the river," Jill says. "Tris' is making lunch, so I'm going to see if I can find them."

"I'll come with you," Hannah says, folding her book and jumping up. "I haven't been down there yet."

Hannah pulls on her sandals and then the two women climb over the fence at the rear of the property and start, in single file, along the track.

"You have to keep your eyes open for snakes," Jill calls back.

"You've seen snakes?"

"No," Jill says. "But Pascal said to watch out."

Hannah frowns at this. "How?" she asks. "How did he warn you?"

"What d'you mean?"

"In what language?"

Jill stops in her tracks. She points at her eye, then at the track, then makes a slithering motion with her hand. "Sssssss!" she says.

Hannah laughs and gives her sister a push. "Get on with you," she says.

"It's true," Jill insists. "Keep your eyes peeled."

Hannah starts to pay attention. The grass either side of the track is elbow-high and humming with insect-life and, no doubt, silent, lurking, snakes. She wishes she hadn't worn sandals.

As they turn onto a wider path heading down the hill, Hannah spots a wooden chalet farther down the first track. "Is that where he lives?" she asks.

"Yeah," Jill says. "Well, it's where his mother lives in summer. It's quite pretty isn't it?"

148

"It looks nice," Hannah says. "Presumably they have their own access? I take it they don't have to trip along that track every time?"

"No, there's a road the other side."

"Anyway, I thought you made the mother up. Or am I getting confused?" Hannah asks.

Jill laughs. "*Intentionally* confused," she says.

Hannah tuts. "Can you please just tell me," she says. "I'm getting bored with all these confused versions of your stories."

"I'm sorry," Jill says genuinely. "I don't mean anything by it. It's just habit."

And Hannah knows it's true. Jill has been weaving multiple contradictory realities around her since she was fourteen. Because fourteen was when Jill started having sex. And the only way to dissimulate what she was really up to was to keep her father and older sister permanently guessing by alternately exaggerating or denying her sins. Poor Hannah has been in a state of confusion as to what really goes on in Jill's life ever since.

"So how *do* you manage to communicate with him?" she asks.

"Like I said," Jill says, making the snake gesture again. "Sign language, mime, drawings . . . it's quite fun really."

They reach a set of steps cut into the hillside and have to revert to single file. As they enter the shade of the canopy of trees that have grown up along the line of the stream, Hannah says, "Ooh, it's lovely and cool down here."

"I know," Jill says. "Mozzies though."

"Yes," Hannah says, swiping at her arm. "Yes, I just found that out."

The "river" is in reality no more than a tiny stream, a

trickling brook, but with the speckled patterns of sun and shade from the trees above, the water sparkles and dances magically.

Hannah shouts Luke's name twice, then Aïsha's. Her voice echoes vaguely from the rocks on the other side of the brook but there's no sign of the kids.

"It's lovely down here," she says again, sitting now on a large stone.

"Isn't it?" Jill says, squeezing in beside her.

"So tell me about Pascal," Hannah says. "Tell me the truth."

"Pascal?" Jill says. "Well . . . He's quite nice really. I mean, as far as I can tell. We do have some comms issues as I said."

"And you're sleeping together?"

"We are now," Jill says. "But only the last two nights."

"So you *didn't* do anything when you went off with him that first time?"

Jill wrinkles her nose and shakes her head.

"You are such a wind-up merchant," Hannah says.

"His mum lives there. And she really did make horrible Turkish coffee."

"And then?"

"He came back the next day. To do the pool."

Hannah pulls a face as she struggles to remember when this might have happened, so Jill explains, "You were at the water-park place."

"Oh, of course."

"And Tristan was here, so he translated. We were able to talk a bit. And it turned out he was nice."

"Right," Hannah says, nodding thoughtfully.

"What?"

"Well, that was the bit I couldn't fathom," Hannah says.

"How you got from holding his bucket to . . . you know."

"Holding his bucket sounds like a euphemism," Jill says.

"It does rather."

"But, no, it was all quite sweet and innocent to be honest. Coffee with mum. He spent the afternoon with me and Tristan. I showed him my room but he didn't take the bait. Only he did give me a peck when he left."

"And then?"

"He was outside my shutters the night before last. Said he couldn't sleep. So we came down here. Had a kiss and stuff. And he came back to the house with me and . . ."

"OK, OK," Hannah laughs. "I can imagine the rest."

"You are strange," Jill says. "I mean, you want to know, and then you don't want to know."

"I don't want to know the sordid details, that's all," Hannah says.

"It's not sordid," Jill says. "That's your whole problem."

Hannah laughs. "It's just a figure of speech. But you may be right."

"So what about you?" Jill asks.

"Me?"

"Yes, how are you feeling about the whole James thing now?"

Hannah takes a deep breath and exhales loudly. "I don't know really," she says. "I've been kind of blocking it out. I've been pretending he isn't really coming. After all, we're not exactly sure that he is, are we?"

"No, I suppose not. I still think he will, but . . . So *were* you in love with him?"

"I don't know, Jill," Hannah admits. "That's the truth. It was fifteen years ago. I don't really remember."

"I think you remember pretty well," Jill says.

"Well, of course I do. I had a mad crazy crush on a guy called James. I'm just not sure I trust my memories. I mean, we only kissed a couple of times. We never even . . . you know, slept together. We kissed, and I spent half the night wondering what to do in the morning, but by then he was gone."

"What to do?"

Hannah swipes at a mosquito on her arm. "Why do they always go for me?" she asks.

"My sun cream has insect repellent in it," Jill says. "So you're the bait."

"Ahh," Hannah says.

"So you were saying?" Jill prompts. "You were wondering what to do . . ."

"I was supposed to be marrying Cliff, wasn't I?"

"Oh God, yeah. The first time around. I forgot about that." Jill slides her arm around Hannah's waist and gives her a squeeze. "That was horrible," she says. "I can't believe I forgot."

"That's probably no bad thing," Hannah says. "I wish *I* could forget."

"So when you say you were worrying what to do, you mean you were thinking of calling the wedding off? Even then? Even before . . ."

Hannah nods. "Maybe," she says. "I'm not sure."

"But that means it was a bit more than a crush," Jill says.

"Maybe," Hannah says again.

"Oh, sweetie," Jill says, giving her another squeeze before releasing her. "So what does Cliff say about it all?"

Hannah picks up a small stone and throws it into the water. "Nothing," she says.

"Nothing?"

"We don't really talk about stuff like that. We don't really know how to. Does that make any sense?"

Jill nods. "Most men don't," she says. "That's why finding one who doesn't speak a word of English is something of a relief. No expectations, you see."

"But it's not just Cliff," Hannah says. "It's both of us. Neither of us could ever talk about feelings really."

"You talk to me," Jill points out.

"Well, that's different, isn't it," Hannah says. "You're my sister."

Jill laughs. "I suppose," she says. "I don't really tell anyone else my secrets either."

"You do, you tell Tristan."

"That's true actually," Jill says. "But you're the only two. Talking of Tris', I suppose we should get back. Lunch will be ready."

"Yes," Hannah replies, scratching at her leg. "Yes, I'm getting bitten to death here as well. Luke? LUKE! Aïsha?"

TWENTY-SEVEN

At the house, Luke and Aïsha are already seated: lunch has been served.

"Wow, that looks good," Hannah says. "Quiche?"

"Yep. Well, a tart really – salmon, asparagus and goat's cheese," Tristan says. "I stole it from Hugh Fearnley-Whittingstall."

"It looks gorgeous."

"You put asparagus in everything, don't you?" Jill comments.

"Well, it's such a lovely summery flavour, isn't it?" Tristan replies.

Hannah turns to Luke next to her. He is slumped, uncharacteristically, in his chair. "Are you OK?" she asks. "You look a bit peaky."

Luke nods.

"We went looking for you down by the river," she tells him. "Where were you?"

Luke shrugs. "Here," he says.

Hannah glances at Aïsha, who is looking equally glum, and wonders if her moods are finally rubbing off on her usually buoyant son. Heaven forbid that these two weeks together should be the final straw that nudges Luke into adolescence.

"You all right, champ?" Cliff, returning from the kitchen with a salad bowl, asks.

Luke nods again, but wrinkles his nose and shrugs at the

same time. It's one of Aïsha's favourite combinations of gestures.

"Cliff made the salad," Tristan says as he takes a seat, reaches for the salad bowl and passes it to Jill. "Dig in, folks."

"I don't think I've ever seen you cook," Jill says, serving herself and passing the bowl on to Hannah.

"Cook!" Cliff laughs. "I'd hardly call washing a few leaves and peeling a few avocados cooking." But he looks, and feels, quite proud. He enjoyed making the salad and mixing dressing with Tristan. He has today made a decision to get more involved in the kitchen from now on. Against all expectation, food preparation is relaxing.

"Do you want some of this?" Hannah asks.

Luke shakes his head.

"But you like avocado," she says.

Luke shakes his head again and says, "I'm not hungry."

Hannah cuts a sliver of quiche and puts it on his plate. "Well, just eat this then," she says. "You have to eat something."

"So you went down to the river?" Cliff asks.

"It's lovely," Hannah tells him. "Beautiful. Put insect repellent on first though. There are loads of mosquitos."

"It is really nice," Jill agrees. "It's shady and cool."

"We're lucky we don't have them up here really," Hannah says. "The mosquitos, I mean."

"I've been bitten here," Cliff says.

"Me too," says Tristan.

"Luke, eat something," Hannah says. "Sit up straight and eat something."

"I'm not hungry," he says again.

Hannah puts down her fork and touches her son's forehead. "You do look pale," she says. "Please try to eat something."

With visible effort, Luke sits up and forks a mouthful of quiche.

"So are we going to Cannes this evening?" Cliff asks.

"I thought after lunch," Jill says. "I want to get out and about. I feel the need to move."

"Hum. I'm getting quite used to having a siesta after lunch," Cliff says. "Plus I may have had a couple of glasses of wine whilst we were cooking."

"We could take two cars," Tristan offers. "Meet up in Cannes."

"We have to take two cars anyway," Jill points out.

"Sure," Tristan says. "You know what I mean."

"*Luke!*" Aïsha whines. She sounds disgusted.

Everyone turns to look at Luke who is bent over his plate, spitting out the mouthful of masticated tart.

Hannah shoots Aïsha a questioning glance and then peers in at Luke. "You're not OK at all, are you?" she says, and Luke, at that instant, confirms her diagnosis by vomiting onto his own lap.

"Jesus," Cliff says, jumping up and joining Hannah, now crouched at Luke's side.

Luke retches again, so Hannah stands, grabs his arm and pulls him upright, then tugs him towards the bathroom. "You had better come inside," she says.

"It's her fault," Luke mumbles as she drags him into the house. He is pointing at Aïsha's seat, now, mysteriously, empty.

Once Luke is in bed with a bucket by his side, Hannah returns to the dinner table.

"Where is she?" she asks. "Where's bloody Aïsha gone?" Her voice has the staccato rhythm of a machine gun.

Tristan shakes his head. "We don't know," he says.

"That'll teach them not to dip into our stash at any rate," Jill says. She sounds amused.

Hannah turns so that she can aim the full force of her anger at her sister, but can't, for a second, find the right words to express herself.

Jill pulls a face. "Hey, it's not my fault," she says.

Hannah gasps. "How?" she says. "How is this not your fault? You spend your entire life taking drugs in front of Aïsha . . ."

"It's only dope," Jill says.

"Jesus! You spend your entire life taking drugs in front of your kid," Hannah repeats. "You bring the stuff on holiday. You leave it lying around."

"It's actually mine," Tristan volunteers.

"Shut up, Tristan," Hannah tells him. "This is between Jill and me."

"O-K!" Tristan says, pedantically. He stands, gathers a few plates, and heads into the house.

"I didn't make your son smoke dope," Jill says. "So, just chillax, OK?"

"No, Jill, I will not *chillax*. And you're right, you didn't make Luke smoke dope. Your daughter did."

"So Luke says," Jill snipes.

"Yes, so Luke says. But you never told Aïsha not to do *anything*, did you? Ever? That's the problem here. You smoke around them all the time, you don't teach her right and wrong, you . . . You shrug off all responsibility and your daughter is out of control and as a result my son is stoned and crying and vomiting."

Jill laughs bitterly. "For fuck's sake, calm down, Hannah," she says. "It was just a bit of dope."

Hannah lets out an exasperated gasp. "Cliff!" she says, turning to her up-till-now silent husband. "Backup please."

Cliff opens his palms skywards and exhales loudly. "It's pretty irresponsible leaving the stuff around," he says. "You have to admit."

Jill pulls a face and points at Tristan, who has returned to gather the dirty glasses and cutlery. "Tell him," she says.

Cliff turns to Tristan. "Tris'?"

"Sure. Whatever. But it wasn't lying around," Tristan says. "It was in my room in my jacket pocket. Aïsha must have gone into my room and gone through my pockets."

"Or Luke," Jill says.

"Oh, come on!" Hannah says. "You know who's behind this."

"Yes," Cliff says. "It's far more Aïsha's style than Luke's."

"Whoever it was," Jill says, "it still wasn't me, was it?"

"Aïsha's your daughter," Cliff says.

"Which makes it my fault?"

"Well, yes, of course it does."

"I don't see *you* taking any responsibility for the fact that your son has been smoking dope," Jill spits.

"*We* didn't *bring* the stuff here!" Hannah says. "You did!"

"Oh, I don't have to sit here and listen to this," Jill says, pushing her chair back and standing. "Aïsha may be out of order but your precious son is the one who's bloody gone and got himself stoned."

Hannah watches Jill enter the house, then turns to Cliff. "Unbelievable!" she says.

Cliff opens his palms at the sky again. "It's just Jill," he says.

Hannah rubs her brow. "How long does it last?" she asks, after a moment's pause. "Do you remember?"

Cliff shakes his head. "I only ever took it twice, I think. And then I threw up like Luke. Never cared for the stuff."

"I used to smoke Jill's," Hannah says. "When we were at college."

"It's the same thing," Cliff says. "Don't worry too much. It's just one of those rites of passage. He'll be fine in a couple of hours."

"He's eleven, Cliff."

Cliff nods. "Sure," he says.

"Wait till I get my hands on Aïsha," Hannah says, then, "And where the *hell* do you think you're going?" Jill and Tristan are leaving the house. Tristan is jangling his car keys and looking embarrassed.

"We're off to Cannes," Jill says.

"You're *what?*"

"We're off to Cannes," she repeats belligerently.

"And your daughter?"

"I'm sure she'll reappear," Jill says. "And I'm sure you'll have a go at her too. You're good at that."

They start to walk towards the Jeep, so Hannah stands and runs after them. "Jill," she says. "Jill!"

As Jill reaches the passenger door of the Jeep, Hannah reaches them and grabs her sister's sleeve.

Jill shakes Hannah off, then raises her palm in a stop sign. "Just . . . just step away from me, Hannah," she says. "You're making me seriously angry now, so just, you know . . . back off!"

Hannah glances at Tristan, now starting the engine. He shrugs and mouths "sorry" at her, and there's nothing that Hannah can do except stand, fuming and forlorn, as she watches Jill climb aboard and the car reverse urgently out of the gate.

Cliff meets Hannah at the corner of the house. "Come here," he says, opening his arms.

"She's just . . ." Hannah says.

Cliff hugs her tight. "I know," he says. "The most shocking thing is that you're still surprised by it after all these years."

Over Cliff's shoulder, Hannah sees Aïsha, sidling towards them across the garden, her hands in the pockets of her shorts. She breaks free from Cliff's hug and strides across the gravel. "Aïsha!" she shouts. "Aïsha! I am so bloody angry with you . . ."

But as soon as she reaches her, her anger melts.

Because Aïsha is crying. "Where's Mum gone?" she asks. "I don't feel well."

TWENTY-EIGHT

By five, both Luke and Aïsha are up again, both well enough, in theory, to go to Cannes. But Hannah feels that rewarding their bad behaviour with a treat would be a parenting faux pas of massive proportions. So when Aïsha finally plucks up the courage to ask the question she says, "No, Aïsha. We *aren't* going to Cannes. I'm furious with both of you, so you had better just stay out of my way today."

Both Luke and Aïsha immediately make themselves scarce.

"The trouble with that of course is that we get punished too," Cliff comments.

"I know," Hannah says, nodding sadly. "But the truth is that if I bumped into Jill living it up in Cannes, I might just punch her, so it's probably just as well."

Hannah is changing for bed that night when she hears a car pull up. She thinks that it's the sound of the Jeep, but she can't be sure, so she pulls her clothes back on and heads outside, crossing paths with Cliff heading for bed.

"Tristan and Jill?" she asks.

Cliff nods. "I wouldn't bother though, Han'," he says.

"Don't tell me what to do, Cliff," Hannah says, immediately regretting having sounded so sharp. "I'm sorry. I just mean, well, she is my sister," she adds as she advances down the corridor. "This is kind of between me and her."

When she gets to the patio, however, she sees what Cliff was trying to say. Jill is standing in the doorway smoking a joint, and swaying, gently, from side to side.

"Are you pissed now, on top of everything else?" Hannah asks.

Jill wobblingly turns to look at her. The remains of her joint slips from her fingers and spins to the floor. She attempts to stub it out with her toe but misses and grinds the floor just to the left of the smouldering butt instead.

"Oh, *fuck off*, Hannah," she says as she unsteadily passes her, supporting herself against the wall, and then, more falling than walking, she vanishes through the door of her bedroom.

Hannah steps outside to recover the still-glowing butt, and finds Tristan sitting. He's pouring the dregs of their bottle of wine into a glass.

"She's drunk then," Hannah says when he looks up.

"You noticed," Tristan says.

"I'm fuming," Hannah says as she squashes the stub out in the ashtray.

"I'm sure," Tristan replies. "Is there any more of this?" he asks, tapping the neck of the empty bottle. "I haven't had a drink all night because I was driving. I've had to put up with your sister sober. Can you imagine?"

Hannah makes a trip to the refrigerator and returns with a fresh bottle of rosé and a corkscrew.

"So are you angry with me too?" Tristan asks as he opens the bottle with professional flourish.

Hannah sighs and perches on the edge of a chair. "I guess not," she says. "It's just Jill. But even beyond the whole Aïsha getting Luke stoned affair . . ."

"So that is what happened then?" Tristan asks.

"Yes. But even beyond that, the fact that she then pissed off and left me nursing both children . . ."

"Aïsha was sick as well?"

Hannah nods. "She was worse than Luke. Jill should have stayed. It's not right. It's not fair."

Tristan pours himself a glass of wine and then points the bottle vaguely at Hannah. She shrugs and pushes a nearby glass across the table. "Oh, just a drop," she says, pulling her chair up and settling into it more permanently.

"Jill can't cope with conflict," Tristan says as he pours the wine. "So if you shout at her, *ever*, well, she'll just run a mile. You must know that by now, right?"

Hannah frowns at him and sips her drink. Though she has obviously noticed this on many occasions, she has never heard it put into words. "You're right," she says. "That's true actually."

"She says she feels physically afraid," Tristan says. "She feels like she's in danger. As soon as anyone starts shouting, she has to run. It's instinctual."

Hannah laughs bitterly. "Well, that's just ridiculous," she says. "I have never hit Jill. I have never hit anyone, and she knows it."

"She knows it's stupid," he says. "But it's something to do with her childhood. When people start shouting she feels scared. She reckons your dad used to slap her."

"He did. It's true. He slapped both of us plenty."

Tristan shrugs. "Well, there you go," he says.

"But she was uncontrollable. You have no idea, Tris'."

"All the same," Tristan says.

Hannah nods. "It was a different generation, wasn't it. That's what people did then."

163

"But that doesn't make it right."

"No, I suppose not."

"You never hit Luke, I bet."

Hannah creases her brow as she tries to remember. "I think I slapped his legs once. He ran into the road. He was about six. And I slapped his legs. But that was more in fear than in anger. And I felt terrible afterwards."

Tristan nods. "My dad used to take his belt off to me."

"God."

"But anyway. Just give her some space and she'll come apologise. That's what I reckon."

Hannah runs her finger around the rim of the glass. It sings briefly but then stops, and she can't get it to do it again. "Well, that would be a first," she says. "Jill never apologises."

"It's not easy being Jill, you know," Tristan says. "I'm not sure you really get that."

Hannah pulls a face. "You're right!" she says. "I don't."

"She's a single parent. She's broke. She's lonely . . ."

"But that's all her fault, Tristan."

"Fault," he repeats flatly.

"Well, it is. She could learn to compromise. She could learn to apologise. She could stick in a relationship. She could get a bloody job."

Tristan shrugs. "Maybe that's not all her fault though," he says.

"I don't see who else . . ."

"Maybe it's not entirely her fault if she's not very good at those things. At compromising. At relationships . . . We all have different skill-sets."

Hannah rolls her eyes. "If you go down that road, then maybe it isn't the serial killer's fault that he's a serial killer."

164

"Well, maybe it isn't," Tristan says. "We're all damaged. We're all damaged in different ways."

Hannah sighs deeply and takes another sip of wine. A tiny gust of air moves across the patio, making her shiver. "It's cooler tonight," she says.

"It is. Storms tomorrow."

"Really?"

"So says the weather forecast."

"That's a bit hard to believe," Hannah says.

"It is," Tristan agrees. "But going back to Jill, you know she's jealous of you, right?"

"Jill? Jealous? Now that *is* ridiculous."

Tristan nods exaggeratedly. "It's true. She sees you as this perfect grown-up who has everything sorted while she's wallowing around in the mud like an adolescent. Those were her actual words."

"She should just stop wallowing," Hannah says. "And she really was drunk if that's what she told you. I'm nothing to be jealous of, and Jill knows it."

"You have a stable relationship with someone you love. You have a great house, a job you enjoy . . ."

"It's only a few hours at the school."

"Even better," Tristan says. "A part-time job that you enjoy."

"But Jill could get all of that, Tristan, that's the point," Hannah says. "But she's never known how to . . . how to *forego* anything so that she can reach a further goal. Do you know what I mean? She's never known how to compromise."

"I know," Tristan says, now rolling a cigarette. "She has certain . . . limitations. We all do. But that's not necessarily her fault. And it doesn't mean that she isn't jealous."

165

"I suppose," Hannah says, unconvinced.

Tristan pops the cigarette into the tobacco tin and stands. "Well, I'm shattered," he says. "Are you coming to bed or . . ." He laughs. "Sorry, that sounded weird. I meant . . ."

"It's OK, Tris'," Hannah says. "I know what you meant. And no, I think I'll sit here for a bit. It's nice and quiet. You don't have a cigarette for me, do you?"

Tristan turns back from the doorway. "For you?" he asks, shocked. "I've never seen you smoke. Ever."

"I know," Hannah says. "I gave up when I met Cliff. So it was a very long time ago. But I just fancy one for some reason."

Tristan pulls his tobacco tin back out of his pocket and proffers it.

"Could you roll me one, do you think?" Hannah asks. "I never was very good at rollies."

"There's one in there," Tristan says, shaking the tin at her. "It's just a cigarette though. That is what you want, right?"

Hannah nods. "Thanks, Tristan," she says, taking the tin. "Goodnight."

"Night."

Hannah lights the cigarette, and though it makes her feel a little dizzy, it does exactly what she had hoped. The taste, the smell, the sensation of smoking takes her back to when she was twenty-one, to before she met Cliff, to a time when a million different life trajectories seemed possible.

And now here she is. At thirty-eight she could easily be halfway through her life. Her mother died at sixty, so she could very well be more than halfway through. What a terrifying thought.

She thinks a bit about the concept of Jill's being jealous

and figures that if you could somehow add Jill's life to her own it would make up one complete whole instead of the two half-lives that each of them are making do with. But there's no way to do that, is there? Choose romance and adventure and excitement and crazy sex adventures and you exclude, by definition, security, safety, comfort and calm.

Yes, she thinks, as she smokes her cigarette. *Yes, you can have whichever half you want, but you can't have both.*

Jill, surprisingly, is up before Hannah the next morning. She finds her sitting in the cool shadow of the lounge, nursing a pint of water.

"What are you doing in here?" Hannah asks, wondering at the change of routine. It is only after she has said it that the full horror of yesterday comes back to her. She realises that her first words should perhaps have been angrier.

"It's a bit bright out there first thing," Jill says.

"Ah," Hannah says. "Hangover then?"

Jill nods.

"Good," Hannah says. "I'm glad."

She makes herself a mug of instant coffee – she can't be bothered with the machine this morning – and walks back past Jill and out onto the patio. The sun, still low enough in the sky to pass beneath the eaves, is blinding but she turns her chair to face it and closes her eyes. The warmth on her eyelids feels wonderful.

"Look, I'm sorry, OK?" Jill says. Her voice, coming from the doorway behind her, makes Hannah jump.

Hannah doesn't move. She doesn't open her eyes. She simply shrugs.

"So you're still angry, huh?" Jill says.

Hannah snorts in derision. "Even when you apologise you sound belligerent," she says.

Jill doesn't say anything for half a minute. "It's because I'm embarrassed," she says.

"Embarrassed," Hannah repeats.

She hears Jill move to her left and take a seat at the table. She casts her a glare and then turns to look back out at the garden. "Aïsha was sick too," Hannah says. "Just in case you wanted to know."

"Aïsha? Really?"

"Yes, I had both kids vomiting while you were swanning around having fun in Cannes."

"I didn't have fun," Jill says. "For what it's worth."

"Aw, poor Jill."

"I was crying if you must know," Jill says. "I was crying by the time we got to the end of the road."

"That must have been really awful for you," Hannah says.

"God, you're harsh sometimes."

"Jill, you told me to fuck off last night," Hannah says. "So don't talk to me about harsh."

"Did I really?"

"Yep."

"Oh."

"Yes, 'Oh.'"

"I don't remember that."

"No," Hannah says. "Well, just to make sure you haven't missed any of the other joys of yesterday, your daughter stole Tristan's dope. She and Luke got stoned and vomited all over the shop. You went out and left me to deal with it alone. And then came back drunk and told me to fuck off. So if I sound a little harsh this morning, that'll be why."

"I'm sorry, Hannah," Jill says. "Really I am."

Hannah shrugs again and throws another brief glare at her sister. "What's new?" she says.

"So James didn't come?" Jill asks.

The attempt at changing the subject is so transparent that Hannah just laughs.

"I still think he will," Jill says. "If it's meant to be."

"Just . . . *don't*, Jill, OK?"

"I'm sorry."

"And stop saying you're sorry. It isn't any use to me. It isn't any use to anyone."

They sit in silence for a few more minutes before Jill says, "It *is* a bit hard to know what to say to you when you're like this."

Hannah chews the inside of her mouth before replying. "It's not about saying anything, is it, Jill?" she finally says. "It's about being. It's about doing."

"Yes," Jill says.

"What would be really lovely, for example," Hannah continues, "would be if just for a bit, say, just to the end of the holiday, you could behave like a responsible adult instead of some chavvy teenage lush." She glances over at Jill, who has flushed red as if she has been slapped. Hannah fully expects Jill to now stomp off, probably throwing some random insult over her shoulder as she leaves. Such is the ritual between the sisters.

Instead, Jill says, "Yes, I get that."

It's such a surprise that Hannah has to check Jill's face to see if she is mocking her.

"Really," Jill says, nodding. "I get it."

"Well, good," Hannah says, disarmed by the unexpected

departure from their script. From the interior, she can hear the echo of doors opening and closing. "Sounds like people are stirring," Hannah says. "I had better get this table cleared and breakfast on the go."

Jill stands and touches Hannah's shoulder. "I'll do it this morning," she says, starting already, to gather last night's glasses from the table. "You have a break. I owe you."

Hannah sits back and watches Jill clear the table. At the sound of cupboard doors and the opening and closing of the refrigerator drifting from the kitchen, Hannah pushes her lips out and nods thoughtfully. "That's new," she says quietly.

The window to the kitchen opens, and Jill leans out. "Where's the coffee?" she asks. "I can't find it anywhere."

"It's in the freezer," Hannah says. "Tristan says it keeps better."

"Oh, of course," Jill says.

Hannah listens to the sounds of the freezer opening and closing, then the clatter of random cupboard doors.

"And the tea?" Jill shouts.

"In the tea-caddie on the counter."

"Oh, right. Cheers."

Hannah rolls her eyes.

"Are we using these baguettes from yesterday, or the sliced stuff?" Jill asks.

"*Not* so new then," Hannah murmurs, as she stands and heads into the kitchen.

TWENTY-NINE

After breakfast, Hannah takes to the hammock, where she dozes for another hour. She has a strange dream where Cliff gets into the Jeep and drives away, leaving her stranded with Tristan (who for some reason has James' face) and Jill (who looks like their mother).

She's awakened, shockingly, by Aïsha grabbing her arm. "Hannah!" Aïsha is shouting. "Hannah! Hannah! Hannah!"

Hannah drags herself from the dream and focusses on Aïsha's panicked features, then, powered by a surge of adrenalin, she rolls from the hammock (her leg has gone to sleep) and then starts with difficulty to run after the girl. "What is it? What's happened?" she calls.

As she reaches the gravel of the car park, she hears the sound of Luke's wailing and switches from a run to a sprint.

Luke's voice turns to a piercing scream as his mother rounds the corner. She reaches the poolside, already scanning the scene for indicators of what might have happened here. Luke's mask is lying shattered on the floor. A mixture of blood, water and tears are running down his face in long, pinkish streaks.

"Jesus, Luke!" she says as she reaches her son and crouches down before him. "What's happened here?"

Luke is crying almost hysterically now, so Hannah glances at Aïsha for answers. "Well?"

"It was an accident," she says. "We were just playing."

Hannah tips Luke's face towards the light. He has multiple cuts around his closed eye and blood is running thick and fast around and into it and perhaps from it.

"*Jesus!*" Hannah exclaims. "Get Cliff! Now!"

"I got him out of the pool," Aïsha says.

"Yes. Get Cliff."

"I think he's asleep," Aïsha says, on the edge of tears herself.

"Then *wake* him! Quickly. Go!"

"Is he gonna be OK?" Aïsha asks.

"Go!" Hannah shrieks.

Aïsha runs off, and Hannah lifts Luke and carries him over to the garden tap, where she tips his head downwards and washes around his eye in the hope of removing any remaining broken glass.

"It hurts," Luke wails.

"I know, baby," Hannah says, her voice trembling. "But you're gonna be fine."

Cliff – still in his underpants – and Tristan and Jill all arrive together in a confusing medley of "What's happened?" and "Is he all right?" and "Oh my God!"

"His mask smashed," Hannah says, sidestepping the question of cause for the moment for expediency's sake. "He's got glass all around his eye. Maybe in it too."

Cliff crouches down next to them and peers in at Luke's face. "Can you open your eye, Luke?" he asks. "Can you see out of it?"

"I can't," Luke sobs. "It hurts."

"It's bad, isn't it?" Hannah says, her own eyes watering in sympathy. "I think it's really bad."

"I don't know," Cliff says. Looking between Jill and

172

Tristan's faces, he asks, "Do either of you know how to call an ambulance here?"

Jill shakes her head. Tristan too.

"Cliff?" Hannah says, her voice pleading.

Cliff shrugs. "I don't know," he says. "Isn't there an international number or something?"

"Cliff. We need to do something," Hannah says. "Maybe go get a neighbour."

Tristan pulls out his phone. "Wait," he says. "I've got this."

"What can I do?" Cliff asks.

"I don't know," Hannah says. "Who are you calling, Tris'?"

But Tristan is talking in French. He raises one hand to tell them to let him do whatever he is doing.

"So how did this happen, Aï?" Jill asks. Aïsha is clinging to her leg looking pale.

"It was an accident," Aïsha says. "But I helped him out of the pool. I thought he was gonna drown."

"Just leave the hows and whys for now, Jill," Hannah interrupts. "Please. We just need to work out what to do."

Tristan hangs up. "The nearest hospital's in Grasse," he says, urgently. "It's fifteen minutes max. I know where it is. I think it's quicker to take him to A and E than to wait for an ambulance."

"Really?" Hannah says.

"That's what Jean-Jacques says," Tristan tells her. "And he is local. He says the pompiers take ages. It's eighteen – the phone number's eighteen – but he says it's best to go to the hospital."

"OK, we'll do that then," Hannah says.

"I'll get the keys," Tristan says, sprinting off.

"Can you get his clothes, Cliff?" Hannah asks. "And a towel."

173

Hannah lifts Luke – whose crying is reaching a new crescendo – and carries him to the front of the house, where she meets Cliff coming the other way with a random assortment of the boy's clothes.

Together they dry and dress him, then Cliff picks him up and they run to the Jeep.

"In the back," Hannah directs. "I'll get in the back too."

"I'll get dressed and follow on," Cliff says as he lifts Luke into the car and buckles his belt for him. "You go. I'll be there as soon as I can."

"Daad!" Luke wails as he realises that Cliff is stepping away from the car.

"I'm coming," Hannah says, climbing next to him. "I'm with you. You're gonna be fine."

Fresh blood is still running down Luke's face. "Give me the towel too," Hannah says, and Jill runs back, scoops it from the floor and hands it to her.

"I'll call you," Tristan tells them, already starting the engine. "I'll call you as soon as we get there."

The traffic is light, and it takes them less than ten minutes to reach the hospital.

During the journey, Hannah holds Luke in her arms and strokes his hair, and perhaps because of this or perhaps because he's simply exhausted, his wailing fades to a series of quiet, whiny sobs.

In Grasse, Tristan drives to the entrance to the Accident and Emergency dock and parks next to a red pompier's truck. Someone berates them – in French – for parking where they have, but Tristan says, with irony, "I didn't understand a word of that, did you?" and they push on into the emergency ward.

The rows of plastic chairs inside contain only two other people: a single Arab man with his arm in a sling and an old grey-haired woman who looks like she may have been living, for some years, under a bridge.

The receptionist takes one look at Luke and uses the tannoy system to call for a nurse. The nurse, in turn, takes one look at Luke and trots off in search of a doctor. The rapid escalation confirms what Hannah thought – that this is serious. Her heart starts to race.

Tristan, in fact, is reassured by their rapidity. "It certainly beats England," he says. "When I broke my finger in London, I had to wait two hours before anyone even spoke to me."

"But this isn't a broken finger, is it?" Hannah says.

"No," Tristan agrees. "But you get my point."

"I do."

"Do you want me to phone Cliff?" Tristan asks. "I didn't even give him the address yet."

Hannah shakes her head. "There's no point yet. Wait till they tell us something." It seems to her, at this instant, that adding another stressed adult to the mix would be more of a hindrance than a help.

In just over a minute, the nurse reappears with a young doctor in tow. He crouches down in front of Luke and points a torch into his eye whilst attempting to lift his eyelid. Luke shrieks and begins to cry again.

"OK," the doctor says. "Emmène-le directement en ophtalmologie."

"I'm sorry," Hannah says, "but do you speak English?"

"We must take you upstairs," the nurse says. "Come."

She leads them to a lift and on up to the third floor. "You

175

have very good chance," she tells them in the lift. "The Doctor Graffin is 'ere today. Surgeon. He is very good. Really."

The word 'surgeon' makes all of the hairs on Hannah's neck stand on end, which is the exact opposite of what the nurse intended.

When the lift doors open, she leads them along a seemingly endless corridor and through multiple sets of double doors, and finally into a small room where the surgeon is standing with his back to them talking on the phone.

Hannah places Luke on one of the two chairs in the room and places her palm at the base of her back and stretches. One more year and she won't be able to carry him at all.

The doctor ends his conversation quickly and turns to face them. He is over six feet tall with olive skin and deep-brown almost black irises. An imposing presence, he shakes Hannah's and Luke's hands, and then crouches down in front of Luke.

"Ils sont anglais," the nurse tells him.

"English, huh?" the surgeon says, his accent a mixture of American and French.

"Yes."

"So we 'ave a little accident, huh?"

"Yes."

"How this 'appen? You tell me, please?"

"A diving mask," Tristan says. He is met with blank looks from both the doctor and the nurse. Lacking essential vocabulary, notably the words for mask and diving, Tristan performs a rather impressive charade involving putting on a mask and diving into a pool, swimming, and whacking himself in the face. Were the circumstances not so dire, it would be pretty funny.

"I understand," Doctor Graffin says, restraining a smirk

176

and reaching into his desk drawer to pull out a pair of powered magnifying goggles, which he clips across his eyes.

"Superpower goggles," Tristan says. "What do you think of those, Luke?"

Luke, apparently paralysed by fear, remains silent.

The surgeon then grasps Luke's head with one hand and pulls back his eyelid with the other, provoking a quivering round of sobs.

"He needs to look and see what's wrong," Hannah whispers. "Try to be still for him. You're being amazingly brave, Luke."

The doctor straightens almost immediately. "OK, my little friend," he says. "You have glass in your eye. We will 'ave to take that out and very quick is better. How long this 'appen?"

"About half an hour now," Tristan says, checking the time on his phone. "Maybe forty-five minutes."

"It's good. You are very quick."

"Is that difficult?" Hannah asks, "to get the glass out, I mean. Will he be OK?"

The doctor gives her a Gallic shrug. "It's a little operation. 'E should be. But you know, the eye is a delicate *organe*. You are the mother, yes?"

Hannah nods. She feels a wave of shame, as if this question is in fact some accusation of responsibility. And she fears that the accusation is reasonable. She should have been watching them.

"Good," he says. "The nurse will get the form. I 'ope we can do it right now." He glances at his watch. "You are lucky. Is quiet today. Very quiet. Is strange."

He rattles off some French at the nurse, who leaves, then says, "I return. Please, stay," and follows her through the door.

"He sent her to get consent forms," Tristan says. "And something or other financial forms."

"I need to get Cliff to bring that card thing in," Hannah says.

"The E111? Have you got one of those?"

"They don't exist anymore. It's a European Health Card or something now," Hannah says. "But yes. We got one before we left. Didn't you?"

Tristan shrugs. "Didn't cross my mind."

"I'm not even sure what it covers," Hannah says, "But to be honest, I don't care. When he says operation, that's not with a general anaesthetic, though, is it? They're not going to put him to sleep?"

"I don't want a general anaesthetic," Luke says. "Don't let them put me to sleep."

Hannah realises that the only time Luke has ever heard the term 'put to sleep' was in reference to their previous cat. She regrets the turn of phrase immediately.

"A general anaesthetic is just when they give you something to make you snooze for half an hour," Hannah says. "So they can fix things without it hurting while you're asleep. But it's not always necessa—"

At that moment the nurse reappears with a wad of paperwork on a clipboard.

"Can you ask her, Tris'?" Hannah says.

"I don't know what general anaesthetic is in French," Tristan says.

"Anaesthesie generale," the nurse says.

"And will Luke need one?" Hannah asks.

"Yes," the nurse says. "Yes for the kids, with the eyes, always. Otherwise they are moving too much."

178

"I won't move," Luke says. "I promise."

"Is it really necessary?" Hannah asks.

The nurse nods. "Yes," she says. "Is necessary."

"It's better really, Luke," Tristan says. "If I had the choice, I'd have one too. Have a nice little snooze in a comfy bed and when you wake up we'll be next to you watching over you and it will all be fixed."

With the nurse and Tristan working together, they translate and answer almost fifty questions about Luke's medical past, his allergies, drug histories and blood type, and then the nurse leaves Hannah to read and sign the other forms: an admissions request, a financial resources form and a consent form.

"I can't translate half of this," Tristan tells her, studying the first page.

"It doesn't really matter, does it?" Hannah says as she puts her initials on each page. "There isn't really any choice, so . . . But call Cliff for me, would you?"

When she has finished the forms, Tristan dials Cliff's number and hands Hannah the phone.

She tells him that they are going to operate, and that she is randomly signing anything that they put in front of her. She asks him to agree that this is the right thing for her to be doing.

"I guess so," Cliff says. "Unless you want me to phone Europe Assistance and see what they say."

"What could they possibly say?" Hannah asks.

"I don't know. They might tell us if it's a good hospital or not, or if it's better to fly him home, or . . ."

"There's no time, Cliff," Hannah says. "They said it's urgent that they get the glass out. And it is a good hospital. I can tell."

"*How* can you tell?"

"I just . . . I don't know. I just can. It's clean and friendly and we've been here less than an hour and we've already seen the surgeon."

"Well, just go with the flow then," Cliff says. "You know best. Give me the address and I'll come and join you. And I will phone Europe Assistance just in case."

"Oh, the nurse is here. We have to go. Don't come now. I'll . . . I'll phone you when we've stopped rushing around." Hannah hands Tristan's phone back. "Thanks," she says.

The nurse leads them to a pre-op ward, where they lay Luke fully clothed on a gurney, take a blood sample to confirm his blood type, and inject him with a sedative.

"You're being so brave," Hannah tells him. "I'm so proud of you."

"It didn't really hurt," Luke says of the injection.

"This *is* amazing service," Tristan comments. "I mean, we've only been here an hour, and they're prepping him for s—"

Hannah raises her hand, silencing him. "Scary word," she mouths.

Tristan nods. "Sorry," he says.

"How are you doing there?" Hannah asks Luke.

"Sleepy," he says, his head already lolling.

Yet another nurse appears, checks over Hannah's paperwork, and then she and Hannah wrestle Luke's floppy body from his clothes and into a hospital gown.

"OK, je le prends," she says, kicking off the brakes on the trolley. "À tout à l'heure."

"She says she can take it from here," Tristan translates.

"Sure," Hannah says, reaching out to grasp the rail of the

trolley as a wave of panic sweeps over her. "I can go with him, right? Tell me I can go with him?"

Tristan translates Hannah's question, but the nurse's reply is clear enough. "Non."

"But he's eleven," Hannah says. She's breaking out in a sweat at the idea of abandoning her son to these strangers.

"I think it's normal, Han'," Tristan says. "It's an operating theatre."

"S'il vous plaît," the nurse says, nodding at Hannah's whitened knuckles, and so she slowly releases her grip.

"How long, Tristan? Ask her how long it will be," Hannah says as the nurse pulls the trolley from her, expertly spins it, and then begins to push it towards the double doors.

"One hour." The nurse casts the words over her shoulder as she pushes through the doors. "Maybe one hour and half. You wait here, and I come get you for wake up." She points at the waiting room, and then she and Luke vanish beyond the closing doors.

In the small, empty waiting room, Hannah sits, then stands and paces to the window, then walks back and sits and sighs before standing up all over again. "I just don't know what to do with myself," she says.

"I know," Tristan says, chewing a fingernail. "It's horrible."

"He'll be OK, won't he?" Hannah asks.

Tristan's honest reaction would be to shrug, but he suppresses this and nods. "Of course he will," he says. "They said it was good that we got him here so quickly. And the nurse said that the surgeon is a good one."

"But she would say that, wouldn't she?"

"I'm not sure," Tristan says. "I have known a few nurses in my time – of the male variety of course – and they rarely

181

had a good word to say about the doctors. So I think that it's a good sign."

"This is my fault," Hannah says. "So stupid of me leaving them in the pool unattended. Anything could have happened. Anything *has* happened."

"If it's anyone's fault, it's mine," Tristan says. "I should never have bought him that mask."

"You couldn't possibly know that this would happen," Hannah says.

"No, well . . . Nor could you."

"I think Aïsha smashed it," Hannah says. "She seemed guilty. That girl so needs some discipline."

"But she got him out of the water," Tristan points out. "That can't have been easy. Luke's almost as big as her now."

"Yes," Hannah says with a sigh. "Yes, I suppose so."

A series of images of Luke with a missing eye spontaneously manifest on the projection screen of Hannah's mind – an empty eye socket, a sewn-up eyelid, a glass eye pointing the wrong way – and the weight of tears that have been building since the day's drama began suddenly overwhelms her. She sinks into the nearest chair and puts her head in her hands and lets the tears roll down her face. Her body shudders.

Tristan crosses the room and sits next to her and drapes one arm around her shoulders.

"God, I hope he's OK," Hannah says through snuffles. "I love that boy so much. I just couldn't bear . . ."

"I'm sure he will be," Tristan says again. "Do you want me to call Cliff?" he asks, unsure as to how best to deal with Hannah's tears. He doesn't really know her *that* well.

Hannah nods, but then as Tristan pulls his phone from his pocket, she snatches it from him, says, "Actually don't," and then hands it back. They sit in silence for a moment as both Hannah and Tristan wonder why she just did this.

"Is everything OK between you and . . ." Tristan starts.

But Hannah interrupts him, saying simply, "Bathroom, sorry."

In the women's toilets she stares at herself in the mirror for a moment. Her mascara has run. She looks a mess. *What is happening here?* she thinks numbly. And then she shakes her head, lowers her face to the sink, and washes away the tears.

When she returns, Tristan looks up at her expectantly. "Cliff phoned," he says.

"Is he coming?"

"I told him to come in an hour," Tristan says. "At twelve."

Hannah glances at the clock. "Right," she says.

"I said that was best."

"Right."

"Is that OK?" Tristan asks.

Hannah nods.

"Aïsha can't stop crying apparently."

"No, well . . ." Hannah says.

For fifteen minutes they sit in silence interrupted only by an occasional set of heals clip-clopping along the corridor. And then, out of the blue, the culmination of some private thought process, Tristan says, "It must be amazing to have a child. To know that he's your own flesh and blood."

"It is," she says. "And at times, like today, it's really painful. It's hard to describe."

"Yes," Tristan says. "Yes, I'm sure."

"It's like his pain is your own. Only worse. Because you can't do anything about it."

"Yes," Tristan says. "I get that."

"Did you ever think about children of your own?" Hannah asks.

Tristan tuts. "It's not really an option, is it?" he says.

"I suppose. Though people do manage it, don't they? Like the gay couple on that TV show, *Modern Family*."

"Sure," Tristan says. "There are ways. If you're determined enough. But I've never been able to keep a boyfriend for more than a week, so . . ."

"A week?" Hannah says. "Really?"

"No," Tristan replies. "*Not* really."

"Oh."

"You know that anyway. You know I was with Paul for two years."

"Yes. I'm sorry. My mind's, you know . . . elsewhere."

"Understandable."

"So what happened with Paul?" Hannah asks. "I don't think I ever really knew. He just vanished one day. And you were with . . . Mark? Mike?"

"Matt. But it's OK," Tristan says. "We don't have to talk about me."

"No, it's good," Hannah says. "I swear that clock moved a whole minute when you were talking."

"It's the world's slowest clock, isn't it?" Tristan says.

"Torture," Hannah agrees.

"Well, Paul was lovely," Tristan says. "Kind, thoughtful, generous . . ."

"Yes, I liked him, I must say."

"But kind of boring."

"Really?" Hannah says. "I thought he was pretty funny."

"Oh, he was funny. But I missed all the stuff I did before, I guess. Going out, clubbing, drinking, dancing. Even dating.

I actually missed all the cruising and chatting people up online and the wondering if . . ."

"The excitement of the chase," Hannah says.

"Exactly. We'd be in of an evening, and you'd just know that all that was going to happen was *Corrie* and a glass of wine."

"*Corrie?*"

"*Coronation Street*. He's from Manchester, so . . ."

"Of course."

"And though, in a way, it was all I ever wanted – you know, someone to snuggle with on the sofa – I just kept feeling this *is this it* kind of feeling. I don't suppose that makes any sense to you."

"It does," Hannah says. "More than you can imagine. But you can't have both, can you? That's the point."

"Both?"

"Yes. I mean, you can't have the excitement *and* the stability. It's life's great dilemma. That every choice excludes something else."

Tristan nods thoughtfully. "After Paul, I thought I wanted to be single forever more, but then I got bored with that too, so I thought maybe I needed someone really adventurous. An extreme sports enthusiast or a mountaineer or something mad like that."

"Right," Hannah says. "And?"

"Well, it's a bit of a tall order, isn't it?" Tristan says. "I mean, I can't even find someone who wants a relationship most of the time. It's never really going to happen."

"No."

"So I went out with Matt. But Matt was just a butterfly. You know, flitting from one thing to the next. So he flitted on elsewhere. And now I think that I should have stayed with

Paul really. I think that leaving Paul was my greatest error probably."

"And is he still . . . I mean, couldn't you get back with him?"

"Nah, he's married now. Well, civil partnered. To a really nice guy. A bit boring too. They watch *Coronation Street* together and eat too many doughnuts. It probably wouldn't have suited me anyway."

"Life's complicated," Hannah says.

"And there's no instruction manual, is there?"

"No. I guess you always regret the choices you didn't make, because you imagine that they would have been better choices, that's the thing. But in the end, you just have to choose something and get on with it. Because if you hedge your bets forever, well, you end up with nothing, don't you?"

"Like me?" Tristan says.

"No, I was thinking of Jill to be perfectly honest."

"Yes. We're very similar that way, Jill and me," Tristan says. "Never satisfied. I often think that people all have different genes or skill-sets or whatever and, you know, perhaps, I just didn't get the one called '*making a relationship work*'. Maybe that's just bad luck for me. But maybe I can't really do anything about it."

"I suppose," Hannah says.

"You don't sound convinced."

"I'm not sure it's a skill," Hannah says. "Or a gene. And I'm not sure it comes down to luck either. I tend to think it's a choice. I tend to think most things are a choice."

Tristan chews his lip as he thinks about this.

"God, it's only twenty past," Hannah says, nodding at the clock.

"I know."

"I saw a drinks machine down the hall," Hannah says. "Have you got any change? I haven't got a penny. Or a centime or whatever."

Tristan stands and jingles his pocket. "Sure," he says. "I'll go. What do you want?"

"Coke I think," Hannah says. "I could do with some caffeine."

"Diet, or . . ."

"Normal. I think I need some sugar too."

When Tristan returns, he hands Hannah her bottle of Coke. "Open it carefully. The machine shook them up a bit during delivery," he says, lifting his half-empty bottle to show her. "Mine went all over the place and I had to get someone to mop it up."

"I hate that," Hannah says. "It happened to me in a super-market once."

They stand side by side at the window and sip their drinks. "Crazy to build the whole town on the hill like that," Hannah comments.

"I suppose it was so they could see the enemy coming or something," Tristan says.

"Yeah," Hannah says vaguely – she's thinking about something else. "Last night you said that Jill is jealous of me," she says.

"Did I?"

"Yes. You did. Is she really?"

Tristan nods. "Yes," he says. "Yes, she is a bit."

"It's funny," Hannah says. "I was thinking about that last night after you went to bed. We're all jealous of what we haven't got, aren't we?"

"Well, except those of us who have got it all," Tristan says, nudging Hannah vaguely with his hip.

"Me?" Hannah says. "You have to be joking."

"A husband, a son, a house . . ."

"A dishwasher. Three bedrooms. A Dyson," Hannah continues.

"Exactly. So what's missing from your life?"

Hannah shrugs. "I don't know," she says. "I guess a proper career, a daughter, passion, excitement, adventure, travel."

"We're in France. Doesn't that count?"

"If you knew how hard I had to twist Cliff's arm . . . But you can always find something to feel dissatisfied about I suppose. It's like you say, maybe none of us can help wondering if this is really all there is. If this is really *it*."

"There's Cliff," Tristan says.

"Yes, Cliff . . ." Hannah says. "I'm not sure what I . . ."

Hannah belatedly realises that Tristan isn't *discussing* Cliff, he's pointing at him in the square below. "Oh! Yes!" she says.

They watch him cross the pavement and then attempt to pull a door open before realising that it opens the other way, then he enters the building and vanishes from sight.

"I'll go down and meet him," Tristan says. "I wonder where he p—. Shit!"

Hannah turns and she and Tristan stare into each other's eyes, and then, in unison, they say, "The car!"

Despite Tristan's directions, it takes fifteen minutes for Cliff to find the opthalmology waiting room. He crosses the floor and hugs Hannah, and notices, but doesn't comment on, the brevity of the embrace. "Any news?" he asks.

Hannah shakes her head. "Nothing new yet. Only what I told you on the phone. He's still in there."

"Tristan's car got towed," Cliff announces. "Apparently he left it right in front of the ambulance bay."

"I know, I was there."

"Daft bugger."

"Well, we were kind of in a hurry."

"Sorry, I know that. I just meant . . ." Cliff's voice fades out.

"Poor Tris'," Hannah says.

"He's gone to get it from the pound – is it called a pound? Anyway it's walking distance, so . . ." Cliff says.

"We must give him money to pay the fine or whatever," Hannah says. "I don't know what I would have done without him."

Cliff vaguely resents what he perceives as the implication that Tristan succeeded where he himself has failed. "I don't think Tristan is short of a few bob," he says.

"Neither are we," Hannah says.

"No."

"Well then."

"I could kill Tristan for giving him that shitty mask," Cliff says.

"Don't, Cliff," Hannah says. "He feels terrible about it already. Personally, I could kill Aïsha for smashing it."

"Yes, she did too."

"So do we know what actually happened? How, I mean."

"She dive-bombed him in the pool – put her foot through it."

"Stupid little bitch."

"Quite. She cut her ankle too. Nothing major. She didn't even notice till later. But, yes, proof if any were needed."

189

"That girl needs some proper discipline," Hannah says.

"She does," Cliff agrees. He crosses to where Hannah is standing and looks out at the window. "That's a view," he says.

"It is."

"Did they give you any prognosis whatsoever?"

Hannah sighs. "I *told* you all this, Cliff," she says.

"I know, I'm sorry. It's just been difficult, not being here. I keep feeling like I'm missing some vital piece of information."

"I know, I'm sorry," Hannah says. "They vaguely said that he should be fine. But in that bland way hospital staff always do."

"Under-promise, over-deliver," Cliff says.

"Well, hopefully."

"I contacted the assistance people. They said they'll pay part of the cost."

"And the Euro-thingie covers the rest?"

"Part of it," Cliff says. "They were a bit vague about that. I'm not sure they knew to be honest. They said that we might have to pay it all and claim it back. It could run to thousands, they said. They wanted to know if I had the funds."

"And you do."

"Of course."

"Thank God for that," Hannah says.

Cliff slides one arm around her and says, "See, I am good for something."

Hannah shrugs him off. There's something unsavoury about the comment that she can't quite put her finger on, but something about it displeases her profoundly.

"We will be OK, won't we?" Cliff asks.

"What do you mean?" Hannah asks, mainly to gain extra thinking time.

"I mean with Luke and Aïsha and all this hassle and James maybe arriving."

"Yes? And?"

"Well, you won't let it . . . you won't let it wreck everything?" Cliff says. "You won't let it wreck *us*. Not when Luke needs us? Not when he's depending on us."

Hannah's feelings about Cliff, which have been a maelstrom of confusion for the last few days, solidify at that second into hatred. She has never liked it when people attempt to manipulate her feelings – no doubt because her mother was such an expert – but such blatant use of their injured son strikes her as beyond the pale.

"Of course I won't," she says sharply.

"You promise?" Cliff asks.

"Of course I promise," Hannah says. But childish or not, she has her fingers crossed behind her back.

Just as Cliff starts to lurch towards her for another attempt at a hug she is saved by the appearance of a short, black female nurse pushing through the double doors. She continues along the corridor past them and then suddenly doubles back. "Monsieur et Madame Parker ?" she asks.

"Yes," Hannah says. "Oui."

"Il est sorti," the nurse says. "Il est en salle de réveil. Tout va bien. Il . . ."

"Sorry, do you speak English?" Hannah asks, interrupting her.

"Est-ce que je parle anglais ?" the nurse says. "Non. Je suis désolée – vous êtes en France. Nous parlons français ici."

Hannah shrugs. "I'm sorry," she says. "We don't speak French."

The nurse rolls her eyes, pushes her lips out, makes a short sharp "pff" noise by blowing through her lips, and then spins on one heel and returns from whence she came.

"She seemed stroppy," Hannah says.

"What was all that about?" Cliff asks.

"I don't know," Hannah says. "I don't, as you know, speak French."

"I expect she's gone to get someone else," Cliff says.

"Do you think Luke's OK?" Hannah asks. "She didn't look happy."

"She didn't look like anyone's died either," Cliff says.

"Don't!" Hannah says, genuinely shocked.

"I didn't mean . . . I only meant . . ."

Hannah starts to pace the floor anew. At one point she approaches the double doors and peers through, but there is nothing but another stretch of endless corridor on the far side.

After ten minutes of this, and specifically when Hannah says, "God, I wish Tristan were here," Cliff – despite the bilingual *Staff Only* sign – pushes through the doors, but within seconds the same black nurse as before appears to march him back to the waiting room.

"Can you please find someone who speaks English?" Cliff asks. "We need to know how our son is."

"Non, non, non !" is all the nurse says.

It's another half an hour – half an hour that stretches like a day – before another nurse, a man this time, comes to speak to them.

"Vous ne parlez pas français ?" he asks.

"Sorry," Hannah says.

"Luke is waked up," he says. "He ask for you. Why you 'ere? Come!"

"No one told us," Hannah says as they follow him back down the long corridor again. "Is he OK?"

The nurse doesn't answer their question, but leads them back to the lift, up one floor, and then down an identical corridor to an individual room which Hannah guesses must be almost exactly above where they were standing before.

Inside the room, Luke is lying in bed, his eye bandaged. "Is he awake yet?" Hannah asks.

"Mum?"

"I'm here, baby," Hannah says, running around the bed so that Luke can see her with his good eye.

"I didn't know where you were," Luke slurs, his pronunciation that of someone who has just left a dentist's chair.

"I'm sorry, baby," Hannah says, pulling up a chair and taking his hand. "They didn't tell us you were awake. We came as soon as we knew. We're here now. Is he going to . . .?" Hannah begins to ask, but as she looks up she sees that the nurse has already gone.

Reassured that his parents are there, Luke ceases fighting the anaesthetic and falls asleep again. While Hannah strokes his hand, Cliff makes repeated sorties in an attempt at getting some information about the success, or otherwise, of Luke's operation, but succeeds only in annoying the staff nurse so seriously that, reminding him that he's outside visiting times, she threatens him with eviction. Returning to the room, his tail between his legs, he tells Hannah, "I think we had better just shut up and wait or they'll kick us out."

"He woke up again," Hannah says. "Just for a few seconds."

"Any pain?" Cliff asks.

"No, I don't think so," Hannah says. "I just hope that behind that bandage . . ." She pulls a face.

"I know," Cliff says.

It's not until Tristan returns at four-fifteen that they are able to get fresh information.

"We don't know anything," Hannah tells him, her voice panicky. "Can you do something, Tris'?"

"Sure," Tristan says, "I'll go give them hell."

"I tried," Cliff says. "But they won't know anything until the surgeon does his rounds."

When Tristan returns less than a minute later with a perfectly informed, English-speaking male nurse, only Cliff's solace at getting some information counteracts his desire to punch Tristan.

"Is good," the nurse tells them, and Hannah gasps with relief.

"He have three little glass in his eye, but is OK now. All gone."

He fumbles in his pocket and pulls out a tiny plastic jar. "Glass," he says.

"God," Cliff says, taking it from his grasp, shaking it, then holding it to the light. He tries to hand it back, but the nurse says, "You can keep. But not for the boy. Is dangerous."

"Sure," Cliff says.

"So he'll be OK?" Hannah says, slightly frustrated by all this boyish gloating over the fragments of glass.

"Perfect," the nurse says.

"And his sight?" Cliff asks. "Will that be affected?"

"Perfect," the nurse says. "La rétine . . . retina?"

"Yes, retina."

194

"The retina was not affected. Nor the . . ." he points vaguely to his eye. "The *lentile*," he says. "So it's good."

"Oh thank you," Hannah says, sensing fresh tears forming. "And the eye-patch?"

"I'm sorry?"

"This?" she says, pointing.

"Ah, quarante-huit heures."

"Forty-eight hours," Tristan translates.

"And before we can go home?"

"Non. This . . ." the guy mimes an eye-patch. "Is for forty hours. Two day."

"So we can go home when? Now?"

"Non !" he laughs. He checks his watch. "Twenty hours."

"In twenty hours?" Hannah asks, trying to calculate what time that will be.

"I think he means at eight o'clock," Tristan says.

"Yes at eight clock. I'm sorry, my English is not so good," the nurse says.

"No, it's very good," Hannah says. "Thank you!"

"So now I go get you some *ordonnance* for antibiotics . . ."

"Yes."

"And someone must come with me for . . ." He makes a money gesture.

"Right, that'll be me," Cliff says, eager for an opportunity to prove his worth in all of this.

"Sorry, do we need to come back for a check-up?" Hannah asks.

"Checkap? What is checkap?"

"Must we come back here? In a day, a week? To see the doctor?" Hannah paraphrases.

The nurse shakes his head. "No. It's not *néccessaire* . . ." he says. "OK." He turns towards the door, but then hesitates. "I'm sorry, but only one person in the room," he says. He looks at Hannah. "Maybe you are staying?"

"Yes," Hannah confirms. "I'll stay."

"I'll come with you," Tristan tells Cliff. He turns to Hannah and adds, "Just in case he needs help with the forms or *something*," and winks.

"So I can't come back here when I've paid?" Cliff asks.

"No, I'm sorry. Only one person in this room."

"It's fine. Go home. Have a rest. I'll meet you downstairs at eight," Hannah says.

"At the reception? In A and E?"

"Yes."

"I'll be there," Cliff says. "And if there's some delay, don't worry, I'll wait."

"Thanks."

"You don't have a phone, do you?" Tristan asks Hannah.

"No," Hannah says. She left her battered Nokia in England.

"Here, have mine," Tristan says, proffering his iPhone.

"It's better if I take Cliff's, isn't it?"

"No," Cliff says. "Take Tristan's. My battery is nearly dead."

Tristan hands his phone over. "The code is two-four-six-four," Tristan says.

"Two-four-six-four," Hannah repeats. "Got it."

"And don't go chatting the boys up on Grindr."

"No . . . no, well, I wouldn't even know how."

Tristan flashes the whites of his eyes at her, and then the three men file from the room.

Hannah sits for a moment thinking about Tristan's strange glance. What did it mean? And then she realises, and shakes her head at the fact that even here, even in the midst of this mayhem, Tristan has spotted a cute male nurse.

She peers in at Luke. He is still sleeping. She strokes his forehead gently, then kisses it and pulls her chair a little closer so that she can lay her head next to his body.

A single final tear of relief slides down her cheek, and then against all expectation she falls asleep.

THIRTY

Luke, still vaguely under sedation, falls asleep in the car.

"He has been amazing," Hannah says, glancing back at him.

"Yes," Cliff agrees. "Yes, I'm so proud. Can you imagine what Aïsha would have been like?"

"No," Hannah says. "No, I can't. Tristan said she couldn't stop crying as it is."

"This morning? Yes. It's true."

"Is her heel OK?"

"I think so. It was nothing really – just a scratch. They've gone," Cliff says. "You know that, right?"

"Gone?"

"Uh-huh. Tristan took them to the station when we got back. I think there were too many bad vibrations for her or something. That's what Tris' said."

Like boiling milk, Hannah's anger froths, rises and overflows. "What a cow," she says. "She didn't even wait to see if Luke was OK!" Hannah hesitates, then asks, "When you say, *gone*, you mean . . . ?"

"Oh, just for one night. They went to Nice. Change of scene, she said."

"Oh, right," Hannah says, swallowing, and trying to force herself to calm down. "God, I thought you meant that she'd gone completely. As in gone home."

"All the same, she could have phoned," Cliff says. "She might have shown a little concern."

Hannah shakes her head and sighs. "I think I'm getting to the point where . . ." she says.

"Yes?"

She shrugs. There's no point feeding Cliff's Jill-phobia. "Oh, nothing. It's just Jill, isn't it. So they've gone to Nice, huh?"

"Yes."

"A nice little treat for Aïsha to reward her for all her good behaviour."

"Well, quite."

They drive in silence for a moment until an advertisement for new-build apartments with a price displayed in euros prompts Hannah to ask, "So, how much did it cost? Are we broke?"

Cliff laughs. "The hospital? No, it was fine actually. I had to pay the, what is it they call it? The, you know, patient's contribution."

"The co-pay."

"Yes, that's it. It was twenty per cent. And apparently we can even try to claim that back."

"And how much was that then?"

"Three hundred-ish. Out of one thousand two hundred and sixty or something."

"That's pretty reasonable," Hannah says.

"Quite interesting seeing the bill – I'll show you later. The anaesthetist was almost half of it. It's a good job you got the Euro-card before we left. Otherwise we would have had to pay the whole lot."

"Good old Europe," Hannah says.

"Yes, for once," Cliff agrees.

As Hannah climbs out, the sudden movement makes her feel so dizzy that she has to lean against the car to steady herself. "God, I just realised. I haven't eaten all day," she says.

"I'll carry Luke in," Cliff says.

But Luke is awake. "I'm fine," he says, already emerging from the car.

Tristan comes to greet them. "Hey, kids," he says. "Everything OK?"

Hannah, still leaning against the car, looks at him and smiles weakly. "I think my blood sugar's low," she says. "I forgot to have lunch. Could you make me a quick sandwich or something?"

"I can do that," Cliff says. "What do you want? Ham? Cheese? Tuna?"

"There's no need, Cliff," Tristan says. "I . . ."

"Just let me make my wife a sandwich, will you?" Cliff says.

Hannah notes, but chooses to ignore, the tension between the two men. She simply doesn't have the energy to care right now.

When they reach the patio however, it's clear why sandwiches aren't needed. The table is covered with food.

"Oh, Tris'," Hannah says. "You didn't have to do all of this." The truth is that she would rather have had a quick sandwich and gone to bed.

"If you'd rather just have a sandwich, I'll make you one," Cliff offers, and Hannah wonders briefly if he has read her mind.

"No, it's fine," Hannah says. "This is lovely."

"I thought you'd be hungry," Tristan says.

"Yes, well, I am, I'm starving."

"I'm hungry too," Luke says.

"So tell me what happened?" Hannah says, once they are all served and seated. "I still don't really know."

"Aïsha dive-bombed me," Luke says.

"So it is Aïsha's fault entirely, or . . . ?"

Luke shrugs. "Well, I kind of dive-bombed her first," he admits.

"Right."

"She was asleep on the air bed like you was when I squirted you."

"Like you *were*," Hannah says.

"Yeah."

"So you sort of started it, did you?" Hannah asks.

Luke shrugs again. "Yeah," he says. "I suppose so."

Dinner over, Luke, unusually, admits that he is tired, so Hannah takes him to bed. "You were so, so brave today," she tells him as she undresses him.

"I wish we took photos," Luke says. "For school. Stephen Hill had his appendix out, but this is way cooler."

"I didn't think. I'm sorry," she says, arranging the bedclothes over him.

Luke yawns. "It's weird having only one eye though," he says.

"Well, it won't be for long," Hannah tells him. "You're lucky it's not for life."

Hannah sits for thirty seconds watching him breathe, then says, "I was so proud of you, you know. You were so brave."

But Luke is already asleep.

"Wow, that was quick, even for you," she says quietly.

She sits and watches her son sleeping for five minutes, and then, without undressing, or even brushing her teeth, she climbs onto the bed beside him. He's almost too old for her to do this now. Indeed, if he were awake, it's fifty–fifty these days whether he would snuggle against her or tell her to leave. But today counts as special circumstances. She loves him so much she simply can't bring herself to go.

When Hannah wakes up the next morning, Luke is gone. She drags herself from his bed and staggers to the bathroom. She feels as if she has been sedated herself.

In the mirror she examines her face: she has a deep imprint from the seam of the pillow right across her left cheek. "Foxy," she murmurs with irony. She runs a finger along the indent before bending over the sink and washing her face vigorously.

Outside on the patio, she finds Cliff, Luke and Tristan having breakfast.

"You're up before me," she says, kissing Luke's head as she passes behind him. "How is my little soldier this morning?"

"Tired," Luke says.

"That will be the anaesthetic," Hannah says.

"No, it's your fault. You took all the bed. I had to sleep with Dad. And he snores."

"Oops," Hannah says. "Sorry. I meant to move but I fell asleep."

"That's what you always say," Luke says. "I couldn't even wake you up."

"Sorry," Hannah says, pulling a guilty face.

"Tris' says I look like a pirate," Luke says proudly.

Hannah laughs. "He's right. You do."

"So do you a bit," Tristan says.

Hannah runs a finger across her cheek. "What this?"

Tristan nods.

"I know," she says. "It's awful, isn't it."

"I went to the pharmacy," Tristan tells her, pushing a paper bag across the table towards her.

"I was perfectly happy to go," Cliff says. "But Tristan wouldn't let me."

"Well, you don't speak French," Tristan points out.

"I would have managed."

"I doubt that. I had a ten-minute argument to get these," Tristan says.

"Really?" Hannah asks, peering inside the bag. "Why?"

"Lack of ID," Tristan says. "My name didn't match with the prescription or something. But I used my famous powers of persuasion on them. No one can resist."

"My ID would have matched, wouldn't it?" Cliff says. "I wouldn't have had that problem."

Hannah yawns and rubs her brow. She looks between Tristan and Cliff's faces and wonders why they are being so competitive this morning and vaguely recalls some bitchiness last night.

"I'd like to have seen you try," Tristan is saying.

"Boys. Boys!" Hannah interrupts. "It really doesn't matter who got them, does it?" She fishes in the bag and pulls out a box of blister-packed pills, then a bottle of eye-wash, another of eye drops and a package of fresh eye-patches.

"The pills are two at breakfast today," Tristan says. "He's already taken those . . ."

"Antibiotics?"

"Yes. And then one every morning. You have to do the eye drops and change the dressing three times a day."

"Will that hurt?" Luke asks.

"No, I don't think it will hurt at all," Hannah says. "And anyway, it's only today and tomorrow, right, Tris'?"

"Right. Just two days the guy at the hospital said."

"He did," Cliff agrees. "I remember. I was there too."

After breakfast, Cliff carries a batch of plates in and begins to unload and then stack the dishwasher. Tristan continues to carry the rest of the breakfast things back indoors.

"So what's going on with you two?" Hannah asks him quietly when he returns. The kitchen window is closed and Hannah's pretty sure that Cliff cannot hear them.

"Who?" Tristan says, pausing with a jar of marmalade in one hand.

"You and Cliff."

"Nothing," Tristan says. "Why?"

"Nothing," Hannah says.

"Nothing!" Tristan repeats more definitively. "Anyway, why ask me? Ask Cliff."

Hannah sighs. Until that last phrase, she had been prepared to believe him. Now she knows something's wrong. "Luke! Where are you going?" she shouts. Luke is heading off in the direction of the pool. He's wearing swimming shorts.

"The pool," he says. "I won't wear the mask."

"Well, you can't, can you?" Hannah says. "It's broken and binned."

"So is it OK?"

Hannah stands. "Come with me and let me change that

204

dressing. And then you can as long as you don't get it wet. You'll have to keep your head out of the water, OK?" She ushers Luke back indoors.

As they pass the kitchen, Cliff looks up from the dishwasher and asks, "Is everything OK?"

"Fine," Hannah replies. "I'm just going to change Luke's dressing."

"I can do that if you want," Cliff says.

"No thanks. We're fine," Hannah says, pulling a puzzled face as they continue down the corridor.

Luke's bedroom is already too hot – the sunshine is streaming in. She pulls the shutters closed with a *clack* and then sits him on the bed and gently starts to pull back the dressing.

"Ouch," Luke protests.

"I'm sorry, it's a bit stuck," Hannah tells him.

"Owww!" Luke says in a voice that confirms to her that it doesn't really hurt at all.

"There, that's it. How's that?"

Luke shrugs.

"Well, open your eye," she prompts.

Luke opens his injured eye and closes the good one. "It's all blurry," he says.

"Yes, it's a bit gunky," Hannah tells him, fiddling in the paper bag. "That's why we have this to clean it."

She opens the bottle of eye-wash and fills the plastic eye-bath with the solution. "So tip your head forward onto . . . that's right," she says. "And now tip your head back. That's it. And now open your eyes and hold this in place . . . that's right."

"Do I open both of them?"

205

"Yes."

"It's cold," Luke says.

"Yes."

"Like swimming underwater."

"Yes. It doesn't hurt though, does it?"

"Only here," Luke says, using the hand that was supposed to be holding the eye-bath in place to point to his eyebrow and spilling the solution down his chest.

Hannah and Luke both laugh. "Sorry," Luke says.

"It doesn't matter," Hannah tells him, scooping a dirty T-shirt from the floor and using it to dry Luke's chest. "So how's that now? Can you see better?"

"Yeah. It's OK," Luke says.

"OK, *OK*?" Hannah asks. "Or OK, perfect?"

"OK perfect. Like normal."

"Good."

"So do I still have to have the patch?"

"You do, I'm afraid. But only until tomorrow night."

"That's OK," Luke says. "I don't mind."

Hannah opens the box containing the eye-drops. "Now, tip your head back and keep it there," she says, fiddling with the plastic seal around the bottle.

At the sound of a car door, followed by their gate opening and closing, Hannah stands, and, still fiddling with the packaging, she crosses the room and peers out through the slats.

She sees a grey hatchback parked beyond the gate and a man closing the gate behind him. He turns and looks straight at her, but she can tell from his blank expression that he can't see her.

He has gone grey. That is the first thing that she notices. She could have deduced as much had she thought about it.

After all, Cliff has been grey for years. He has grown a little goatee beard as well. It suits him.

Beyond the shutters, Hannah watches as James crosses his arms behind his head and stretches. He's wearing what looks like hiking gear. Walking boots, lightweight shorts with lots of pockets, a sleeveless checkered shirt. He looks fit and rugged and to her eyes – in a *Brokeback Mountain* kind of way – a little bit gay.

"Mum?" Luke says.

Without averting her gaze, Hannah raises one hand behind her and says, her voice distant, "Yes. Just wait a minute, sweetheart. I can't get this open."

She watches James as he peers inside the Mégane, no doubt looking for clues to confirm that he's in the right place. He must see something which reassures him, because he then crosses the gravel until he's standing just feet away from her – she actually sniffs the air in case she might catch the scent of him.

He cross-links his hands, stretches again, purses his lips, exhales slowly, and then, starting to walk towards the front of the house, calls out, with theatrical bravado, "Hello? Hello? Anybody home?"

"Mum!" Luke says again.

Hannah turns back to see Luke with his head still tilted back.

"Sorry," she says, returning to the bed and finally wrestling the cap from the bottle of eye-drops. "So open your eye and look up at the ceiling . . . There."

"Yuck," Luke says. "I can taste it."

"Yes, that's funny, isn't it," Hannah says.

"It's stingy."

"Yes, just a bit. But it will be OK in a minute."

"Who was that?"

"Who was who?"

"I heard someone outside."

"I'm not sure," Hannah lies. "Let's get this dressing on and then we can go and see. How does that sound?"

Luke's eye re-bandaged, Hannah says, "OK, Luke. Off you go. I'll just put these things away and I'll be out. And don't get it wet, OK?"

Luke runs off and Hannah sits back down on the bed and rests her temple against her fingertips. She sits and stares at her feet. She wiggles her toes.

From the other side of the house she can hear the men's voices but not their words.

She takes a series of long deep breaths, and then, on an exhalation she breathes, "OK!" and stands.

Out on the patio, Cliff, Tristan and Luke are standing with their backs to her, almost as if to prevent James, opposite, from entering. It looks like some kind of rugby defence.

James, facing her, is the first to see her arrive, and she sees him look past Cliff; she sees his eyes wrinkle as he smiles.

". . . that you found it," Cliff is saying.

"I just used the GPS," James replies. "Brought me straight here."

James nods at Hannah and grins, and Cliff turns to see her. "Ah, there she is!" he says, stepping to one side to make room.

Hannah moves forward so that she is between Cliff and Tristan and bristles a little at the implied possession when Cliff lays an arm around her shoulders and says, "My wonderful wife."

"Hi James," Hannah says. "You're looking very . . ."

"Yes?"

"Very *alive* actually."

James laughs. "Why thank you?" he says. "You're looking very *alive* too?"

"Gosh, you *do* sound Australian," Hannah says.

"Well, it has been ten years?" James replies. "More than ten years?" His voice goes up at the end of each sentence as if, perhaps, he's unsure of what he's saying, as if it's a question.

"Yes," Hannah says. "Yes, I know. Well, *now* I know."

Why am I being so bitchy? she thinks. "Would you like something? Tea? Coffee? Juice?"

"Keep going?" James says/asks.

"Beer, wine?" Hannah offers.

James nods. "Sure, a beer would be great?"

Hannah heads to the kitchen and pulls a single beer from the chill-box at the bottom.

She pauses and watches through the window, now ajar, as the men discuss the pros and cons of GPS. *Men*, she thinks. *Fifteen years apart and they're discussing GPS.* She studies James' face as he talks animatedly, notices again the incredible blue of his eyes, and then he glances indoors and sees her watching and, slightly flustered, she returns outside and hands him the beer.

"You aren't expecting me to drink alone?" James says.

Cliff glances at his watch. "It's a bit early for me," he says.

"For me too," Tristan agrees.

"I'm still on Ozzie time," James says. "Hannah! Have a beer with me so I don't feel so lonely?"

"Hannah never drinks beer," Cliff says.

"Actually," she says, "I will." She heads back to the kitchen and returns with a second can.

"I can't even remember the last time I saw you drink beer," Cliff says once she has reappeared, the can in her hand.

"No," Hannah agrees as she pulls the ring-pull and chinks her can against James'. "I'm glad I still have the power to surprise. Cheers, James. Welcome back. Welcome back from the dead."

THIRTY-ONE

Tristan makes a fresh pot of coffee for Cliff and himself and the adults settle around the large table on the patio. Luke, intrigued by the newcomer, soon joins them as well, saying, "The pool's kind of boring on your own. When's Aïsha coming back?"

"Should be today," Cliff says. "Maybe even this morning."

"Is it more interesting when Aïsha's dive-bombing you?" Tristan asks.

"No, not really," Luke replies, with a sheepish grin.

"So what happened to your eye, Bud?" James asks.

"I smashed my mask and got glass in it," Luke explains.

"We had a day of drama yesterday at the hospital," Hannah tells him. "You missed all the fun. He had a general anaesthetic – the works."

"That's a quick recovery then," James says.

"It is," Hannah agrees, stroking Luke's head.

"So how did you get down here?" Tristan asks James. "Did you drive all the way, or . . . ?"

"No, I flew to Nice with some low-cost outfit," James says.

"EasyJet?"

"Yep. That's the one. It wasn't very low cost at all, in fact."

"Well, you have to book in advance," Tristan says. "If you buy your ticket three or even six months beforehand, it can be very cheap. Otherwise it's pretty much the same price as everyone else. More sometimes."

"I'm not really a six-months-in-advance kinda guy," James says.

"No," Tristan agrees. "I know what you mean. Nor am I. And the car is a hire car then?"

James nods. "A rental. Yes. I picked it up at the airport. I guess I should bring it inside," he says, standing. "It's still parked out on the road."

When he returns, he changes seats so that he is directly opposite Hannah and Luke. "So where's your sister, Luke?" he asks.

"My sister?" Luke says.

"Aïsha, is it?" James says. "She must be, what, fifteen?"

Luke shakes his head. "She's not my *sister*," Luke says, with what sounds like disgust.

Cliff frowns and catches Hannah's eye.

"Aïsha's Jill's daughter," Hannah explains. "My sister's daughter. They're here with us on holiday, but they've gone off to Nice. They should be back soon."

"Oh," James says, looking confused. "So how old are you, Luke?"

"Eleven," Luke says. "Aïsha's thirteen."

"Oh," James says. "OK."

Hannah can see him counting, calculating. She can see him trying to understand. "They're like brother and sister really," she says, trying to head off any more embarrassing questions. "Which is nice for them, being only children."

"Sure," James says, nodding thoughtfully.

"So you live in Australia?" Hannah asks, attempting to change the subject. "That must be nice."

"Yes," James says. "Yes, I'm Australian now. I took the nationality."

"Why did you do that?" Cliff asks.

James shrugs, and swigs at his beer. "I had my reasons," he says.

Tristan nods at James' hand. "So is that a wedding ring?" he asks. "Did you find yourself an Australian beauty?"

Hannah's stomach lurches. Which is absurd. She can't work out how she managed to not notice the ring.

"This?" James says, using his other hand to turn the ring. "Yes. I was married. Not now though. I just . . . I can't really imagine taking this off," he says.

"Any children?" Hannah asks.

James physically winces at the question. They all see it. "I . . ." he says. He closes his eyes for a second, and then reopens them and adds, "Hey, let's not talk about me. Tell me what you guys have been up to all these years."

"Is he gay, do you think?" Tristan murmurs when he catches Hannah alone in the kitchen.

"I haven't the foggiest, Tristan," she says, only barely hiding her irritation at the frivolous nature of the question. "He wasn't fifteen years ago, but who knows. Why don't you ask him?"

Luke runs into the kitchen at that moment and announces, "Jill's here. She wants to know if you've got any money."

"Money?" Hannah asks, drying her hands on a tea-towel.

"To pay the taxi guy."

"I've got fifty euros, I think," Hannah says, heading to her room for her purse.

"I've got some cash too if you need it," Tristan calls after them.

Out at the gate, she finds Jill standing next to the open

cab-driver's window, a circle of expensive-looking shopping bags at her feet.

"Hi Han'," she says. "Can you please pay this guy for me? He doesn't take credit cards."

"Where's Aïsha?" Hannah asks.

"She went inside," Jill says, nodding towards the back of the house.

"I've got fifty," Hannah tells her. "Is that enough?"

"It's ninety-seven," Jill says. "I haven't got any cash left at all."

"Ninety-seven?!" Hannah exclaims, turning back to the house. "I'll see what Cliff has."

The taxi paid, Jill heads to her room to shower and change. When she returns, she makes a bee-line for the new arrival. "So you must be James," she says, interrupting a conversation between James and Tristan.

"Yes," James says, holding out his hand.

"I'm Jill," she says, grabbing it and pulling him in for an embrace. "We spoke on the phone."

"Right," James says. "So that was you."

"So you found it OK?" Jill asks. "My directions were spot-on then?"

"You gave me the address," James says. "That was spot-on."

"Yes, of course," Jill says, wondering why she even said that. "So is everyone looking after you?"

"They are."

Jill nods. James' expression is a mixture of wry amusement and confusion. It's a very attractive look, she decides. "Anything you need?" Jill asks.

"Another stubby would be good," James says.

"A what?"

"Sorry, a beer," James explains.

"Coming right up," Jill says.

Hannah, who has been watching this exchange from the doorway, follows Jill into the kitchen. "Please don't flirt with him," she says as her sister stoops to pull a beer from the fridge.

"Why?" Jill asks. "Do you want him for yourself?"

"No," Hannah says.

"Well then! Anyway, I wasn't flirting with him. I was just being hospitable."

Hannah raises one eyebrow and sighs. "I just think that the dynamics around here have been complicated enough the last few days, don't you? It would be nice to have a normal, relaxing time for a bit."

"I'm just being friendly," Jill says.

"Sure," Hannah says, then, "I still can't believe you spent nearly a hundred euros on a taxi."

"Well, if you choose not to invest in your own environment-wrecking, carbon-pumping box of metal then sometimes a taxi is your only choice," Jill says.

"I just meant that if you had phoned, one of us would have come and got you."

"You'll get your money back," Jill says.

"I'm not worried about the money," Hannah says.

"In which case you *won't* get it back," Jill laughs.

"I knew I wouldn't anyway," Hannah says. "You never honour your debts."

Jill puts one hand on her hip. "Oh, come on, Han'," she says. "Lighten up, will you? This is supposed to be a holiday."

"It's been a stressful couple of days, Jill," Hannah says. "I don't feel very *light*."

215

"I know. I was here. Remember?"

"You were here until you decided to swan off to Nice for a little shopping trip," Hannah says, pointedly.

"Ah, *now* we're getting to the point."

"Honestly, Jill. I'm in the hospital wondering whether my son is going to lose an eye, and you take your daughter – who caused all the trouble in the first place – off on a shopping spree to Nice? Did you even wonder how Luke was doing? Did you even care?"

"That's so unfair!" Jill protests, her voice louder now. "And you know it."

"I don't think that's unfair at all."

"We knew Luke was fine before we left."

"Did you? How?"

"Tristan told us when he got back. He said everything was fine and that you'd be home in a few hours."

"Oh. I got confused. I thought you left before then, but of course you didn't."

"And we had been worried sick all morning. Aïsha couldn't stop . . ."

"Crying, yes, I heard," Hannah says.

"So when we found out everything was OK I decided it would be better for us, and for you, if we all had a bit of space."

"OK," Hannah concedes. "I still don't think rewarding Aïsha by taking her shopping was—"

"And it wasn't a reward. I wanted some time alone so that I could talk to her. And I did. We stayed in a horrible little hotel, if you must know, and we had a good long talk about the dope and the mask and how serious it could have been and I made her fully aware that she was out of order and that she had better buck her ideas up."

216

"Right," Hannah says. "And then you took her shopping."

Jill shakes her head. "I hate you sometimes, Hannah," she says.

Hannah blinks slowly. "I know," she says. "It's fairly mutual, actually."

"The shopping was Aïsha's idea . . ."

"I'll bet it was."

"Those are gifts. For you. We bought holiday gifts for all of you. We thought it would be *nice*."

Hannah swallows with difficulty.

"So . . ." Jill says, tiling her head sideways momentarily.

"I see," Hannah says.

"You see, do you?"

Hannah shrugs.

"This is where *you* say sorry," Jill tells her.

"OK, I'm sorry," Hannah says. "Look, I *am*. It's just all this . . ." she says, gesturing vaguely around her. "But you see how it looked, right? We got back from the hospital and you'd gone off on a jolly to Nice. Then you reappear with a pile of shopping bags and ask me to pay for the taxi."

"God, are we back to that again?" Jill asks, wide-eyeing her sister. "Shall I go and get some cash out now?" she asks, pointing. "Is that what you want me to do? I could get Tristan to drive me to a bank and be back within an hour if that's what's required here."

"No," Hannah says. "No, really. That's not what I'm saying. I'm just trying to explain how it *looked*."

"Right," Jill says. She looks down at the countertop for a moment, takes a deep breath, and then says, "OK, I get that. And I get that you're stressed out by . . . you know who . . . and I'm sorry Aïsha got Luke stoned, and I'm sorry she smashed

217

his mask. And I'm even sorry the taxi driver didn't take credit cards, OK?"

"OK."

"So can we now, please, just, move on?"

Hannah nods gently and smiles sadly. "It's me," she says flatly. "I'm just so stressed out at the moment."

"So don't be," Jill says. "Have a beer and chillax."

"I hate that word," Hannah says.

"Actually, so do I," Jill agrees. "So, have a beer and *relax*."

"I had one this morning already," Hannah says.

"You devil you," Jill laughs. "Have another." She proffers the beer and Hannah laughs and takes it from her grasp.

"I do love you," Hannah says. "You do know that, right?"

"Of course," Jill says.

"You annoy the hell out of me, but I love you."

"That feeling's mutual too."

James pokes his head around the door. "I guess I shouldn't count on that being for me," he says, nodding at the beer can.

"This?" Hannah says. "No, this one's mine. Get your own."

"I'm sorry, sweetheart," Jill says, turning to face James and sticking her hip out. "Hannah's need was greater than yours." She wrenches open the door to the refrigerator. "I'll get you another," she says. "There's plenty more where that came from."

Because James' presence flusters her in a way she can't quite put her finger on, Hannah chooses to help Tristan prepare lunch rather than remain on the patio.

They are running low on provisions – someone needs to go shopping – so they end up serving a trio of salads: potato and chives; tomato, cucumber and goat's cheese; and last night's pasta salad – recycled. (Tristan replaces the slices of tomato in it with fresh, a "dodgy restaurant trick" he says.)

At one point during the preparations when he's standing right next to Hannah at the sink, Tristan says, "He's nice."

Hannah looks up and sees James talking to Jill while she swings Aïsha in the hammock.

"Yes," Hannah says. "He is, isn't he?"

"So what do you think happened to the wife?" Tristan asks.

"I really don't know," Hannah says. "But I'm sure we'll find out before the holiday is out. I expect you're hoping that he left her because he decided he was gay, aren't you?"

"Something like that," Tristan laughs. "Cheeky! Just dump those chives on the potatoes and then pour the dressing over, OK?"

"Don't you want me to cut them up?"

"Well, of course," Tristan says.

Over dinner, James regales them with tales of his travels: his trip to Thailand, his time in India, his summer in Bali, and finally his arrival in Australia.

"How did you finance all of this?" Hannah asks. "I mean, if it's not an impolite question . . ."

"We got our inheritance," James says. "When Mum died."

"Of course you did," Hannah says.

"Cliff was sensible with his half."

"I bought our house," Cliff reminds her. "Best investment we ever made."

"Exactly. Whereas I blew mine."

"All of it?" Cliff asks.

James nods. "Pretty much," he says. "But it was worth it."

"So how did you end up owning a farm?" Cliff asks.

"Farm?" Hannah says. She has no recollection of anyone mentioning a farm.

"Yes, um, James here, was, um, telling me he has a farm," Cliff stammers.

"Yes," James says, looking confused. "Well, I sort of inherited that too. It was in my wife's family. It was falling apart when we took it over. But as I say, that's a long story."

"We have all night," Jill says. "We have all week for that matter."

"Maybe another time," James says.

"So how long *are* you staying?" Jill asks.

"Where are you staying, more to the point?" Cliff comments.

James shrugs. "I haven't really got that far yet," he says.

"You must stay here," Hannah says automatically, unsure once she has said it if she regrets it or not.

"That would be great," Cliff says, "obviously. But I can't really see where. What about that little auberge place down the road?"

"Rubbish," Hannah says. "There's plenty of room here."

"I could double up with Mum," Aïsha offers, clearly on her best behaviour.

"Well, there you go," Hannah says. "You can have Aïsha's room. And if she gets fed up with it, we can all take turns on the sofa bed."

"I'm totes happy with the sofa bed," James says.

"There's no need," Jill says. Then suddenly wondering if she will still be able to sneak out to see Pascal, she adds, "Not for tonight anyway. Aïsha says she's happy in with me."

"So what kind of farm is it?" Tristan asks. "Is it livestock? Are you a cowboy?"

James laughs. "It's a bit of everything. It's the only way

220

to survive these days. We grow sugar cane and wheat and sorghum."

"Sorghum?"

"Hay to you. So not really a cowboy, no."

"Is it big?" Hannah asks.

"Not really," James says. "Thirty acres, so not huge. But it's pretty beautiful. We have palm trees out front, and a view of the Glasshouse Mountains out back. The sunsets are pretty cool."

"Sounds lovely," Hannah says.

"It is."

Hannah sits and listens to James' smooth baritone voice, so similar to Cliff's, but now, because of the accent, so much more exotic. Tristan keeps topping up her glass, which means that she drinks more than she intended, but she feels that it's doing her good. It's helping her relax.

It's a funny thing, because though it is all new to her, nothing James says actually surprises her. He has led exactly the kind of life she thought he would have all those years ago, a life filled with changes and challenges and achievements and exciting adventures and warmly described friendships. It's such a big life, she can't help but compare it with her own fifteen years living in the same house in Surrey, working at a local school. She feels a bit like she has failed in some fundamental way.

As James tells them about his bionic leg (he was trampled by horses and has metal pins in it that caused him much hassle going through airport security) and about the killer spiders and crocs and snakes of Queensland (Luke and Aïsha are, for once, both gripped), lunch merges into afternoon tea, which merges, as the sun sets, into high tea.

Tristan, throughout, manages to continue rustling up snacks, seemingly from nowhere, and at one point James tells him, "You'd make someone a great wife, Tristan, has anyone ever told you that?"

"Do you know, no one ever has?" Tristan laughs. "Though *I* have been trying to tell everyone that for years."

"He has," Jill says. "He even has it printed on a T-shirt."

"Tristan's a chef," Hannah explains. "Which is why the food's so good."

"Ah, I guessed as much," James says.

"Come to my room later, and I'll show you just how well I fulfil my other wifely duties," Tristan comments. He has had a bit too much to drink as well.

Hannah fears that the comment might be a little too much for an Australian farmer, and says, "You'll have to excuse Tristan. He likes to shock."

James, though, appears to already have Tristan's measure. "I'm afraid I don't bat on your side of the fence, mate," he tells him. "But I'm one happy guy as long as the food keeps coming."

"You know what they say," Tristan says. "If you like it, try it. If you don't like it, try it, you might like it. My room's the one at the end of the corridor on the left."

Everyone laughs.

"Anyway," Tristan says. "Who wants a slice of dessert? I knocked up a little raspberry charlotte earlier on."

"You did?" Hannah asks. "When?"

Tristan sends Hannah a theatrical glare. "OK, *evil* one," he says, putting one hand on his hip and camping it up. "So it's frozen, OK? It still looks pretty tasty though."

"Can we do the thing after?" Aïsha asks.

"The thing?" Cliff asks.

"Yes," Jill says. "Yes, we have little surprises for everyone. Go get them. They're in my room."

That night, in bed, lying plank-like, side by side, Cliff says, "That was nice of Jill to buy us all gifts, wasn't it?"

"Yes," Hannah says. "Yes, they were nice gestures."

"Not sure I'm ever going to wear skimpy orange Speedos, but it's the thought that counts."

"Yes."

"And James is a nice guy, isn't he?"

"He is," Hannah agrees. After everything that has happened, there's something not right about discussing James with Cliff in a polite manner, so she adds, "I'm glad he's not dead."

After a minute's silence, during which Cliff considers rising to that particular challenge but decides against it, he continues, "You maybe shouldn't ask him about his wife though."

"Why not?" Hannah asks. "Do you know something?"

"No," Cliff says. "I just get the feeling he doesn't want to talk about it. I don't think it's a very happy story."

"Yes, I picked that up for myself," Hannah says.

For ten minutes Hannah lies thinking about James sleeping next door in Aïsha's bed, about Australia, about farms, and horses, and crocodiles and combine harvesters, and about how alien the life he leads is, compared with their own suburban existence.

She's assuming that Cliff is asleep, but he suddenly says, "So how do you feel about him? Seeing him after all these years, I mean."

She waits a full three minutes before she makes what she considers to be a pretty convincing snoring, snuffling sound and rolls onto her side. But Cliff isn't fooled one bit.

THIRTY-TWO

It's five a.m. To be precise, it's five *thirteen a.m.* Hannah has been awake for forty-two minutes.

She had hoped that, by lying very still and concentrating on her breath, she would be able to get back to sleep, but now her back is aching and she feels hungry and thirsty – too hungry and thirsty to stay in bed.

In the kitchen, she finds James eating a cheese sandwich. "James," she says quietly. "Gosh, you're up early." She closes the kitchen door behind her. Should she kiss him good morning? Of course not. The British don't kiss each other. Why did she even think that?

"I have jet-lag," he says wearily. "What's your excuse?"

Hannah fills the kettle and plugs it in, aware that James is watching her as she moves around the room. "I don't know really," she says. "I just woke up feeling hungry. It happens sometimes."

"D'you want a sandwich?" James asks. "This cheese is really good."

Hannah shakes her head. "No, I'll stick to muesli thanks." Once she has made two cups of tea and filled her bowl with cereal, she adds, "I'm going to take this outside. It's lovely out there first thing."

"I'll join you," James says. "Unless you want to be alone with your thoughts."

"No, please feel free."

Outside the air is still cool and vaguely misty. The grass is covered with dew and the low sun is cutting atmospherically through the trees.

"So how has life been?" James asks once they are seated.

Hannah smiles and shrugs. "Oh, it's been fine," she says. "Just normal life really. You know how it is."

James nods.

"I think yours has been more exciting by the sound of it," Hannah says.

James copies her shrug. "Well it's been a mixed bag," James says. "Plenty of joy and a shed load of sadness." He has to clear his throat before he can continue. "It's good to be away," he says. "It's good to be elsewhere frankly."

Hannah nods, detecting something in his voice, yet understanding nothing.

She eats in silence with only a pair of warring birds in one of the olive trees for accompaniment.

"So how long before the rest of the mob wake up?" James asks once Hannah has finished her cereal.

She leans back in her seat in an attempt at checking the kitchen clock, but the reflection of the sun on the window makes this impossible. "I'm not sure what time it is now," she says, "but they generally wake up between eight and nine at the moment. Luke's usually first, but after yesterday, well, it wouldn't surprise me if he sleeps in. Why?"

"I thought we might have time for a walk," James says.

Hannah stares at him. "Yes," she says. "Yes, we do. I'll show you the stream if you want."

"We have a stream?"

"We do. It's lovely down there."

Once they have sprayed each other with insect repellant, Hannah leads James past the pool to the back of the house and over the fence. "You have to beware of snakes apparently," she tells him.

"Venomous snakes?" James asks.

"I don't know really," Hannah admits. "Just keep your eyes open."

As they walk single file along the track, the sun is warm on her face and contrasted against the cool, damp morning air, it feels quite special.

After the intersection of the two paths, they are able to walk side by side once more.

Hannah is hyper aware of James' hand swinging mere inches from her own as they walk, but rationalises that the desire to take it is as absurd as her desire to embrace him at breakfast. She's amazed though to discover that the attraction between their two bodies is still here after all these years.

"So you must really like Australia," Hannah says.

"Must I?" James laughs.

"Well, you took Australian nationality," Hannah says. "And you never came back."

"Yes, I guess so," James says.

"So why now?"

"I don't know," James replies. "I think I needed to touch base with my roots, if that makes any sense."

"Maybe," Hannah says.

"I had a bad few years. I think sometimes you need to remember who you were before. Remind yourself that you even *existed* before, so maybe you can survive now, on your own again . . ." James' voice fades.

"Are you talking about your divorce?" Hannah asks.

"There was no divorce," James says as they reach the climb down to the riverbank.

As they file down the steps Hannah thinks about James' words, about the fact that if there has been no divorce then she is about to be cast in the role of confidante. She promises that she will be generous. She promises to herself that she will help James and his wife get over whatever their problems are. She is not Jill. She does not see every man as a potential conquest.

Once they reach the riverbank, they start to walk slowly downstream. The babble of the brook combined with the screeches of the birds makes the place sound like a tropical rainforest this morning.

"Marriage is tough," Hannah says. "There are always problems. You always have to fight for it if you want it to survive."

"Yes," James says. "Yes, I suppose so."

"So what happened, James?" Hannah asks, eventually.

"A car accident," James says, and Hannah's heart lurches in two directions at once. "They were both killed outright."

Hannah stops walking, and turns to face him. "Both of them?" she says.

James closes his eyes briefly and nods his head. He swallows and licks his lips. "A truck driver . . . he was texting," he says. "She had broken down and he . . ." he shrugs. "He just drove into them. He didn't brake at all apparently."

Hannah takes James' forearms in her hands. She shakes her head. "I'm so sorry, James," she says. "I . . . I don't know what to say."

"There's not much *to* say," James says.

"No."

"But I needed to remember, you know? I needed to remember who I was before."

"Yes, that makes perfect sense."

"She . . ." James pauses and looks up at the sky. When he returns his gaze to Hannah his eyes are watering. "She was six . . ." he says, his face screwing up. "Hannah, she was only six."

Hannah's eyes are watering too now. She leans in and takes James in her arms and hugs him tight. "I'm so sorry," she says again.

It is James who ends the embrace. He pushes Hannah to arm's length, and smiles sadly. "Let's walk," he says, swiping at a tear on his cheek. "I'm tired of blubbing. Honest I am."

Beyond the bend, the path is blocked by a fallen tree, so James climbs on top and pulls Hannah up and then lowers her down the other side.

"When was it, James?" Hannah asks. "How long ago did this happen?"

"Two years last February," he says.

They continue to walk and then after a while, Hannah says, "Losing a child is the worst thing of all."

James nods. "You can just never get your mind around that one really."

"No."

"Is that what happened to you as well?" James asks.

"Kind of," Hannah says.

"I did wonder," he says.

"Because I was pregnant?"

"Yes. It looks like this is it," he adds, nodding at the way the riverbank they have been walking vanishes just ahead.

"There's a path up there," Hannah says, pointing higher up the bank.

"Let's do that then," James says.

"So how old was yours when . . ." James says once they have scrambled to the higher path.

"It was before she was born," Hannah says. "It was a miscarriage."

"God," James says. "I'm sorry. I didn't know."

"Well, no," Hannah says. She shrugs. "It was a long time ago now," she adds.

"Sure."

"It was the day after you left," Hannah tells him.

"Really?"

Hannah nods.

"It wasn't . . . you know . . . the stress of . . . all of that?"

Hannah shakes her head. "No," she says. "No that wasn't it. It was just one of those things, I think."

THIRTY-THREE

James V

I waited for Cliff to leave for work before I got up. As soon as I heard his car drive away, I dressed and went downstairs. My stomach was fluttering weirdly as I made two cups of tea and carried the one I had made for James upstairs.

I hesitated outside his bedroom for a moment – I had no idea what was going to happen but a compressed sensation of excitement seemed to fill me. Life seemed full of possibilities, both terrifying and exciting. I felt as though I was reading a novel and couldn't wait to see what would happen next. I knew we needed to talk about what had happened. I suspected that we might end up kissing again, and that with Cliff out we might even end up sleeping together. But I also knew that it might all simply be imaginary. James would perhaps apologise for his behaviour and I might feel nothing more than silly and the whole story could end right there and then. I was convinced that the second I saw him I would know, that the instant our eyes met, everything would be clear one way or another. There was only one possibility that I hadn't imagined.

I opened the door and was surprised to see that the room was lit – the curtains were still open.

I threw the door wide open and saw that James' bag was no longer on the floor. The bed had not been slept in.

I put the mug down on the dresser and ran downstairs, still hoping that I might find James in the lounge, watching TV and smiling up at me. When he wasn't, I walked nervously to the window and looked out. The Volvo was gone.

I sat on the sofa and tried to imagine a reasonable scenario in which James would have had to leave so early but I couldn't come up with one at all.

I went back upstairs to the bathroom where the lack of James' toothbrush finally convinced me that he had really gone, that he had left in the night.

I waited a full hour before I phoned Cliff at work. In a rehearsed voice, feigning casual interest, I said, "James seems to be missing this morning. Any idea where he is?"

"James has gone," Cliff replied, and I wasn't sure if he was repeating my phrase in surprise or confirming it.

"Do you know *where* he has gone, Cliff?"

"No, I have no idea," Cliff said.

"So do you know when he'll be back?"

"No," Cliff said.

"I just need to know how many people I'm catering for," I told him.

"Two by the sounds of it," Cliff said. "You and your fiancé."

"OK. See you this evening."

The house was entirely silent. I sat on the sofa and stared at the wall until a postman pushed something through the letterbox, making me jump. And then I started to cry.

I don't think I did anything that day. I made a sandwich at lunchtime and ate it and drank tea and stared into the middle distance. Occasionally I would look out at the street and hope and pray that the orange Volvo would reappear.

Dinner was not ready when Cliff got home that night. He was pretending that everything was normal, that everything was fine, but I could sense that he was lying – I could tell that he was angry.

He spoke about his day at work and I pretended to listen, and then he asked what was for dinner, and I silently went through to the kitchen where I boiled potatoes and sliced carrots and fried pork chops. I felt like a robot performing to a script. I felt as if the part of my brain that controlled emotion had been surgically removed.

I was just serving up when Cliff came into the kitchen. "Is that going to be long?" he asked. "I'm starving."

"It's ready," I said, moving my body so that he could witness that I was in the process of serving up.

"Good."

"So do you have *any* idea where James went?" I asked without looking up from the plates.

"None," Cliff said.

"But why would he leave like that?" I asked.

"I think you know the answer to that," Cliff said.

He picked his plate up and carried it through to the dining room and I followed.

We sat in silence, and began to eat.

"Presumably he'll be back," I said, aware that this was dangerous, but unable to stop myself. "I mean, our shed is full of all of his stuff."

Cliff put his knife and fork down. As he stared at me he started to redden. His head seemed to swell, and for a second, I became worried about him – I wondered if he was having a heart attack or a seizure or something. And then his arm twitched violently to the right, and his plate slid across the table like an ice-hockey puck and flew into the wall. Without a word, he stood and left the room.

I sat for fifteen minutes looking at the stain on the wall before I got up, picked up the broken plate and the food and went through to the kitchen for a sponge.

Outside in the fading light of the garden I could see that Cliff was lighting a bonfire.

I finished cleaning the stain from the wall and then I took my coat and left the house. I went to the park, where I sat on a bench until the sky was dark. I still felt entirely numb.

When I got home, the bonfire was still burning. Cliff was sitting on a fold-up chair swigging at a can of beer, his face lit by the flames.

I brushed my teeth and went to bed, and pretended, an hour later when Cliff arrived, that I was asleep.

He undressed, got into bed, and then reached over to pull me towards him. "Kiss me," he said.

I told him that I wasn't in the mood.

"Kiss me," he said again, more insistently.

"No, Cliff. I'm tired," I said. "I just want to sleep."

Then he pulled me towards him and rolled on top of me. He did a lot of sports in those days – he was strong. And I don't think I fought either. I don't remember actually fighting.

But I did say "no". I did turn my head away. I did say, "Please, don't."

"You're my fiancée," he said, forcing his legs between mine. "You're *my fucking* fiancée."

And as he started to fuck me, I began to cry.

As soon as it was over – and because I was crying, he gave up quite quickly – I went to the spare room. Cliff didn't follow or try to stop me.

I locked the door behind me and crawled into the single bed. And there, in sheets that still smelt of James, the ceiling still flickering from the flames that outside were slowly consuming his every possession, I cried myself to sleep.

The next morning I awoke at dawn to find that the sheets were cold and clammy – there was blood on them. I lifted the covers and saw that there was blood everywhere, pints and pints of it, and knew that the worst thing possible was happening.

Paralysed by fear – I was convinced that if I moved it would make things worse – I screamed and then screamed again, specifically screaming for Cliff to come.

He had to kick in the door to reach me.

THIRTY-FOUR

Brisbane, 7th February 2010

Dear Cliff and Hannah,
Whatever shall I do now?
  James.

HORROR ON THE BRISBANE
VALLEY HIGHWAY

Two victims were dragged yesterday (Tuesday) evening from the wreckage of a Holden Commodore on the Brisbane Valley Highway just north of Ipswich.

Judy Parker (32) of Brisbane was trying to push the car to the roadside after apparent engine troubles when the accident happened.

Witnesses, who had stopped just after the junction and were returning to help, watched horrified as a petrol tanker appeared over the brow of the hill and without braking ploughed into the Holden.

Judy Parker died on impact, Hannah Parker (6 years old) died later in Brisbane Central Intensive care.

The driver of the truck and the two witnesses, currently unidentified, are all currently being treated for shock.

Police and ambulance services were on the scene of the accident within twenty minutes, which Chief Constable Dower of the Brisbane police pointed out was extremely fast considering the location. "We have launched a full investigation into the cause of this horrific accident," he said.

The Brisbane Times sends its condolences to James Parker, husband and father of the deceased.

THIRTY-FIVE

By the time James and Hannah return, everyone except Jill is up. Luke and Aïsha are sitting on the edge of the pool with their feet in the water.

"Hannah, can you tell Luke the new mask we got is OK?" Aïsha asks as Hannah passes. "He won't use it."

"It is OK, because it's plastic," Hannah confirms. "So it can't smash. But you can't use it until the dressing comes off anyway. Did Dad change it yet this morning?"

Luke nods. "And I took my pill," he says.

"Good," Hannah says.

James crouches down beside the children and tests the water with one hand. "It's warm!" he says.

"It's heated," Aïsha tells him.

"I might go for a swim later, then," James says.

Hannah continues to the front of the house, leaving him talking to the children. As she reaches the front door she hears echoey voices drifting from within. Angry-sounding voices.

She pauses and holds her breath. ". . . tell her." Tristan is saying.

"It's none of your fucking business," Cliff replies.

"Fine!" Tristan says, and then a door somewhere slams.

Hannah does her best to fix a neutral expression and then heads indoors.

"Morning," Cliff says when she reaches the kitchen. "Where were you?"

"I couldn't sleep; I showed James the river."

"Nice," Cliff says, and she's not sure from his voice if he's being genuine or facetious. "How long's he staying anyway?" Cliff continues.

"I don't know," Hannah says. "Don't you like him being here?"

"I'd just rather we got back to normal."

"Normal," Hannah repeats. "Yes."

"Meaning?"

"Meaning nothing, Cliff. Anyway, what was all that about?"

"All what?" Cliff asks. His voice sounds neutral but Hannah notices that he averts his gaze. She sees that he busies himself with the coffee machine. It's hard to dissimulate after fifteen years of living together.

"You were arguing with Tristan," Hannah says.

"Oh *that*," Cliff says. "That was nothing."

"It didn't sound like nothing."

"Just politics," Cliff says. "You know what he's like."

Hannah stares at her husband's back and frowns. Because yes, she knows what Tristan's like, and she knows what Cliff is like, and two less political animals would be hard to find. "OK," she says quietly, then, "Well, I'm going to shower."

At breakfast Hannah sips her coffee and watches everyone eating. She tries to decode the multiple tensions within the household and is surprised to note that the hub seems to be Cliff, who is prickly with not only James but with Tristan as well. Even Jill, when she arrives, gets greeted with, "So you finally deigned to join us, huh?"

Jill just laughs this off. "I didn't know there was a schedule we had to stick to," she says.

By the time breakfast has been cleared it becomes apparent that the early morning mist is not clearing but intensifying. "Are they still predicting storms on the forecast?" Hannah asks Tristan.

He nods. "But they've been saying it for days," he says.

"Can we go somewhere today?" Luke asks. "Can we go to Nice like what Aïsha and Jill did?"

Hannah rolls her eyes. "When you can phrase that question correctly I might think about answering it," she says.

"Could we please go to Nice in the same way as what Aïsha and Jill have done yesterday?" Luke says, and everyone laughs at his convoluted attempt at correct grammar.

"Cliff?" Hannah says.

Cliff shrugs. "Why not?" he says. "I wouldn't mind a dip in the sea."

"How about we do it tomorrow?" Hannah says. "Then Luke can swim without worrying about the eye-patch."

"Sure," Cliff says.

"But what about today?" Luke says. "I'm bored."

"Why don't you get one of the board games out?" Hannah suggests.

Luke pulls a face.

"I could put the badminton net up," Cliff offers. "How would that be?"

Luke glances at Aïsha, who shrugs. He turns back to Cliff. "OK," he says.

★

239

Cliff ties the net between two trees and Hannah watches from the hammock as he thrashes first Luke, then Jill, and then Tristan and Aïsha at badminton.

She tries to imagine, for the first time, Cliff's feelings in all of this. He still assumes, she knows, that she and James slept together all those years ago. He has never said as much, but it was the only explanation she ever came up with for his overflowing anger at the time. Anger, which, judging from his badminton performance, is still very much alive today.

She thinks about the fact that they have never discussed those events, initially because she was so angry herself that she was happy for him to think the worst, and then later because it had become such a dangerous taboo that no one ever dared mention it again.

But watching Cliff swing angrily at the shuttlecock as he hammers James at badminton, she wonders if the time hasn't come to release the pressure from that particular boil. But how to have that conversation now?

By twelve, the sun has vanished entirely behind a dark bank of cloud. It still feels hot; in fact the oppressive nature of the weather makes it seem even hotter. Even the flies seem angry.

With Cliff now forcibly removed from the badminton tournament – no one wants to play him – Aïsha and Luke are playing doubles against Jill. Cliff is reading on the porch, James is floating in the pool and Tristan has gone to his room. Hannah levers herself from the hammock and heads indoors determined to interrogate him.

As she passes Cliff, he looks up from his novel and asks her if she would like him to perform Luke's midday change of eye-patch.

"No," she says. "It's fine. I'll do it."

"Luke!" she calls out. "Dressing!"

Luke – provoking protests from his badminton partner – drops his racket and runs to Hannah's side. "You're keen," she says.

"It's the last one, isn't it?" Luke says.

"You're right," Hannah confirms. "When you go to bed tonight, it's all over."

She leads Luke through to his bedroom, sits him on the bed and pulls back the dressing. "How's that now?" she asks.

Luke blinks repeatedly and then looks around the room. "Fine," he says.

"Your eyebrow has healed too," Hannah says, tracing it gently with her fingertip.

"I hope I get a scar," Luke says.

"I hope you don't," Hannah counters.

"So where's Tristan going?" Luke asks as Hannah fills the eye-bath with solution.

"I'm sorry?" Hannah asks, applying the plastic cup to his eye and tipping his head back.

"Tristan," Luke says, pointing behind her. "He looks like he's going out."

Hannah puts Luke's hand on the eye-bath to hold it in place and turns to look out of the window. Beyond it she can see Tristan loading suitcases into the boot of the Jeep. She stands and crosses to the window, then opens it and shouts, "Tristan!"

Tristan turns and smiles at her. He looks a little sad.

"Where are you going?"

He shrugs and mimes driving.

"OK, that's enough, Luke," Hannah says. "Just . . . just hang on a minute. I'll be back to finish it."

Hannah bursts from Luke's room and runs to the patio, past Cliff, and around to the front of the house, where she finds Tristan in the driver's seat of the Jeep, already fastening his seatbelt.

"Tris'!" she says breathlessly. "Wait!"

She grips the edge of his door and Tristan, whose hand had been on the ignition key, relaxes his grip and drops his hand to his lap. "I thought I'd managed the perfect getaway," he says.

"Where are you going?" Hannah asks.

"Sitges."

"In Spain?"

Tristan nods.

"For good?"

"For good?" Tristan repeats, looking puzzled.

"I mean, are you coming back here?"

Tristan shrugs. "Maybe. To pick Jill and Aïsha up. We haven't worked out the details yet."

"But why?" Hannah asks. "Has something happened?"

Tristan shakes his head. "Nah," he says. "Not really. You know what I'm like around hetties."

Hannah tuts. "I thought you were getting bored," she says. "I'm sorry it hasn't been too exciting."

"It's all a bit *too* exciting to be honest," Tristan says. "It's all getting a bit tense for me."

"The James thing?" Hannah says.

"Amongst other things."

"Have you fallen out with Jill?"

"No," Tristan laughs. "No, not at all. But she's busy with Aïsha, and when she isn't, she's busy with Pascal."

"Is that still going on?" Hannah asks.

"I'm just feeling a bit superfluous to requirements."

242

"And Cliff?" Hannah asks.

She sees a hint of a shadow cross Tristan's features before he masters them and morphs his expression to one of benign indifference. "Cliff?" he says.

"You were arguing about something," Hannah says. "I heard you. You're not leaving because of something Cliff said?"

He shakes his head. "Not at all," he says.

"OK," Hannah says, unconvinced. "So how is Jill getting home?"

"As I say, we haven't got that far yet. She's going to look at flights. But I might swing by and get them on my way home."

"OK," Hannah says, twisting her mouth sideways to express disappointment. "Well, I'm sorry to see you go."

"Sorry, babe," Tristan says. "I might be back in a few days. But I just need some time with my own people."

"Sure. Well, drive carefully," Hannah says, leaning in to kiss him on the cheek. "You're important to me, you know? So look after yourself." As she says it, she realises that this is true and feels strangely tearful at his departure.

Tristan blinks slowly. "Thanks," he says.

Hannah releases the door and steps back. She watches as Tristan starts the engine and performs a three-point turn on the driveway.

As he edges towards the gate, Hannah follows the car with the intention of closing the gate behind him, but then the car stops. "Hannah?" Tristan calls back.

When Hannah catches up with him, she leans in the passenger window. "Yes?"

"I think James is a really great guy," he says.

"Yes?"

"Yes. Just so you know."

Hannah frowns. "He's not gay, Tristan," she says. "I would put in a good word for you but . . ."

"I don't mean for me," Tristan says. "I mean for *you*."

Hannah inhales sharply. She stares into Tristan's eyes, which seem to be filled with meaning, only she isn't sure exactly what that meaning is.

"I *care* about you," Tristan says, "that's all. And you deserve to be happy."

"OK," Hannah says, her brow creasing. "Thanks. I *think*."

"James is a great guy. And he likes you a lot."

Hannah laughs lightly. "Thanks," she says, "but so is Cliff."

"Is he?" Tristan says.

Hannah laughs again. "Well, yes."

"Do you know that?"

"After fifteen years . . ." Hannah says, "yes, I think I know that."

"OK," Tristan says. "Well . . ."

Hannah turns to see Cliff rounding the corner of the house and heading towards them.

Tristan follows her gaze and says, "OK, well, I've said enough. See you in a few days maybe."

And then just as Cliff reaches her side, he engages first gear and, spitting gravel, drives away.

"Everything OK?" Cliff asks. "I had to finish Luke's dressing."

"Of course," Hannah says, patting his arm briefly, then turning towards the house. "Tristan's gone away for a few days, that's all."

"Right," Cliff says flatly.

They jointly close the gates and then Hannah heads to the pool, currently unoccupied. She removes her sandals and

244

lowers her feet into the water. She reruns the conversation with Tristan through her mind over and over as she tries to decode any hidden meaning. It is, she decides, truly one of the strangest conversations she has ever had.

Less than five minutes later, Aïsha appears at her side. "It's Tris'," she says, brandishing her phone. "He wants to talk to you."

"Really?" Hannah asks, taking the phone.

"Don't drop it in the pool, will you," Aïsha shouts back as she runs away.

"No," Hannah tells her. "No, I won't."

She raises the phone to her ear. "Tris'?" she says.

"Yes."

"I'm glad you phoned, I've been trying to work out—"

"Listen, Hannah," he interrupts.

"Yes?"

"I shouldn't really say this, but . . ."

"Yes?"

"But I like you, so . . ."

"Right. Well I like you too, Tris'."

"So check his phone, OK?"

"Whose phone?"

"Cliff's."

"Check it?"

"Yes."

"Check it for what exactly?"

"Just check it," Tristan says. "Discreetly."

"Why? What's wrong with . . ." Hannah starts, but Tristan interrupts her.

"OK, gotta go," he says. "There's a police car and I'm driving."

The line goes dead, and so Hannah lowers the phone from her ear and stares at the screen until it turns black, and then she sits and stares at her own face reflected in it.

After a few minutes, she stands and returns to the patio, where Aïsha reclaims her property. "Has Tristan gone?" she asks.

"Yes," Hannah tells her. "Yes, he has."

"Bummer," Aïsha says.

"Yes," Hannah agrees. "It is a bummer. Where's Jill?"

"She's gone to shower. We got all sweaty playing badminton."

"Thanks," Hannah says, heading indoors.

Hannah goes to Jill's bedroom, where she sits and waits. The room feels cooler. Is it cooler, or is it just because it's painted blue?

"Ugh!" Jill exclaims as she steps into the room. "God, you gave me a fright."

"Sorry," Hannah says.

Jill pulls the towel around her middle a little tighter and skirts around the bed until she is out of Hannah's line of sight. "Don't turn around," she says, when Hannah starts to turn her head.

"I think I've seen what you look like before," Hannah laughs.

"Of course you have," Jill says. "But not for a few years."

Hannah raises one eyebrow and turns to face the dresser, where she realises she can watch Jill in the mirror just as well. "So what happened with Tris'?" she asks.

Jill drops the towel and finishes drying herself. "I don't think anything happened, did it? You know what he's like. He got bored. He's gone to Sitges to get some man-love."

"Why didn't you tell me?"

246

"Tell you what?" Jill says, stepping into a sexy pair of panties.

"That he was leaving."

"I thought he told you. Didn't he tell you? Didn't he say goodbye?"

"Yes, but . . ."

"Well then."

"But only because I caught him sneaking off," Hannah says.

Jill pulls on a pair of shorts and walks back around the bed. "There," she says.

"So you stopped waxing," Hannah says.

"You peeped."

"Erm, big mirror Jill," Hannah says, nodding at the dresser.

Jill rolls her eyes, and pulls a halter top from the drawer. "Yes, I stopped waxing."

"You used to have such a go at me about that," Hannah says.

"Well, we were young then," Jill says. "It was the fashion. Whereas letting it grow wild is all the rage now."

"Is it?"

Jill shrugs. "Apparently so. Shaven is the new unshaven or something. I mean, unshaven is, oh you know what I mean."

"So Tristan," Hannah prompts.

Jill starts to dry her hair with the towel. "What about him?"

"I still don't get why he left so suddenly."

"I told you," Jill says.

"He was bored then, that's it?"

Jill pauses and peeps out through the towel at Hannah. "I think so," she says. "He's always been like that."

"Like what?"

"I don't know. Independent," she says, starting to rub her hair again. "A free sprit. He does what he wants."

Hannah nods and glances out of the window. "I think it might actually rain today," she says after a moment.

"I think that might be a good thing," Jill says, now sitting down in front of the mirror. "This heat is horrible."

"I heard them arguing, you know," Hannah says. "Tris' and Cliff."

Jill fumbles in a drawer and retrieves her lipstick. "Really?" she asks, taking a seat at the dressing table and looking back at Hannah via the mirror. "What about?"

"I don't know," Hannah tells her. "I was hoping you'd be able to enlighten me."

"Sorry, babe," Jill says, stretching her lips, and swiping the lipstick expertly across them. "When was this?"

"This morning. Before you were up."

"I doubt that," Jill says. "I was up at four."

"Really?"

"Uh-huh. I went over to see Pascal."

Hannah nods. "So that's still current then?"

Jill shrugs. "Yeah, it's nice," she says. "I think it's just a holiday fling, but it's nice."

"But Aïsha's in with you. In here, I mean."

"Yes."

"So she knows."

"Well, of course she knows. She's not blind."

"And she doesn't mind?"

"Why would she mind?"

Hannah shrugs, but then realises that Jill isn't looking at her – she's applying mascara. "I don't know," she says.

"She quite likes him I think. Well, as much as anyone can like anyone who speaks a foreign language."

"When did they even meet?"

"When we went to Nice. We had dinner together," Jill says.

"Oh. He didn't stay with you though? In the hotel?"

"Of course he did," Jill says. "We all slept in the same bed."

"You said you weren't going to do that anymore," Hannah says. "You said you were going to stop trying to confuse me."

Jill looks back at her and rolls her eyes. "Of course he didn't. What do *you* think?"

Hannah frowns confusedly.

"What now?" Jill asks.

"I'm just trying to imagine dinner for three when one of you doesn't even speak English," Hannah says.

"We got an app for Aïsha's iPhone," Jill says. "It's really good. You type in a phrase and it translates it to French."

"So you spent the meal passing the phone back and forth."

"Something like that," Jill says. "But really. Aï's fine about it."

"She's actually been amazing since . . . you know . . . the accident. I don't know what you said to her, but it worked."

"She has," Jill says. "But you know it won't last. So just make the most of it."

"I will," Hannah says. "So have you *really* no idea what Tris' and Cliff were arguing about?"

Jill massages her brow with one finger, rubs her lips together, and then turns to face her sister. "Nope," she says. "So how do I look?"

"Hot," Hannah says.

"What shiny, sweaty hot?" Jill asks, turning back to the mirror.

"No. Hot as in sexy. Have you got a date or something?"

Jill shakes her head. "Not really," she says. "But we are going shopping."

"Again?"

"Food shopping," Jill says. "He's taking us to some big supermarket. Says it's cheaper."

"How domesticated."

"Isn't it?"

"So you really have absolutely no idea?" Hannah asks again.

"About Tris' and Cliff?" Jill says. "None. I can phone him if you want."

Hannah wrinkles her nose. "No," she says. "No, I just wanted to know if he'd said anything."

"I would guess it was about James if it was about anything," Jill offers.

"James?"

"Well, Cliff hasn't exactly been being nice to him, has he?"

"Hasn't he?"

"Well, no," Jill says. "I mean, there's not much brotherly love going on there, is there?"

"No," Hannah agrees with a sigh. "No, I suppose not."

"Still, I expect he's a bit jealous," Jill says. "Don't you think?"

Hannah laughs sourly. "God, they don't call you Sherlock for nothing, do they?"

"I wasn't aware they did," Jill says, spraying on perfume.

"It's a figure of speech."

"Yes," Jill says, "I got that."

"Do you know what aftershave Tris' uses? I really like it."

Jill shrugs. "Not sure. Ungaro something or other, I think."

"It's lovely. I thought I might get some for Cliff."

"Not sure he'd appreciate being made to smell like Tristan," Jill laughs.

"No," Hannah says. "Maybe not."

"So how *do* you feel about James this time around?"

"How do I *feel*?"

"Yes. I mean, he's pretty hunky, isn't he?"

Hannah laughs sadly. "Hunky," she repeats.

"Well, he is."

Hannah nods and fingers at the hem of her shorts. "You're right, of course," she admits. "He's very hunky. And he's friendly, and sweet and rather lovely."

"But . . ."

Hannah shrugs.

"He's still married?" Jill asks. "Is that it?"

"He's widowed," Hannah says. "His wife and child were killed in a car accident two years ago."

Jill pauses brushing her hair, then flashes the whites of her eyes at her sister. "God, that's awful," she says.

"I know."

"And you're not even a bit tempted to, you know . . ."

Hannah pulls a face indicating incomprehension.

"To . . . *console* him?" Jill says.

Hannah laughs. "I know you don't really get the whole concept of monogamy, Jill, but I'm *married*."

"So you are then?" Jill says, poker faced. "Tempted, that is."

"I'm married to Cliff," Hannah says pedantically.

"Yes, to *Cliff*," Jill says, pulling a face.

"God, you're terrible," Hannah says. "You're like . . . like some kind of little devil sitting on my shoulder."

Jill smiles wickedly. "I know," she says. "I can't help it."

When Jill and Hannah step outside, they find Pascal sitting with Cliff, waiting, silently. He is wearing normal clothes – white shorts and a blue short-sleeved shirt – and looks relaxed and boyish. "Bonjour," he says, rising to embrace both Jill and Hannah.

"Tout va bien avec la maison ? Avec la piscine ?" he asks.

"I'm sorry," Hannah says. "I don't speak any French."

"I think he wants to know if the house and pool are OK," Aïsha says.

Hannah raises one eyebrow and shoots an astonished look at her.

"He's told me some words," she says. "Piscine is pool and maison is house."

"Very impressive," Hannah says. "Oui. Bien. Merci," she answers. "I'm afraid that's about the limit of my French."

THIRTY-SIX

Once they have cobbled together a shopping list and Hannah has given Jill the code for her Visa card, Jill and Pascal climb into the little red Fiat and drive away.

With James in the bathroom and Luke and Aïsha arguing about points through the badminton net, Hannah finds herself alone on the patio with Cliff, seemingly for the first time in days.

"She seems happy," Hannah says.

"Jill? Or Aïsha?"

"Both. Aïsha's being amazing at the moment. Long may it last. But I meant Jill. I think she really likes that Pascal guy."

"Aïsha's probably up to something, and Jill likes anything in trousers," Cliff says.

"A little unfair," Hannah says. "He seems OK."

"Sorry. Yes. He seems nice enough."

"Not that we'd know really."

Cliff shrugs. "He's smiley. He's taking her shopping . . ."

"It's a shame the kids couldn't go with them. But we're taking them to Nice tomorrow, right?"

"That's what we said. I hope the weather will be OK."

"It looks stormy over there," Hannah says, pointing at the horizon, where the sky is an even darker shade of grey.

"And it's coming this way," Cliff says. "Anyway, they could have taken the kids, couldn't they? I expect they just didn't fancy going shopping."

"No, they wanted to go," Hannah explains, "but the Fiat only has two seats. It's a commercial vehicle."

"Oh," Cliff says. "I didn't know. They should have taken ours. It's insured for any driver."

"Well . . ." Hannah says. "They seem happy enough playing badminton for now. Well, arguing about badminton. I wish Tristan had stayed though."

"No more haute cuisine," Cliff says.

"No," Hannah agrees. "No, we're back to Hannah-cuisine now."

"I didn't mean . . ." Cliff says. "That's not what I meant."

"I know. But you're right. I prefer it when Tristan's cooking too." Hannah clears her throat, and then adopting a casual tone of voice, asks, "So what did you two argue about?"

"With Tristan?"

"Yes."

"Nothing."

"Nothing?"

"It's of no importance," Cliff says, picking up his novel from the table and opening it.

"To you maybe. But Tristan has gone."

Cliff sighs and closes the book again. "What did he tell you?"

"Nothing," Hannah says. "But I have eyes to see. And ears to hear. I'm not totally blind to what's going on around me, you know."

Cliff snorts dismissively.

"What?"

"Nothing," he says.

"No, go on, what?"

"Well, you're not the only one," Cliff says.

254

"The only one who . . . ?" Hannah ends the phrase with a tiny questioning upward nod of the chin.

"The only one with eyes to see," Cliff says.

"OK, that's enough. You've been weird for days. Please stop being cryptic. You know how I hate it."

"I just wish Tris' had taken James with him," Cliff says.

Hannah is momentarily aware that Cliff has dodged the subject of his argument with Tristan by mentioning James, but then her frustration at his relationship with his brother takes over and she forgets. "He's your brother, Cliff," she points out.

"Really? Gosh! Hold the front page," Cliff says.

"You haven't seen him for fifteen years. You could at least try to be nice to him. Try to get to know him."

"I *do* know him," Cliff says. "That's the problem."

"I don't get you two," Hannah says. "You have one brother. You pretend he's dead for fifteen years. And when he turns up . . ."

"When he turns up, he's the same selfish bastard he always was."

"I haven't seen any selfishness. I haven't seen any sign of that at all."

"No, you don't see anything, Hannah," Cliff says. "But James is the same as he always was. This is what he does."

"This?"

"This . . ." Cliff says, gesturing in an all-encompassing manner. "He comes in; he takes over; he spoils everything; and then he fucks off leaving the wreckage behind him."

"What has he taken over? What has he spoilt? You're not making any sense at all."

Cliff snorts again. "I see the way you two look at each other," he says.

So there it is out in the open. Hannah inhales sharply. "And what way is that, Cliff?" she asks.

"You know full well."

"You're being ridiculous," Hannah says, simultaneously angry, guilty and embarrassed.

"You know what's ridiculous?" Cliff says. "What's ridiculous is having your brother come spoil your party even now. It's having your brother *still* trying to steal your stuff at forty-two."

"Your *stuff?*" Hannah says in disgust. "Your *stuff?*"

"It's a figure of speech," Cliff says.

"When you say *your stuff*, do you mean me?" Hannah asks, wiping her forehead, now damp with perspiration.

"No, it's just what he always did," Cliff says, "when we were kids."

"I am not your *stuff*," Hannah says. "How dare you!"

"That's not what I meant, Hannah, and you know it."

"It's exactly what you meant. *And I know it.* How dare you! I'm your wife, Cliff. Your *wife*. Do you know what that means? It mea—"

"It clearly doesn't mean much to James," Cliff interrupts.

"Is that so?" – a voice from the doorway. They both turn to see James standing in the shadows. He takes an extra step forwards onto the doorstep.

"Oh, just . . . go away, James," Cliff says.

"Go away?"

"Yes, just *fuck off*, will you," Cliff says.

"Oh, fuck off, is it?" James repeats, laughter in his voice. "Nice."

"Yes," Cliff says. "Fuck off back to Australia or wherever it is you hide out when you're not trying to steal my wife."

256

James stares at Cliff, his amusement fading and being replaced by an expression of eyebrow-raised shock. "Maybe I will," he says, quietly. "Maybe that's the best thing here."

As he heads back into the house, Hannah stands. "Really, Cliff! For God's sake, what is wrong with you?"

Hannah heads inside in pursuit of James. "James? James!" She finds him in Aïsha's room stuffing clothes into his rucksack.

"You don't have to leave, James," she says. "Don't listen to him."

James looks up. His face has turned pink.

"He's just . . ." Hannah says.

"An asshole?" James offers.

"No, don't say that."

"Well, he's *what*, Hannah?"

"I don't know. He's jealous," Hannah says.

James laughs bitterly.

"Don't leave."

James sighs and releases the handle of his bag. "I don't know, Hannah," he says. "What's the point?"

"The point?"

"I just seem to be causing a load of shit for everyone. Isn't it better if I go?"

Hannah shakes her head. "No," she says. "No, I don't think it is. If you leave, this will never get sorted out."

James sighs deeply.

"Please?" Hannah says.

James shrugs. "You're sure you don't want me to leave?"

"It's the last thing I want," Hannah says.

James nods, pushes the bag from the bed to the floor and then sits on the edge of the bed. "You need to talk to him then,

Hannah," he says. "You need to calm him down. Because I can't."

"I'll try," Hannah says running a hand through her hair. "Just give us a little space and I'll try."

She heads to the bathroom and washes her face in cold water, then pats it dry and heads back outside. The time has come, she decides. She will tell Cliff that she never did sleep with James. Her failure to do so has been shameful, she now realises. It's been the cause of an unbridgeable gap between her husband and his only surviving family, and it's time to fix it.

She pauses in the kitchen to drink a glass of water, and then, steeling herself for the next round, heads back out to the patio, but Cliff is no longer there.

She walks around the grounds, past the exit to the track, past the pool, past the Mégane, still parked. Finally when she reaches the hammock, she finds Luke and Aïsha lying side by side playing with their phones. "Any idea where Dad is?" she asks Luke.

"He went for a walk, I think."

"Are you two OK?"

"We're on Facebook," Luke says. "I'm letting Aïsha use my phone. But only for a bit."

"That's nice," Hannah says, absent-mindedly. As she carries on back towards the porch, she sees Aïsha nudge Luke sharply but it only barely registers, and she doesn't even stop to wonder why. She has other things on her mind.

Back in the house, she finds James in the kitchen opening a beer. Seeing her arrive, he offers her the can. "Beer?" he says.

Hannah nods and takes the can from his grasp.

"Well?" James asks, opening the door and reaching for another one.

"I don't know where he is," Hannah says. "He's gone for a walk, apparently."

"Right," James says.

Hannah sips at her beer and then rubs the cold can against her forehead. "He still thinks we slept together," she says out of nowhere. "That's the thing."

"I'm sorry?" James says.

"Cliff. He thinks we slept together. Fifteen years ago."

"Oh," James says. "Why does he think that?"

Hannah shrugs. "I never explained. It's my fault. I'm so sorry."

James shakes his head and swigs at his beer. "Can I ask why?" he asks. "Can I ask *why* you didn't explain?"

"I was angry," Hannah says. "It's stupid, I know. But he assumed that we had slept together, and that hurt me. So I let him carry on thinking it. And then he was . . ." She closes her eyes briefly at the almost physical pain the memory still brings, then continues, "He was so awful to me after you left. I really hated him for a while."

"Wow," James says.

"And by the time that was over, well, it seemed better not to mention it. I'm so sorry," Hannah says. "This is all my fault, isn't it?"

James tips his head sideways. "Well, not entirely," he says. "I mean, I guess I did try to steal you. He was right about that at least."

"God, you heard all of that?"

James blinks and nods slowly. "And I'm sorry about that too," he says. "It was wrong of me. It was clearly a mistake."

"What was a mistake?"

"Trying to steal my brother's fiancée," James says.

Hannah laughs sourly. "Well, you didn't try very hard," she says.

"I thought I made a pretty good stab at it," James says. "But you were never going to leave Cliff, let's face it."

Hannah shakes her head. "It's weird," she says. "It all feels like it was yesterday."

"It does," James agrees.

For five minutes they stand in silence, each lost in memories, and then Hannah asks, "Why *did* you leave?"

"Why did I leave?" James repeats.

"Yes. Why did you vanish in the middle of the night like that?"

James clenches his teeth and stares into the middle distance, remembering, then replies, "Cliff told me to go, didn't he."

"He *told* you to go."

James nods. "Uh-huh."

Hannah takes a swig of beer. "I still don't understand though," she says. "I mean, you never did what Cliff told you to do before. Why the sudden . . . I don't know . . . obedience?"

"He convinced me, I guess," James says. "He said you weren't gonna leave him and that all I was doing was making everyone crazy. He said he'd kill me if I stayed, and I kind of believed that a bit too. I was a kid. He was my big brother. But mainly, I thought he was right. I didn't reckon I had much choice but to bugger off."

"God, I wish you hadn't," Hannah says, screwing up her face in an attempt at holding back an unexpected batch of tears.

"You wish I hadn't left?"

"Yes."

"What would it have changed if I had stayed?" James asks. "Honestly?"

260

"Everything. It would have changed everything."

"You were pregnant," James points out. "You told me yourself, remember? You were with Cliff and you were pregnant, and you were about to get married."

"Not by the next day, I wasn't. By the next day I had lost the baby, and I hated Cliff and the marriage was cancelled."

"It was cancelled?"

"We cancelled everything. We had to. I had lost a lot of blood. I was in hospital for a week. I couldn't have got married even if I had wanted to. And I didn't."

"I didn't know," James says. "I'm sorry."

"I kept thinking you'd come back, you know," Hannah says. "For years I thought you'd come back. How stupid is that?"

James pinches his nose as if to prevent a sneeze and then swings his head from side to side to stretch his neck. "So what happened after?" he asks eventually.

"After?"

James nods. "I mean, you got married in the end. Well, I assume you did, anyway."

"We broke up for a while. Three months, I think it was. I stayed with Jill. They had a spare room in her student house, so I camped there. It was miserable. I remember we ate beans and rice every day to save money. And then we got back together. Cliff was pretty tenacious. But even then I thought you'd reappear. For ages, I thought you'd just turn up on the doorstep one day and whisk me away. And then Cliff told me you had died, so . . ."

James' forehead creases. "He *what*?" he whistles.

"He said you were dead. I thought maybe you knew about that."

James shakes his head rapidly from side to side as if to

dislodge this crazy idea. He opens his mouth to speak, but then gives up trying to find the right words and closes it again.

"A motorbike accident, he said. In India," Hannah explains.

James raises one eyebrow. "Well, at least it's exotic," he says.

"Yes."

James shakes his head slowly. "I can hardly believe that," he says.

"It's true. So I gave up hope. And things were OK with Cliff by then, so . . ."

"So you got married after all."

"We lived together for a few more years. I had kind of gone off the idea of marriage. But then I got pregnant with Luke. So . . ."

"So?"

"So it seemed the right thing to do."

"I see."

"So who knows what might have happened if you hadn't left. Or if you had come back."

"I did, you know," James says. "Just once. But I did come back."

"God, did you? When?"

"The day after the wedding. Well, the day after the wedding was supposed to be. I sat outside all day watching the house. I just wanted to see you again. I wanted to congratulate you if you'd got married, or . . ."

"Or . . ."

James shrugs. "I didn't know really."

"The day after the wedding, you say? The Sunday then?"

James nods.

"I was still in hospital then."

James nods again. "If only I had known."

"What would you have done if you had known?"

"I don't know," James says. "But I was so in love with you. I was totally sold on you."

"Were you really?" Hannah asks.

"I was."

"Really?" Hannah asks. "Or was it just . . . I don't know . . . infatuation or something?"

"I think so," James says. "I think it was real."

"Yes, I think it was too," Hannah says, and unable to hold the tears back any longer, her face collapses.

"Here," James says, putting down his beer can and crossing the kitchen towards her. "Come here."

Hannah lets him take her in his arms, then lays her head on his shoulder, and cries. Her angst is so powerful that she can hardly breathe. It feels the same as it did the last time James held her in his arms, fifteen years ago. A mixture of misery at the impossibility of the situation, and yet, even here, even now, a stirring of desire.

When she opens her eyes again she sees that Cliff has returned and is standing outside on the patio, just beyond the open window. He is staring at them – his own eyes red and watery.

She pats James' back, then, when he fails to understand, she tries to push him away. "Let me go," she whispers. "Cliff's back."

"I'm sorry?" James says, pushing back so that he can see her face.

"She said to let her go," Cliff says loudly, his voice almost a shout. "She said her husband's back."

By the time they have separated, Cliff is in the kitchen. "Right, that's enough," he says, seizing James' forearm. "Now, you *really* need to go."

"Cliff, please," Hannah says, stepping towards the two men.

Cliff raises his left arm, barring her path, and even pushes her away with it.

"Cliff!" Hannah protests. "What's got into you? You've got this all wrong, you know."

James prises Cliff's hand from his arm. "Fuck off, Cliff," James says. "You don't get to tell me what to do."

"Actually, I do," Cliff says. "Hannah's my wife. And you're leaving."

"I'll leave when *Hannah* tells me to leave," James says.

"I swear that if you don't butt out of my life, I will fucking punch you out of it," Cliff says quietly.

Hannah watches her husband in disbelief. She has virtually never heard Cliff swear. She has certainly never seen him threaten anyone with physical violence. "Cliff?" she protests.

"Only you can't, mate, can you!" James says, his tone goading. "That's what I didn't realise last time. You may be my big brother, but you're not so big after all, are you, mate? You couldn't punch out a fucking opossum."

Hannah sees Cliff squaring his shoulders as if preparing to carry out his threat, which, faced with James' stature, would be a terrifying and futile exercise. "Please, STOP THIS!" she cries, managing now to step between the two men. "Stop behaving like idiots."

"He has to go," Cliff says, pointing over her shoulder. "Tell him he has to go!"

"No!" Hannah says. "No, I won't. I want you two to sort this out once and for all. But like adults, not like this."

"TELL HIM TO GO!" Cliff says, lunging at James over her shoulder.

"Don't you fucking talk to her like that," James says. "Or I'll bloody punch you out myself."

"People! PEOPLE! STOP!" Jill has returned and is standing in the doorway with one hand on Luke's shoulder. The boy looks pale and terrified. He looks about to burst into tears. "It's OK, Luke," Jill says, then, "Looks like it's a good job I got back, though."

At the sight of Luke, everyone freezes. Hannah steps from between the two men and crouches down in front of him. "We're just having a bit of an argument," Hannah tells him, her voice wobbling strangely. "It's just the same as you do with Aïsha sometimes, sweetheart. But don't worry. It'll all be fine in the end."

"Just don't anybody say a word until I've got these two out of the way," Jill says.

As she leads Luke back outside and indicates through a mixture of mime, English and French that Pascal should take the children down to the river, Cliff and James glower at each other. Hannah pours herself a glass of water and Cliff follows suit.

When she returns, Jill says, "Really! What were you thinking?"

"I'm sorry," Hannah says, touching the bridge of her nose. "Things got a bit out of hand."

"He still needs to fuck off," Cliff says.

"Cliff, just shut up for a minute, will you?" Jill says acidly. "Actually, I'll tell you what. Just go outside for a bit, will you? I need to talk to Hannah."

"Don't tell me what to do," Cliff says.

"Cliff?" Hannah pleads. "Please? Just for a minute."

"This is bullshit," Cliff says, but he obeys all the same.

"You, stay here," Jill says to James. "If you move, I'll slap you myself." Then to Hannah, she says, "Come."

Once she has led Hannah to her bedroom and shut the door, she asks, "So what the hell is happening here, Han'?"

Hannah shakes her head dolefully. "I don't know, Jill," she says.

"It's my fault for inviting him," Jill says. "Shall I tell him to leave? That would be best, wouldn't it?"

Hannah shakes her head. "I don't want him to leave," she says. "I want this all sorted out. This has all gone on for too long anyway."

Jill nods seriously, then sighs. "But that's not all, is it?" she says. "That's not the only reason you don't want him to leave."

"I don't know," Hannah says again.

"OK, well," Jill says, visibly switching into a rarely seen practicality mode. "This place is turning into a war-zone, and it's no good for the kids."

"No. You're right."

"So let me take them to the seaside for the day. We could even stay the night. How does that sound?"

"I guess," Hannah says.

"We might need you to take us to the station or something," Jill says. "Pascal's old banger only has two seats."

"You can take the Renault," Hannah says. "Cliff already said that it's fine. But you will look after them properly, won't you?"

"What do you mean?"

"I mean, no dope. No masks. No . . ."

"Hannah! How many times have I looked after Luke?"

"Lots, I know, but . . ."

"So, he'll be fine. You know he will."

"Sure."

"I won't even drink, how's that?"

"Well, if you're driving, you had better not."

"Are you sure it's OK for us to take the Renault?"

"Absolutely."

"OK, well, we'll do that then. That way you'll have the whole place to fight in. And you'll get it sorted by tomorrow, by the time we get back, OK?"

"I will."

"OK, well, we had better get the shopping in before the frozen stuff melts."

"Sure," Hannah says.

"I might need to keep your card," Jill says. "Mine got refused at the supermarket."

"Sure," Hannah says, with a wave of one hand. "Whatever."

When Hannah opens the bedroom door, she can hear that Cliff and James have already resumed hostilities. Followed by Jill, she runs down the corridor to the lounge where Cliff is prodding James with his forefinger.

"Nothing ever changes with you, does it?" he is saying. "That's the fucking problem. That's why I . . ."

Hannah pushes her way between the two men again. "Just STOP THIS!" she shrieks, pushing them apart. "You're like bloody children."

"You're a bloody psycho, mate, that's your problem," James tells Cliff.

"You come with me," Jill says, grabbing James' arm, and dragging him reluctantly outside.

"He has to go, Han'," Cliff says. "You have to tell him to go."

"Listen," Hannah says. "We need to get the shopping in and . . ."

"Shopping? Are you crazy?" Cliff says. "I don't give a shit about the shopping."

"We need to get the shopping in . . ." Hannah repeats. "And then Jill and Pascal are taking the kids off to the beach so that we can sort this out like adults. And maybe at the end of that James will have to leave."

"He will."

"Maybe. But I want to try. I want to at least *try* to get this sorted."

"He *is* leaving," Cliff says.

"Well, maybe he is. But until the kids are out of the way, please, *please*, just stay out of each other's way."

"How?" Cliff says. "How the fuck am I supposed to do that?"

Hannah rolls her eyes. "Please stop behaving like a ten-year-old," she says. "Just go for a walk, or go to the bedroom or read a bloody book for half an hour."

Cliff groans, then heads back towards the bedroom. "I'll tell you how this ends," he says loudly, as he walks away. "This ends with my arse-hole of a brother leaving. And it ends with him never coming back."

THIRTY-SEVEN

Hannah climbs over the fence and then heads down the track. Hearing the sounds of children coming from the valley, she heads down towards the stream, climbs down the staircase, then follows the flowing water to the first bend, whereupon Jill comes into view.

Luke, Aïsha and Pascal are all paddling; Jill is sitting on a large flat rock watching them.

"God, you haven't left them alone, have you?" Jill asks as Hannah approaches. "They'll knock seven shades of shit out of each other, won't they?"

Hannah shrugs and squeezes onto the rock next to her sister. "Let them," she says. "I'm beyond caring."

"You don't mean that," Jill says.

"You're right," Hannah says. "I don't. But I do wish they'd just behave like adults. Anyway . . ."

"Anyway?"

"I thought you were all off to Nice."

"We are in a bit. But it's nice down here, and the kids are having fun. Luke was really upset before, so this is good."

"The water's freezing!" Luke shouts. "Come try."

"No, I'll take your word for it," Hannah calls back.

"I was wondering if we can take Luke's patch off," Jill says. "It's supposed to come off today anyway, right?"

Hannah nods. "I'll do it when we get back."

"Are you sure this is the right thing?" Jill asks. "I don't need to worry about you, do I?"

Hannah shakes her head. "No, you're right. Get the kids out of the way for a bit. It's perfect. I'm quite tempted to come myself. Shall I go back and pack an overnight bag for Luke?"

"I guess," Jill says. "Actually, I'll come with you and do ours."

Aïsha, who has just splashed up to join them, asks, "Where are we going?"

"To Nice," Jill says.

"Again?"

"Yes. But we're taking Luke this time as well."

"We're not staying in that hotel again, are we?"

"No, I think we might try to find somewhere nicer," Jill says.

"There were these really gross insects in the bathroom," Aïsha tells Hannah.

"Cockroaches," Jill informs her. "There were only two, but all the same . . ."

"Yuck," Hannah comments. "Well, definitely don't go there again."

An hour later, the car has been loaded and Cliff's keys handed over. Jill wishes Hannah luck, and drives the loaded Renault away.

Hannah closes the gate slowly. She's in no hurry to return to the drama of the house.

She heads around the back and crouches to dip her fingers in the pool. She watches the ripples emanating from her hand and then, seeing what she thinks is a raindrop, glances up at the leaden grey sky. But though the air feels almost wet with humidity, it's still not raining – it must have been an insect hitting the water, she decides.

She walks to the rear of the house, past the track once again, past the lavender – she picks a sprig – and finally returns to the porch where she expects to find James.

Seeing that he is absent, she heads indoors to Aïsha's room, but when she reaches the door she changes her mind and decides to tackle Cliff first.

When she enters their bedroom, she finds Cliff sitting on the bed. "You're not reading," she says – an attempt at normality.

"I don't want to read," Cliff says.

"No," Hannah says. "No, I'm sure."

She circles the bed and then perches on the edge of it next to her husband. "Look," she says. "I know that this is all difficult still, but there's something you need to know."

Cliff nods. "Go on," he says.

Hannah sighs. "You need to know that I never slept with James," she says.

Cliff scrunches up his features. "What?" he asks.

"We never slept together," Hannah says again. "It never happened."

"Why . . ." Cliff says.

"Why?"

"Yes, why are you even saying that to me?"

"Because I know that you think we did," Hannah says. "But we didn't."

Cliff shakes his head, half in confusion, half in disgust. "I *know* you didn't," he says. "But you wanted to."

"Oh," Hannah says, a little deflated that her great problem-solving revelation has turned out to be entirely ineffective.

"Jesus," Cliff says, rubbing his brow.

"What?"

"If you're not even going to deny it . . ."

"Deny what?"

"That you wanted to," Cliff says.

Hannah laughs falsely, and stands. She crosses to the window and looks outside. "I don't even remember," she lies. "It was so long ago."

"And now?" Cliff says, sliding off the bed and following her to the window.

"Now?" Hannah asks, glancing at him and then returning her gaze to the olive tree outside. It's covered in tiny green fruits. She hadn't noticed before.

"Yes, now," Cliff says sharply.

"I like James," Hannah says. "I like him a lot. But the question of whether I want to sleep with him doesn't even come up because I'm married to you."

Cliff snorts. "So I'll take that as a 'yes', then, shall I?"

Hannah glances at Cliff again. "Oh, take it how you want, Cliff," she says. "I'm getting to the point where . . ."

"I should have let him stay," Cliff says, cutting her off and taking her arm now in an attempt to make her look him in the eye. "I should have let him have what he wanted fifteen years ago."

"Well, thanks," Hannah says, furious at the implication that this was somehow an option within Cliff's control, but unable to find a way to put that specific outrage into words.

"He would have had his fun and thrown you away like a used tissue," Cliff says.

Hannah shakes her head. "How *foul* you are when you want to be."

"That's all he wanted," Cliff says. "It's still all he wants. It's just because you're mine, you know."

"I'm not *yours*," Hannah says even though she realises that

272

it's open to misinterpretation and risky. "And stop squeezing my arm! You're hurting me," she adds, as she attempts to prise his fingers from her.

"That's what you just don't get about James," Cliff says. "You like the idea that James thinks you're special. But he doesn't. James isn't interested in you. The only thing he ever liked about you was that you were mine."

Hannah shakes her head. Some line is being crossed here, and she's beginning to doubt if they will ever find their way back. She turns her body to face Cliff now. "That's enough," she says. "You're just going to end up saying things that you'll regret because you're angry. And get your hands . . . off . . . me." She shakes him free. "And stop talking about me as if I'm one of your things."

"Why don't you go and fuck him now?" Cliff says.

Hannah stares deep into her husband's enraged eyes and doesn't recognise him at all. "God, have you been drinking? Is that it?"

"No, seriously," Cliff continues. "Why don't you just go and get it out of your system?"

"How dare you!" Hannah spits.

She turns and starts to walk towards the bedroom door, but Cliff follows her and grabs her arm again, spinning her around and pushing her back against the door. "Where are you going?" Cliff asks. "To *James*?"

His face is too close to hers now. In this instant, she hates him as much as she ever has – as much as she hated him that night fifteen years ago in fact. *Everything's the same*, she thinks. *We've come full circle, and we're back here again. Everything's exactly the same.*

"What's the matter, Hannah?" Cliff asks, his voice now a

revolting sneer. "Married life getting you down? Think you want a bit of variety? I wonder if he's still interested. You have aged a bit, put on a bit of weight . . . but maybe . . ."

"I can't deal with you when you're like this," Hannah says. "Let me go."

"Why should I?" Cliff says. "You're my wife, aren't you? Surely this is within my marital rights?"

"You're hurting me again," Hannah says, her voice now trembling as the first inklings of physical fear hit her. "Get off me!"

"Let her go, Cliff." James has appeared at the window and is looking in at them.

"And here he is," Cliff says. "The knight in fucking armour to the rescue."

"Let her go," James says again, his voice still calm.

"Fuck off, James," Cliff says. "This is between me and Hannah."

"Fuck off?" James says. He sounds amused. "Again?"

"You're hurting me, Cliff," Hannah says again. "Will you just stop . . ."

"Tell him to leave," Cliff says, "and I'll let you go. Tell him to fuck off."

Hannah thinks about this for a second, then decides that it's worth saying anything right now to end this crazed conflict. "Leave," she says. "Cliff's right. Please, just go."

But it's too late, because James is climbing through the window, and Cliff is already releasing her and lurching towards him.

Hannah watches in horror as Cliff scrambles over the bed and throws a punch at James, who, still off-balance from climbing in, stumbles against the bed, loses his balance, and falls to the ground.

"Stop!" Hannah screams. "Please, Cliff, stop!"

He throws himself on top of James, now sprawled on the floor, and lands a single punch to the side of James' face before his brother manages to seize both of his hands.

"Ha!" James laughs, as he rolls Cliff onto his back and pins him to the ground. He looks totally un-traumatised by the whole thing, thoroughly amused about it all.

"You're a worm, James," Cliff says, dominated yet un-cowed by his brother's physical strength. "You're a fucking worm, and you always were."

"Not so tough now, are we, mate?" James says.

"It was always the same," Cliff spits. "Anything I had, you stole. When we were kids, it was toys. When we were teenagers it was my records. Every fucking thing I ever had . . . Well, you can't have my wife, you cunt."

"Oh, shut the fuck up, Cliff," James says, now managing to pin down both of Cliff's arms with a single hand. "You sound like a fucking three-year-old."

"So, Hannah," James asks, "what do you want me to do with this . . ." His voice trails off as he looks up, because he sees that Hannah has gone. "Hannah!" he shouts. "Hannah? Shit!"

He slaps Cliff hard across the cheek. "That's for being a wimp," he says, and then, a little unsettled by the fact that Cliff now starts to cry, he releases him and stands. "Hannah?" he shouts. "HANNAH!"

THIRTY-EIGHT

Hannah opens the gate, closes it quietly behind her, then runs away from the house as fast as her legs will carry her. She doesn't know where she is going and she doesn't have a plan. Pure instinct is driving her actions – she's scared and she *needs* to escape. If she can just get to the corner, she thinks, glancing back, if she can just get out of sight, then no one will know where she is.

As she reaches the broken street lamp, she notices a track to her left leading into the forest, so with one last glance back at the house, she ducks down it and out of sight.

Doubled up, she pauses to catch her breath. Sweat is dripping into her eyes, making them sting. Her T-shirt is clinging to her chest. The stormy heat of the day is unbearable.

When her heart has slowed, she starts to stride on into the trees, a cloud of flies buzzing irritatingly around her. The stupid men can beat shit out of each other for all she cares. She has had it with them.

As the neighbours' houses vanish into the greenery behind her, her fear turns to anger, and then as this too wanes, tears start to flow instead. After another twenty yards, her vision is so blurred that she is stumbling, so when she reaches a clearing, she pauses and sits on the trunk of a massive fallen tree.

Her thoughts are a swirling mess. She is thinking about

seeing the two brothers together fighting like children. She is thinking about the fact that this fight has – and, in a way, Cliff is right about this – nothing to do with her. It really is all about sibling rivalry. It's all a childhood ritual played out because that's what these two brothers do when they're together.

From feeling special and loved by both men, she has gone, in a day, to feeling unloved by either of them, and to feeling stupid for having been duped in the first place. Cliff's remarks have hurt her so badly she feels – even though experience tells her that she is probably being over-dramatic – that he may never claw his way back from them. And James? As far as James is concerned, she fears that Cliff may be right. The way he sat on him, the way he pinned him to the ground and gloated about it – maybe it *was* all about competition, about domination, about possession. Maybe she has wasted her life dreaming about something that was never entirely real. And maybe, yes, he *would* have used her and tossed her away like a used handkerchief once he had demonstrated his superiority over his brother.

A second wave of tears hits Hannah, and she lets it happen, lets the tears slide unhindered down her cheeks. It feels like release, and there's no one here to see anyway.

She has had this thing stuck deep within her for years, she realises, a doubt, a fear, pushed aside and squashed down, and compressed until it was an almost unnoticeable lump of darkness, a tiny manageable chunk of coal squashed deep within her chest. It began, she remembers, even before James came on the scene. It began because even compared with selfish, impossible Ben, life with Cliff seemed dull, and that made her doubt her choices, that always made her wonder.

James was a brief gust of oxygen that made that coal burn bright, and for a moment, for those few hours he was in the house all those years ago, she had been able to see clearly that she was making a mistake, that she was *living* a mistake, and that this was not how her life was meant to be. And even after James had left, that doubt had stayed, even after he had "died" it was there, ever present, because during those few hours she had spent with him, she had learned that true love really did exist, that passion and almost irresistible sexual attraction were real things, not fiction, and that this being the case, the train she was on – to Surrey, and marriage, and motherhood and a part-time job in a school – was the *wrong* train to the wrong destination.

But she never found the courage to get off. That was her crime. She had never had the courage to face that doubt. Because what she had felt for James had seemed so rare, so unlikely – so *unreasonable* – that she feared that if she chose it, she would end up with nothing. Had he come back for her she would have perhaps had the courage to jump carriages. But he didn't come back, so she squashed it down, became expert at compressing, at containing, at dousing that doubt, and ultimately became so expert that she managed, for the most part, to pretend that it didn't exist at all.

And now, today, it has expanded again. It has exploded and tainted everything, leaving her life suddenly dark and polluted and dirty and wrong.

She thinks of Luke and wishes she had her phone with her. She feels a profound need to hear his voice, to know that he's OK. Wonderful, beautiful, innocent Luke, the diamond in her life. And how can she allow herself to even think that her relationship with Cliff has been a mistake when something so beautiful has come from it? But they say that coal and diamonds are the same thing, don't they? She read that somewhere – that diamonds are just coal compressed even more tightly.

Hearing the crack of a twig, Hannah turns to see James coming along the forest path towards her.

"You're here," he says breathlessly as he reaches her.

"Yes, I'm here," she replies, wiping her eyes on the sleeve of her T-shirt. She's pretty certain that she must look shocking.

"I was worried about you," James says, swiping at the sweat trickling down his own brow. "I didn't know where you were."

"I needed to get away," Hannah replies. "I needed to be alone."

"Should I go?" James asks. "Do you want me to leave you in peace?"

Hannah swallows and turns away. She looks out at the grey skyline beyond the trees and feels ashamed because, even now what she wants, she realises, is for James to hold her. She has just seen him pin her husband to the floor and humiliate him, and still all she wants is a kiss that might prove to her that something important she once felt was real.

At the lack of reply, James sighs and sits down next to her. He lays one arm loosely across her shoulders.

"Did you hurt him?" Hannah asks.

"Cliff?"

"Yes, Cliff."

"No," James says. "No, I didn't hurt him. I gave him a slap because . . ." He shrugs.

"Because?"

"He punched me, Hannah," James says. "He gave me a fuckin' nose-bleed."

Hannah looks up and sees from the drying blood around James' nostrils that this is true. She reaches out to touch it, but then stops herself in time. "I'm sorry," she says.

"He told me not to come," James says. "I guess I should have listened."

Hannah nods.

"But then I wouldn't have seen you, would I?" James says. "I wouldn't have seen my Hannah."

"Is it true?" Hannah asks. "Is it true what Cliff says?"

"That I'm an asshole?" James says. "Probably."

"No, what he said about me. That it was all just to prove a point."

"Of course not," James says.

"It's OK," Hannah tells him. "If that's it, it's OK."

It's OK, but it would break my heart, she thinks.

"I can see how competitive you are," she continues. "But if that's all it ever was, then I'd rather know. I need to know now. It's time."

James takes a deep breath. "What can I say?" he says. "I fell in love with you, Hannah. I fell in love with you the first time we met."

"The second time," Hannah says. "The first time we met you were too drunk to even know who I was."

James shakes his head. "Nope," he says. "Nope, it was the first time, in the pub. I remember it like it was yesterday."

"Really?"

James nods and squeezes her shoulder. "Why do you think I went off and hid at the bar?" he asks. "Why do you think I never came to visit?"

"I didn't realise. I just thought . . . I don't know what I thought really."

"And then, when I came down from Edinburgh . . . God. Do you remember, you sat in the car with me?"

"I do."

"I wanted to drive away there and then, but . . ." Something about Hannah's expression makes him pause. "What is it?" he asks.

"You just said he *warned* you not to come," Hannah says.

"I'm sorry?"

"You said Cliff warned you not to come and you should have listened to him."

"Ah," James says, pulling a face.

"*When* did he warn you?"

"I'm not supposed to . . ." James says.

"Not supposed to what?"

"I'm not supposed to tell you. Cliff made me promise when I arrived."

"You're not making any sense to me, James," Hannah says.

"I don't suppose it makes any difference now," James says. "You might as well know."

"OK. Know what?"

"I wrote to say I was coming," James says.

"You did?"

James nods and licks his lips. "And Cliff emailed me to tell me not to come."

"So he knew you were coming?"

"Uh-huh. Well, to England. Not here, obviously."

"But he knew the dates?" Hannah asks.

"Yes."

"Cliff knew the dates you were coming to England?" Hannah says again.

"Yes," James says again. "Yes, I sent him my flight details."

281

"Which, of course, is why we're here," Hannah says. James frowns, so she expounds, "Oh, Cliff didn't want to come to France, that's all. But he suddenly changed his mind. And he suddenly wanted to come for two weeks, not one."

"Right," James says. "Well, that figures, I guess."

"God, so you were in contact with him and he didn't tell me. That's unbelievable."

"The thing is, Hannah . . ." James says.

"Yes?"

"I wrote quite a lot, actually."

"You wrote *a lot*?"

"Well, maybe not *a lot*. But I wrote quite a few times, yeah. And I sent a card most Christmases."

"You wrote to us every Christmas?"

"To *you*. I sent you a card most years. You told me you loved Christmas. Do you remember?"

Hannah shakes her head. "I don't remember. I do love Christmas, but I don't remember telling you."

"Well, you did. So I wrote most years."

"And Cliff, what? He stole them?"

"Yes."

"Maybe they got lost. Maybe the address . . ."

"No, he told me, Hannah. He told me he took them."

"He *stole* my letters."

"Yes. He made me promise not to tell you. He said it might upset you. But . . ."

"Upset me?"

"Yes."

"Jesus." Hannah closes her eyes and strokes her eyelids as she rewrites yet another aspect of the last fifteen years. "Did he read them, then?"

James shrugs. "I think so," he says.

"So what did they say?"

"It's kind of embarrassing really," James says.

"Tell me what they said."

"That I missed you. That I loved you. That I couldn't forget you. Stuff like that."

"God," Hannah says.

"I know. I'm sorry. I didn't think he was reading them. I thought you were."

"No wonder he's jealous."

"I wrote other shit too."

"Other shit?"

"You know. About my travels. Where I was at. What I was doing."

"Right."

"And it was more of that as time went on, of course."

"Of course."

"Once I met Judy, obviously I didn't . . . I mean, I wrote more ordinary stuff. I wrote about life on the farm, and about little Hannah. I wrote to tell you about . . ." James clears his throat. "About the accident as well. I really thought you'd reply then. I could have done with a reply back then."

"Hannah?" she repeats, a fresh bout of tears already welling up. "Did you say little Hannah?"

"Yes," James says, his own voice quivering and his eyes glistening. "Yes, I named her after you."

James turns sideways on the log, and the sadness in his eyes makes Hannah melt into fresh tears. He hugs her, and after a few minutes, her sobs fade and she dries her eyes on her sleeve again and stands. "Let's walk for a bit," she says.

They head, in silence, deeper into the forest, and as they do so, the pines become taller and taller, the trunks ever more massive, the air quieter, stiller.

"I love pine trees," Hannah says for no reason other than it feels good to say one normal sentence today.

"Yes," James agrees. "It's always so quiet. Dead almost."

"It is."

"So what happens now, do you think?" James asks.

"I don't know," Hannah says, then after a few seconds silence, she adds, "But I suppose you need to leave. And I need to work out if I can forgive Cliff."

"Forgive him for . . . ?"

"Well, he lied to me about so many things," Hannah says. "He said you were dead. He stole my post. I can still barely believe that. I wonder if he kept them all."

"But you still love him despite it all?"

Hannah can't answer that now. She's not sure right now if she ever loved Cliff, but she's also unsure of her judgement. In the end, she just shrugs and says, "Love . . ."

They walk on a little farther, startling a bird, which screeches in turn startling *them*. As the path narrows, James' hand bumps against hers. The contact is so light, so vague, that it could almost go unnoticed, but it happens again and again, and each time Hannah senses the hairs on the back of her neck prickling. The fifth time, she stops walking and turns to face James. "What are you doing, James?" she asks, her voice flat, almost robotic with constrained emotion.

"I still want to kiss you," he says. "Isn't that crazy?"

Hannah sighs deeply and shakes her head. "No," she says. "That's not crazy at all."

He's going to leave soon, she thinks. *He's going to leave, and I'll probably never see him again before I die.* She glances left and right and leans in.

James half-smiles and then their lips touch and his arms come up to hold her. Momentarily, everything is all right with the world. Just for an instant, she is home.

They kiss delicately and then Hannah opens her lips and lets James' tongue slip inside, exploring her mouth. They start to kiss more passionately, start to grind their bodies together. She becomes aware of James' hands slipping inside her T-shirt, becomes aware of the roughness of his fingers against her shoulders. And then suddenly, James pulls away and rests his head instead on her shoulder. "God, I want you so bad, Hannah," he whispers.

"I know," she replies – her own legs have gone so weak she's struggling to stand.

"Is it too late for us?" James asks, and Hannah, in spite of herself, bursts out laughing.

"Of course it's too late for us," she says. "I've spent half my life with your brother. We have a child."

She senses James' body shudder against her strangely and then he says, "Spend the other half with me, Hannah," and she realises that he is trying not to cry. "Tell that stupid brother of mine to get lost," James says, "and come with me."

Hannah laughs again. She can't help herself. The absurdity of this time-warp they are stuck in strikes her as too ridiculous for words. "I think we both know that's not going to happen, James," she says. "If it was going to happen, it would have happened fifteen years ago."

"But I want you so bad," James says, pulling her tight again, so tight that she's aware of his erection pressing against her through their clothes. She wonders if, just for half an hour, she

285

can be someone else. She wonders if, just here, just now, just for a bit, she can do what Tristan or Jill, or half of the other people on planet Earth would probably do.

She's considering both this and the folly of even considering this when a large, aged Labrador pads up to their feet and starts nuzzling their legs. James breaks free and crouches down. "Hello buddy," he says. "Where have you come from?" and Hannah hates that dog, could kill that dog for destroying the moment.

A few seconds later, the owner, a short man with a vast pot-belly comes into view. "Milou !" he shouts. "Ici !"

Hannah and James smile falsely and nod at the man, and, as he passes, he apologises for the dog. "Désolé," he says, "mais il aime tout le monde."

"He gave me a funny look," Hannah says, once the man has waddled on. "Do I look shocking?"

"Your eye-stuff has gone a bit crazy," James says.

"Panda eyes?"

James nods, then leans in to kiss Hannah again, but this time she turns her head. That moment has passed.

"Hannah?" James asks.

"I think that's enough for now," she says, pushing him gently way.

"For now?" James says.

"For forever probably," Hannah tells him.

"*Probably*," James repeats.

"Just stop it," Hannah says.

"Sorry."

"I think we should go back now," she tells him, suddenly business-like. "And I think you should leave."

James nods sadly and blinks acquiescence.

"This is enough," she says. "This is just . . . *enough*."

"Yes," he says, nodding again.

As they turn to walk back to the house, James reaches for her hand, and she lets him take it.

"We can keep in touch this time though, right?" James says, squeezing her fingers.

"I guess," Hannah says.

"And if, you know . . ." James says, "things change for you."

"Yes," Hannah says. "Yes, if anything changes . . ."

"Do you have email?" James asks.

"I use Cliff's, so, no, not really," Hannah replies.

"Maybe you could get your own?"

"Yes," Hannah says with a sigh. "Yes, that would seem like a good idea, all things considered."

Once they hit the road, they separate and Hannah pauses and asks, "Do you have your keys with you? The car keys?"

"Sure," James says. "But I have to get my stuff from the house."

"Right," Hannah says. "Maybe I can go and get that for you. It might be better if you don't come inside. Just in case it all kicks off again."

"Sure," James says. "I can just wait in the car, if you want. If you think you'll be all right."

"I'll be all right as long as you don't come in," she says, then, swiping at her cheek, "Is it raining?"

"Yes, I just got hit too," James says.

Another drop hits Hannah's forehead and then another her leg, and then suddenly they are running towards the house through a deluge.

When they reach the property they open the gates and

James climbs into his car, calling to Hannah to get in as well.

She jumps into the passenger seat and pulls the door closed behind her. She is already drenched. The rain drumming on the roof gives her a sense of déjà vu that is so powerful it makes her come up in goosebumps.

"God," James says. "Do you remember?"

Hannah nods. "That's exactly what I was just thinking."

"I should have driven away there and then," James says. "I wanted to, you know."

"Yes, you said. But it was a whole lifetime ago now."

"Well, half a lifetime ago," James says.

"Yes. So. I'll go get your bag from your room."

"My wallet's on the side too," James says. "Are you sure you don't want me to . . ."

"Really, no," Hannah insists.

"And you'll be OK. He won't . . . you know . . ." Hannah creases her brow, so James explains, "He was holding you before. He seemed pretty aggressive. Will you be OK?"

"Of course," Hannah says. "He's my husband, James. He's not going to *hurt* me."

"Right. So, my wallet, bag, the phone charger is plugged in next to the bed. My bathroom bag – the grey one. I think that's about it."

"I'll scan around for anything else," Hannah says. "Where will you go?"

James shrugs. "It's getting late," he says. "And this is hardly ideal . . ." he nods at the water cascading down the windscreen.

"There's a bar-hotel place at the end of the road," Hannah tells him. "We went there for drinks the other night."

"This road?"

"Yes. It's half a mile after that bend. Just straight down. You can't miss it."

"I'll go there then," James says, "then head down to the coast tomorrow morning for a few days. My flight back's not until Saturday."

"Right," Hannah says. "So, wish me luck."

"Yes, good luck," James says. "And if you need anything, just shout or something."

"I'll be fine."

She climbs from the car and runs to the house. The raindrops are the biggest she has ever seen, each one almost a puddle of its own.

Inside the house is dark and, with the exception of the white noise of the rain falling outside, completely silent.

She checks the kitchen and then seeing that their own bedroom door is closed, she takes her shoes off and creeps to the bathroom, then to Aïsha's room, where she stuffs James' wallet, phone charger and toiletry bag into the rucksack before heading back to the patio.

Then she heaves the bag over one shoulder, and runs, still barefoot, back across the gravel to the car.

James has the hatchback open, and is standing beneath it, using it for shelter. He takes the bag from her and drops it in the boot.

"Your wallet's in there," Hannah says, aware that the rain is still lashing her legs. "Everything's in there, I think."

"If you find anything else, you know where I am," James says.

"Yes."

"And if you want to see me for any other reason," he says, looking searchingly into her eyes.

Hannah nods and swallows. "Yes," she says. "But I won't. You know I won't."

"If you change your mind . . ."

"Stop it, James. Just leave, will you?"

"Right. Oh! Here," James says, rifling in one of the smaller pockets of his rucksack and producing a business card. "It's a bit formal, but it has my email and stuff on it."

"Thanks," Hannah says, sliding the card into the damp pocket of her shorts. "I'll get an account set up and I'll send you a message – an email."

"Is that a promise?" James asks.

"It is," she says, then, "Right!"

They look into each other's eyes, and then both sigh simultaneously.

"Hannah," James starts, but she interrupts him.

"Don't," she says. "Please, just go, will you?"

James swallows with difficulty, then nods. "Fine," he says. "Right."

He opens his arms, embraces her in a final hug, and then closes the hatch and runs to the driver's door. "Go inside!" he shouts through a gap in the window. "You're soaked."

"I don't care!" Hannah says. "It's warm. It's like a warm shower."

James smiles sadly at her, shakes his head and starts the engine. And then with the tiniest of waves, he is gone.

Hannah closes the gates and leans on them to watch as the Clio shrinks in size, and then finally vanishes around the bend.

In those last twenty seconds before it disappears from view, she considers running after him, she considers screaming, and she considers sinking to her knees to writhe in the mud. But though they all seem like possibilities, she can't imagine herself doing any of them. She is, she realises, a prisoner of her own body, trapped by her genes, or her conditioning, or her upbringing, or expectation or whatever it is that makes Hannah, Hannah.

She's thirty-eight, and if at thirty-eight you're still not Jill and you're still not Tristan, then you might as well get used to it. Because ultimately, that is the greatest revelation of all. That even now, even after all the years of dreaming, of wanting, she is not Tristan, and she is not Jill, and she is not anyone who can recklessly seize unexpected opportunities. She is Hannah. She is Hannah Parker. And standing in the pouring rain once every ten years is about as crazy as it gets.

The water running down her neck makes her shiver. She glances down and sees that her T-shirt is drenched and transparent and is clinging to her breasts.

She looks left and right to check that no one has seen, and then turns and walks briskly back to the house.

THIRTY-NINE

Hannah dries herself in the bathroom. She washes her face and removes her blurred make-up. Not wanting to face Cliff yet, she changes into dry clothes from the laundry basket – the T-shirt and shorts she was wearing yesterday.

She heads through to the lounge, now dark as evening, and sits on the cold leather sofa and watches the rain plummeting from the overflowing guttering beyond the French windows.

For half an hour, she sits like this, and for half an hour she has no thoughts at all.

Eventually, she hears the bedroom door open, then Cliff's footsteps. She doesn't turn around, just continues to sit staring at the rain. She waits for him to speak.

"I take it you were with him," Cliff finally says, still standing behind her.

"Yes," Hannah says, but the word comes out as a croak, so she has to clear her throat and say it again. "Yes."

After a few seconds silence, Cliff asks, "So what are you going to do?"

Knowing that he can't see her face, she allows herself to frown deeply. The question makes no sense to her.

After a while, she hears Cliff head into the kitchen and pull a beer from the refrigerator. As he comes into view he cracks the ring-pull and takes a sip. He sits in the armchair and looks out at the garden. "Rain," he says.

"Yes," Hannah agrees.

"So what are you going to do?" Cliff asks again.

Hannah stares at him blankly. She still doesn't understand the question, but it seems somehow important not to reveal this.

"Are you going to leave me?" Cliff asks.

Still, she stares at him, transfixed. *So that's an option, is it?* she thinks. Presumably if Cliff thinks she might leave him then it's a possibility. "I can't believe how much you lied to me," she says, the first logical sentence that springs to mind.

"He told you then?"

Hannah nods. "Did you keep them?"

"The letters?"

Hannah nods again.

"No," Cliff says. "No, I didn't keep them."

"But you read them?"

"I'm sorry?"

"Did you read my letters, Cliff?"

Cliff shrugs. "He's my brother. I wanted to know he was OK despite everything."

Hannah nods. "I did too," she points out, simply.

Cliff fidgets in his seat.

"And he wasn't OK, was he?"

"Sometimes he was, and sometimes he wasn't."

"You had no right," Hannah tells him. "You had no right to steal my post."

Cliff shrugs. "He had no right to send you letters like that," he says.

"Maybe," Hannah says. "But all the same . . ."

She turns back to watch the rain falling, and sees, from the corner of her eye, that Cliff is doing the same.

"So are you going to leave me?" he asks again. "Are you leaving me for James?"

It strikes Hannah, that every time he says it, it becomes a little more real. That every time he repeats it, the option becomes a little more plausible. She expected him to apologise. She expected him to fight for her. She expected to have no option but to patch things up and carry on, because that, in life, is what generally seems to happen. But instead, he seems almost to be willing her to go. The conversation feels unreal, somehow. Like a bad script from a dodgy TV drama.

"It's weird," Hannah says, "but you don't sound like you care."

Cliff's brow creases. He stands and crosses the room to join her on the sofa. "Of course I care," he says. "I just have this feeling that you want out."

Hannah stares at him beside her. There's something still wrong with the script, something false. But she can't put her finger on it. And she doesn't want him this close. She doesn't want him this close at all.

"Do *you* want out?" she asks, squinting at him as if attempting to peer into his soul. "Is that it?"

"Of course I don't," Cliff says. "We have a son together. I couldn't even imagine . . ."

Hannah nods, vaguely convinced by this.

But then Cliff adds, "But if you're not happy. If you need something that I can't give you . . ." And there it is again. That false note.

As displacement activity, because she simply doesn't know what to say next, and because his physical proximity is somehow embarrassing her, she heads to the bathroom.

She locks the door, lowers the seat, and sits and stares at the door. Beyond the tiny open window, the noise of the rain falling into the pool is impressively loud. The temperature has plummeted since the rain began, and the air drifting from outside is almost cold now.

So, *does* she want something Cliff can't give her? It's almost as if she lacks the circuitry required to work out what she wants, what she needs – as if fifteen years of worrying about other people's needs, of looking after Jill and Luke and Cliff, fifteen years of trying to make sure that everyone else is OK has left her bereft of any sense of what she wants herself, what she herself needs.

And if she *did* want James, rather than Cliff, is that *really* an option? Jill seems to think it is. Tristan thinks so too. James says it is, and now, even Cliff apparently agrees, has virtually offered it up on a plate.

Beside her, on the sink, she sees Cliff's iPhone – forgotten in the bathroom.

She picks it up and plays with it absent-mindedly, but then she remembers Tristan's strange comment. "*Check his phone,*" he said.

She presses the on button and swipes at the screen to unlock it, but sees that, of course, it is protected with a pin code.

She sighs and stares at the screen. One-three-zero-nine, she types – Cliff's birthday. Wrong Password. Two-zero-one-zero – Luke's birthday. Wrong password. Zero-seven-one-two – *her* birthday. Wrong password.

She wonders if there's a limit to the number of attempts. She doesn't want the phone to get somehow stuck, she doesn't want to have to explain that.

And then, suddenly, she's sure she knows what the code is. Two-zero-two-four she types – Cliff's pin number for his Visa card. The phone unlocks with a click.

What to look for though?

She's no iPhone expert – she's not even much of a fan of technology in general, but she manages to find the recent calls list: Tristan, Jill, Aïsha, Luke, Dave (Cliff's business partner), Jenny (his aged secretary), Brian (squash), herself (wife). Nothing to see here.

Next she finds his email account, and decides that that's probably what Tristan meant – he probably knew about Cliff's emails to James. But the phone only holds a few days' messages. There's nothing revealing there either. She finds the contact list and scrolls through it. There are plenty of names she doesn't know there, but they're probably just clients. How would she know?

She sighs and clicks the phone off. She's just about to stand, when it crosses her mind that she can use the phone to call Tristan and ask him. She types in the pin code again and calls him, but it goes straight to voicemail. He's probably driving.

She ends the call and hits the home button. She is debating whether to phone Jill when a little yellow icon catches her eye. Grindr.

She frowns. Wasn't Grindr the gay dating app that Tristan was using the other day in the bar? She clicks on it and the screen fills with the same little thumbnail photos and the phone chirrups to signal that it has new messages. She glances nervously at the toilet door, then switches the phone to silent mode before, with a sick feeling in her stomach, continuing.

Messages are showing from three people. The first is a face-shot of Tristan. She clicks on it.

WILDEMAN: Cliff?
WILDEMAN: Cliff? Is that you?
WILDEMAN: WTF are you doing on Grindr?

She's not sure she understands entirely how the program works, but there don't appear to be any replies.

She returns to the main screen and clicks on the second icon, a balding guy with a full beard.

ACTIF83: SLT. A/P?

She has no idea what that means, but again, she can see no reply.

Finally she clicks on the third conversation. A photo of Jean-Jacques from the bar appears.

HOLIDAYGUY: You speak english?
MECDUSUD: Pics?
HOLIDAYGUY: Sorry, no pics.
MECDUSUD: Why?
HOLIDAYGUY: Married.
MECDUSUD: Tristan? Blageur!
HOLIDAYGUY: Not Tristan. Clive.
MECDUSUD: Sorry. Hello Clive.
HOLIDAYGUY: Hello.
MECDUSUD: Top or bottom?
HOLIDAYGUY: Both. Either. I'm free for one hour, now.
MECDUSUD: Send me a pic and we meet.

Hannah scrolls the screen up and then down, but no further messages appear.

"God," she murmurs. She feels numb.

Perhaps Cliff lent Tristan her phone, she reasons. She had taken Tristan's phone that day at the hospital, hadn't she? But no. That makes no sense. She returns to the previous dialogue. It is clearly Tristan talking to Cliff.

She feels shocked, yet strangely unsurprised, like when

Amy Winehouse died. Someone tells you Amy Winehouse is dead, and you're shocked, but part of you thinks, "Of course she is," as if you already knew. And that's how she feels now. Shocked, but somehow . . . A wave of nausea sweeps over her, so she puts the phone down on the edge of the sink and jumps up. She opens the lid to the toilet bowl and vomits, efficiently, into the pan.

After half an hour of staring at the bathroom tiles, Hannah washes her face, unlocks the door and steps outside.

"I was beginning to think you'd got lost in there," Cliff offers.

Hannah ignores his feeble attempt at humour, and saying, "Here!" she throws him the phone.

"Jesus! Careful!" Cliff exclaims as he scrambles to catch it. "It's made of glass. That cost five hundred pounds."

"Only, I don't care, Cliff," Hannah says, her voice as hard as marble.

"No? Oh, OK."

Hannah walks over to the French windows and looks outside. The rain has slowed now, but the sky is still a deep, devilish grey. "So is there something you want to tell me?" she asks.

"Erm, no," Cliff says. "No, I don't think so."

Hannah laughs bitterly. "Oh, I think there is," she says.

"To do with James?" Cliff asks. "To do with the letters?"

"I know about the letters," Hannah says. "I think we've covered that particular lie." She sounds harsh and bitchy, she knows that, but she can't seem to manage any other tone.

"It's only because I loved you," Cliff says. "Love you."

"What is it they call that?" Hannah asks, turning, briefly to look at him. "A Freudian slip, isn't it?"

"That's not what I mean," Cliff says. "That's not what it was."

"So is there something you want to tell me?" Hannah repeats, in exactly the same hard voice as before.

"No," Cliff says. "Unless, what, do you want me to tell you I lo—"

"Maybe holiday guy has something to tell me then," Hannah says, interrupting that particularly nauseating declaration.

"Holiday guy?"

"Yes, holiday guy," Hannah says.

"I'm sorry, Hannah, but I don't . . ."

"Stop bullshitting me," Hannah says, her voice rising almost to a shout. "I know, Cliff."

"You know what?"

"About Grindr."

Hannah looks back out of the window and waits for Cliff to reply.

When he fails to do so, she turns to look back at him.

He is sitting on the sofa staring at her. His face is pink and his eyes are wide and watery. He looks like a child caught out, a child on the verge of tears.

"So?" Hannah asks.

Cliff shrugs.

"Are you gay, Cliff?" she asks, as gently as she can manage, which sadly isn't very.

He matches her stare, then very slowly shakes his head. "I . . ." he says.

"Yes?"

"I just wanted to look," he says. "When Tristan said about it, I just wanted to look."

"Because?"

"Because . . . I don't know. I just wanted to look."

Hannah holds her hand out for the phone, and because Cliff thinks initially that she is going to delete the app and then, a second later, that she is going to smash the phone – either of which strike him as getting off lightly – he hands it over.

Instead, Hannah returns to the dialogue screen, and reads, "Top or bottom?"

"I'm sorry?"

"Are you top or bottom, Cliff? Or both perhaps. Both apparently."

"It doesn't mean anything," Cliff says.

"I'm free now for one hour," Hannah reads. "How about that, Cliff?" she asks, raising her eyebrows and performing a sharp perfunctory nod. "Doesn't that mean anything either?"

She tosses the phone back to him again, and he stares at the screen, strokes the side of it, and then switches it off. When he glances up at her, his expression is so wretched that she can't bear to look at him.

"When was that anyway?" she asks.

"When was what?"

"*When* were you free for an hour?"

"I wasn't really . . ." Cliff says.

"God, was it when I was at the hospital? Is that it?"

Cliff stands, slips the phone into his pocket, then moves towards her. "Hannah," he says.

"Just . . . just stay away from me, Cliff," she says, slapping away his hand, which was reaching out to touch her arm. "You disgust me."

She pushes past him and walks to the kitchen, but when she gets there, she has no idea why. It feels no better here than the lounge, in fact it's worse. It's a room with only one exit, and Cliff has followed her and is now standing blocking the doorway.

"Hannah, I'm not, you know . . ." he says. "You're getting this all out of proportion."

"You're not what, Cliff?" she asks, turning to look out of the window again, anything to avoid his gaze.

"I'm not, you know, like Tristan," he says.

"You're not like Tristan."

"No. No it was just once or twice. When I was younger. At the beginning. But it all stopped. I promise, it all stopped when we got married."

Hannah spins back to face him now. "When we got married?" she cries.

"Before."

"You were gay, even back then?"

"No," Cliff says, his voice pleading now. "No I stopped, like I said. I'm not gay."

"But you were with other . . . you were with men . . . when we were together?"

"It was when we split up, Hannah. And it never happened again."

"Until now."

"But I didn't do anything," Cliff says. "It was just fantasy. I gave it all up to be with you."

Hannah buries her face in her hands for a moment, takes a deep breath, then lowers them again. "Well, I had fantasies too, Cliff," she says. "And I gave them all up for you. Actually, I didn't even give them up. You took them from me."

Cliff launches himself towards her. "You're getting this all out of proportion, Han'," he says.

"No! Stay away from me, Cliff," Hannah shrieks, raising

her hand. She feels sick. She's scared she's going to vomit again. "You revolt me, Cliff. You disgust me. Just stay away."

As she pushes past him, he pleads, "Don't say that, Hannah. It's not, I'm not . . . it's not like you think. I'm not *gay*."

She pauses and looks back at him. "I don't care what you are, Cliff," she says.

"What do you mean, you don't care?"

"This isn't about you being gay. It's not about that at all. It's about you being a bloody liar. It's about you being a compulsive liar."

She pushes into Aïsha's bedroom and locks the door behind her, then stands with her back against the door, breathing heavily.

After a minute, she hears the front door slam, and then, her strength suddenly exhausted, she slides down to her knees and begins to sob.

Once her tears have subsided, Hannah climbs onto the bed and pulls a pillow to her stomach. Only once she is hugging it does she remember that James has been sleeping in this bed, that James has been using this pillow. She sniffs it but can't find any detectable scent.

For hours, she lies on her side like this, simply staring out of the window, watching as the rain fades, then stops, and then, eventually, the first tentative glimpses of sun appear.

As the weather starts to clear, so do her thoughts. The problem is that *of course* Cliff is gay. Well, perhaps he's not gay per se, perhaps he's bisexual or metrosexual or whatever they call it. He did, after all, manage fifteen years of fairly regular performances with her, and that's not, from what she has been told, something that guys like Tristan can manage.

302

But her biggest shock today is her lack of surprise at the concept that Cliff isn't entirely heterosexual either. She has never once, not in fifteen years, had that thought before, but now that it's out there, well, *of course*! She has never caught Cliff looking at other women, not once surprised him a little drunk in a party flirting with another woman. One of his greatest qualities has been that she has never once felt jealous or threatened.

But she *has* seen him look at men. She always assumed that these discreet glances were him eyeing up rivals, but as she thinks about it now, she can see him peering over his book at the pool guy or hiding behind the book as he pretends not to listen to Tristan's latest conquests, excusing himself from the table whenever the discussion got too intimate, or worse, involved him in some way. That one can spend half a lifetime trying to do the right thing only to find out that it was entirely the wrong thing for everyone concerned is more irony than she can bear.

Then again, if what Cliff has wanted all of these years is a guy, then why would he have gone to such absurd lengths to keep her away from James?

As the sun regains its full force outside, even this starts to make sense to her. She feels strangely centred, unusually calm, and, a unique experience, suddenly wise. For something about her life, something that has forever escaped her is starting to make sense. From the desire she felt for James to the repetitive and increasingly rare sex she has had with Cliff; from their stiflingly "normal" existence – a perfect cover if ever there was one – to Cliff's exaggerated insensitivity towards her moods, towards anything remotely feminine whether it be film, or book, or television . . . Even his dislike for anything gay-themed, his discomfort around Tristan and, yes, even his desperation to beat his brother for her affections, it has all been cover. It has all been a textbook performance of heterosexuality.

She's just toying with the idea of getting up again, when Cliff knocks on the door.

"Hannah? It's Jill for you. On the phone," he calls.

She climbs from the bed, and opens the door just enough to take the phone from him, then closes and locks it again.

"Jill?"

"Hi. I've been worried sick about you. Is everything OK?"

"Yes," Hannah says. "It's all been pretty dramatic but everything's fine now. How's Luke?"

"He's fine. We just had pizza, and you know how Luke likes pizza. Do you want to talk to him?"

"In a minute, Jill. I need to ask you something first."

"Fire away."

"I need to ask you a huge favour."

"Right."

"Can you look after the kids for a while?"

"Sure. For how long?"

"Until the end of the holiday maybe."

"What? Till next Saturday?!"

"Yes."

There's a pause, during which Hannah hears Jill take a sharp intake of breath. "I don't know, Han'," she says. "They're quite a handful, and what if I . . ."

"Jill!" Hannah interrupts. "How many times have I saved your bacon?"

"I know," Jill says. "It's just . . ."

"Jill! How many times?"

"You're right. It's just that . . ."

"And how often have I asked you for a favour? Seriously. How often?"

"Virtually never, I guess."

"So just do this for me, will you?"

Jill tuts. "Where are you going anyway?"

"I don't know. But I need some time alone. If I stay here, I swear I'll explode."

"Are you going away with . . ."

"Not in front of Luke, Jill."

"Sorry. Are you going away with *you know who*? Is he still there?"

"No, he's gone."

"But what if I want to spend some time with Pascal?" Jill says.

"He's there with you now, isn't he?"

"Well, yes, but . . ."

"So."

"Can we come back to the villa tomorrow, or do you want us to stay away?"

"No, you can come back. Cliff's here."

"But that's going to be awkward, isn't it?"

"Not really. You can leave the kids with him while you go off and do whatever you do with Pascal."

"I guess," Jill says. "So you're not going away with James?"

"Jill, not in front of the kids, for God's sake."

"Oops. Sorry. But are you?"

"I have no idea to be honest."

"But you might be."

"Like I said, I have no idea. But I'll phone you tomorrow, OK?"

"OK, I guess. Shall I put Luke on?"

"Sure."

"Luke? It's your Mum . . ."

"Mum?"

"Hi, sweetie, are you OK?"

"Fine. We had pizza. And tomorrow we're going swimming in the sea."

"Good. Well, just be careful, OK?"

"The hotel's all blue."

"Right."

"Are you OK, Mum?"

"Yes, of course I am."

"You're not still arguing with Dad then?"

"No. That's all dealt with now, just like you and Aïsha."

"We're still arguing a bit."

"That's fine too. Just make sure it doesn't go on too long."

"OK."

"When you get back tomorrow, I won't be there, but Dad will."

"OK."

"I'm going to see some tourist things before we go home. Boring things you wouldn't like."

"OK."

"But I'll be back in a few days, OK?"

"Sure."

"Night, Luke."

"Night, Mum."

The conversation over, Hannah sits and stares at the phone. She thinks about Luke, wonders what will happen to him, how he'll react if . . .

But then she stops herself. These what-if equations have kept her life static since adolescence. And if life proves one thing, it's that the best-laid plans don't necessarily lead to the best results. Luke will be fine. Whatever happens, she trusts herself to make sure of it.

She dashes to the bathroom and locks herself in. She showers and fixes her make-up – her eyes are still a bit red, but otherwise she looks OK – then nervously returns to their bedroom. Cliff, thankfully, is elsewhere.

She dresses in clean clothes, throws two further changes of clothes into her smallest bag along with her purse and her passport, then carries the bag out to the lounge.

"Here," she says, and when Cliff looks up she tosses him the phone.

"Jesus, don't do that!" Cliff protests, once he has caught the phone for the third time.

"OK, I won't," Hannah says with meaning.

Cliff notices her bag now. "What's in the bag?" he asks.

"Just some clothes. I'm leaving."

"You're leaving . . ." Cliff repeats.

Hannah dumps the bag on the sofa then crosses the room to her husband.

He stands to meet her, his expression a strange mixture of confusion and fear.

"I don't understand," he says.

Hannah takes his face between her hands and kisses him on the lips, then wraps her arms around him and hugs him tightly. "I love you, Cliff, I do," she says before releasing him. "But life's too short for this. I only just worked that out, but life really is too short for this."

"For what?"

"For all this . . ." Hannah says, gesturing vaguely. "For all this mucking around."

She sighs deeply, then squeezes his arms and releases him. She returns to the sofa and hikes the bag over her shoulder.

"I still don't get it," Cliff says. "Where are you going?"

"I'm off on my holidays," she says.

"Your holidays?"

"Yes, Cliff. For one week I'm going to do whatever the fuck I fancy. I can only suggest that you do the same."

As Hannah turns to the front door, Cliff says, "But I want . . . I mean, I don't want . . . Hannah!"

She pulls the door open and steps out onto the porch.

The storm clouds have moved to the east and the setting sun is streaming out from beneath the band of cloud, making every wet surface shine with its yellowy light. Steam is rising from the terracotta floor-tiles.

As she reaches the gate, Cliff calls out to her, and she pauses and looks back.

"I don't understand where you're going," Cliff says.

"It's OK, Cliff," Hannah tells him. "You don't need to."

"But you can't walk anywhere from here," Cliff says. "You're being stupid."

Hannah wrinkles her nose. "Nah," she says. "Nah, this isn't stupid. The last fifteen years have been stupid, but this isn't. This is fine."

"Well, wait till Jill gets back at least," Cliff says. "Wait until tomorrow, and they can drive you somewhere."

Hannah shakes her head. "Relax, Cliff. It's all going to be OK."

"But what am I going to do here on my own?" Cliff asks.

"I don't know. Do whatever you want to do. Call

Jean-Jacques on your Grindr thing. Knock yourself out. No one cares anymore."

"I'm not gay, Hannah," Cliff says. "I know you think I am, but I'm not."

"Then Jean-Jacques is perfect," she says. "He's not gay either. Enjoy."

And then she closes the gate behind her and starts to walk along the road, steam rising from the puddles around her.

She's imagining James' face when he sees her arrive in the auberge, and that image is, despite all of the trauma, making her smile. She doesn't know quite what will happen when she gets there, but she trusts that instinct will tell her, that instinct for once, unconstrained by conditioning, or genes, or circumstance, will tell her exactly what to do.

Because though she is still Hannah, she feels like an entirely different Hannah right now. She feels as free as the birds that are tweeting so crazily in the wet leaves of the trees; she feels light-footed and wise and centred and reborn.

Whatever happens next, it will be something new, something wonderful. She has, after all, a whole half-life ahead of her.

Find out what happens next in

OTHER HALVES

The hotly anticipated sequel to *The Half-Life of Hannah*
Read on for a sneak preview . . .

ONE

HANNAH

I was in the middle of a family holiday in France when I walked out on my marriage. Some would say that I could have chosen my moment better, but the appearance at our holiday villa of the man I had fallen in love with in my twenties – a man who unfortunately happened to be my fiancé's brother – not only provided the opportunity, but opened the floodgates on a tsunami of revelations that revealed my marriage to be built upon nothing more substantial than a sea of untruths.

My husband, Cliff, had been revealed as a compulsive liar – to keep us apart, he had told me that James had died, when in fact he had simply been living in Australia – and my feelings for James were rekindled with the same intensity as fifteen years earlier.

But though one could explain my walking out of that door in terms of these events – my attraction to James and my betrayal by Cliff – in hindsight, I think that would be somewhat missing the point.

What really happened that day was that my bubble of steely self-control burst. A muscle that I had been exercising, stretched to its limit in order to keep myself centred in the middle of my life, gave way. The desire to break free, to live something new, to change not this, not that, but *everything* about my life became, in an instant, irresistible.

Perhaps it *was* what people call a "midlife crisis". Some buy sports cars, others have affairs, and perhaps it was a similar thing going on here, only in my case, it didn't build slowly enough for me to identify small safety valves that might enable me to get by. In my case, the water suddenly boiled and blew the top right off the pressure cooker.

I blamed Cliff, of course, for making a lie of our marriage, and I thanked James for returning and providing a catalyst and a suitable destination, but the truth is, I think, that both were almost innocent bystanders in a much larger process grounded not in events but in some internal body-clock. I truly believe now that the explosion would have happened anyway; it was just a matter of time.

So, one minute I was sitting on the bed feeling trapped in my marriage and confused about my feelings, and the next I was walking away from the house with a bag over my shoulder – my husband protesting behind me.

I don't know what Cliff was thinking as he watched me walk away, but I expect he thought I had gone mad. Perhaps I had, a little.

As Cliff didn't know that James was staying in the little auberge down the road, it certainly must have seemed crazy of me to head off on foot without any apparent destination.

When I got to the auberge, I asked Jean-Jacques, the barman, if he could put me through to James Parker's room.

"Il est parti," he said, which I somehow managed to understand: James had already left.

I surprised myself by thinking, *"Oh, OK then."*

One part of me watched the other react calmly, and was surprised at the lack of emotion. That was the moment I first suspected that this was bigger than Cliff or James – that this was about escape.

I ordered a glass of wine and, because all the seats outside were wet from the recent rainstorm, I sat in a window seat and watched steam rising from the ground. I thought, "*So, no James.*"

I felt unexpectedly calm and strangely wise. It was such an unusual feeling that I thought, as I sipped my wine, that I might be having some kind of nervous breakdown.

It was a surprise, and I wondered if all the melodrama hadn't perhaps been because I needed to be alone. As a wife and a mother, day after day, you forget to notice just how stifling, how suffocating motherhood and marriage can feel. After the drama of the day, a glass of wine, alone, in an empty bar felt like everything I had ever wanted. It crossed my mind that this might be a momentary need, that perhaps I would want, in an hour or so, to return to the villa to carry on as if nothing had happened.

Jean-Jacques brought me a plate of nibbles and said something that I didn't understand.

"I'm sorry," I reminded him. "I don't speak French."

"Ah . . ." he said. "Will you be stay 'ere? In the 'otel?"

Exactly as he said these words, the door to the hotel lobby opened, James reappeared, and my heart did a little somersault.

At first he didn't see me, and I didn't say a word – I just watched him and thought about my feelings.

Jean-Jacques returned to the desk and retrieved James' room key from a board. Jean-Jacques glanced in my direction and so James turned and saw me sitting with my bag and my

3

glass of wine. He broke into a smile – a lopsided, confused smile – and said, "Hannah?" and my heart fluttered again. So my feelings for him were real, after all.

"Hannah!" he said again, distractedly taking the key that Jean-Jacques was proffering and crossing the room to where I sat. "What are you doing here?" he asked, crouching down beside me.

"I . . ." I stammered.

James raised his eyebrows expectantly.

"I think I've left him."

James nodded. "Wow," he said.

"I thought you'd gone. I thought I'd missed you."

"Nah, I just went to get some food. I didn't think you were coming."

"Yes," I replied. "I know."

"Are you . . . ?"

"Yes?"

"I don't know," James said, looking hopeful and scared at the same time. "Are you . . . here for me? Or just . . ."

"I'm not sure," I said, aware that I was sounding less enthusiastic than I intended. "I think so."

James nodded slowly. "D'you want me to go?"

I shook my head. "God, no!" I said. "I'm just . . . I feel a bit strange. It's all been a bit much."

James glanced at the barman, then back at me. "Do you want to go up to the room?" he asked.

I sipped my wine and stared outside for a moment before I replied, a little robotically, "No, actually, I think I'd like you to take me somewhere else."

James nodded thoughtfully.

"Can we do that? Can we go somewhere away from here?"

4

I asked, with increasing urgency. "Can we just get out of here and go stay somewhere else?" I suddenly needed to be as far from Cliff as possible.

James nodded. "Sure," he said, standing and offering me a hand. "Sure we can."

The hotel in Antibes was beautiful. It was set on the ramparts behind the old town, overlooking the sea.

We had barely spoken during the drive there, just sitting side by side in a weird, numbed silence, but James seemed OK about this. He seemed to understand that the day had been monumental, and that it was perhaps normal that this hadn't been a passionate falling into each other's arms.

The receptionist asked, "A twin room or a double?" and I replied without thinking, "A double." I think that was the moment both of us realised that this was really going to happen.

The receptionist took our names down and assumed that we were married. I was – stupidly – surprised to find that James and I shared the same surname. It hadn't crossed my mind that his being Cliff's brother would make hotel check-ins that much easier. And then we followed the porter up to the room.

Our room had the most stunning sea view, and the afternoon sun was low enough to be flooding through the windows.

While James tipped the porter, I opened the French doors, then stood on the tiny balcony and sniffed at the air. It seemed like the freshest, purest, most oxygenated air I had ever breathed.

James came and stood behind me, so close that I could feel his breath on my neck, and after a moment, I reached for his hands and pulled his arms around me.

He nuzzled my neck and my spine tingled and he said, "I'm so glad you're here."

And like some other, younger, more confident woman I barely remembered from way back, I said, "Yes, I know," and I turned to kiss him.

My newfound confidence lasted precisely until I had to undress in front of him; after all, it had been fifteen years since I had shown myself to anyone other than Cliff. This time around, I was closer to forty than twenty. Plus I had had a baby in the intervening years.

I had never been that sure how attractive Cliff had found me, and though I now realised that this sense of doubt might not have been entirely of my own making, I still felt incredibly uneasy about my body.

I broke free from James' embrace just long enough to pull the blinds and switch the lights off. Daylight was still filtering around the edges, but it was certainly an improvement. If James did notice my stretch marks or cellulite, it certainly didn't put him off his stride and that reassured me sufficiently that I was able to relax – just enough – to enjoy sleeping with him.

We stayed in that hotel for five nights, eating in little local seafood restaurants, wandering the streets of the old town and making love in the semi-shade of our room.

Though occasionally I would think of Cliff and my vision would tint red with rage or blue with guilt, I mainly managed to push every other aspect of my situation from my mind, and for five days and five nights, I let myself live in the moment. I felt a little crazy, but that craziness felt heavenly.

Jill, my sister, phoned a couple of times from the villa, and I reassured her that I was fine, thanked her for looking after my son, Luke, and headed her off when she tried to tell me anything about Cliff. Whatever it was, I didn't want to hear it. Whatever it was, I couldn't *bear* to hear it.

In Antibes, we visited the Picasso museum, which had beautiful floor tiles but little else of note – "It's a bit shit really, isn't it?" was James' comment – and another day we drove along the coast around the stunning shallows of Cap d'Antibes past the millionaires' residences, on to the golden beaches of Golfe-Juan and then Juan-les-Pins, and then Cannes, where, sitting on a sandy beach with James' arms around me, I wept for the mess that, unexpectedly, my life had become.

"It'll all be OK, Hannah," James said, but I didn't believe him. I couldn't see any way that could possibly be true.

Opposite the beach in Cannes we could see two small islands that looked gorgeous, so the next day we returned and took the small ferry out to the larger of them. Here, we wandered around the island, pausing to kiss, or picnic, or sit on the beach and stare back at the mainland, where everything seemed, from this calm haven, so unreasonably chaotic. Armed with pots of lavender honey bought from the monks, and over a rougher sea – the wind had got up – we travelled back, eating in a gorgeous but outrageously expensive restaurant in Le Suquet, before driving back to Antibes.

James was gorgeous throughout: a little abrupt at times, a little vulgar at others, but thoughtful and kind and, above all, undemanding. I think he understood that for our time together to be anything but horrific, reality had to be suspended. And that required avoiding whole areas of discussion, specifically anything pertaining to the future or the past.

At the end of the holiday, I bought a plane ticket so that I could fly home with James.

7

The horrid security personnel at the airport confiscated my pots of honey – apparently they were potentially explosive – and, ridiculously, I worried that, as they were the only thing I had bought with James to take home, this was somehow a bad omen.

It wasn't until we were actually seated side by side on that EasyJet flight that James asked me, rather nervously, "So what happens now?"

"I don't know," I told him. I purposely hadn't projected any further than passport control.

"Do you just go back to Cliff?" James asked.

I shook my head. "I don't think I can," I said.

"Do you like me?" he asked.

I laughed. "Can't you tell that?"

James nodded. "Well, I can hang around, or I can head back to Oz," he said, once the safety demonstrations were over.

I nodded. "Then hang around."

"Yes?"

"Definitely."

"Will you go back to the house?"

"Luke's there," I said, simply. "So, yes, initially at least . . . God, James. I don't know . . ."

"I could just find somewhere to stay then. Somewhere not too far from you. I can stay for a while. Ryan, my manager, is running the farm."

I covered my eyes with my palms, trying to think, then dropped them and said, "Yes. Then please stay."

"And then we just, what?" James asked. "See how things pan out?"

I nodded. "I don't know how else to play it," I said. "I'm sorry."

James nodded. "Suits me fine," he said. "I'm cool with that."

It's strange that those are the only words we exchanged on the subject – I think that it all seemed too vast to think about, the links between everything and everything else too criss-crossed and confusing even to be considered.

I had never been a big *let's-sit-and-talk-about-this* kind of person anyway, and I now realised that this part of my relationship with Cliff – the stilted communication that we had always experienced – had probably been more my doing than his, and would probably follow me wherever I went and whoever I was with.

On arriving home, I braced myself all the same for hysterical arguments with Cliff, but they didn't transpire either.

Cliff knew, through Jill, that I had spent the week with James, and by the time I got to the house he had moved to the spare room. It wasn't the first time in fifteen years that he had slept in the spare room, so Luke, though unusually surly, simply assumed, I think, that we were going through a rough patch.

For a few weeks we lived this strange, brittle silence of non-communication, gliding around each other without any unnecessary word being uttered. It was horrible, tense, unbearable, almost . . . but as the days went by it became more and more obvious, to me at least, that there was no going back.

Things with James, though unscheduled, continued in a relatively easy manner. Considering the horrifically stressful circumstances surrounding us, the fact that we never had a single argument struck me as astounding. He was undemanding and easy to get on with – a model partner. When I looked at him, I felt myself melt with desire, and whenever he was elsewhere, I missed him. My feelings for James were growing stronger by the day and my marriage to Cliff was revealed to be a sham. It was over, and I attempted to make Cliff realise this in the only way I knew how: through my actions.

OTHER HALVES

ebook (ISBN 978 1 84502 767 4)
available for download now

print (ISBN 978 1 84502 764 3)
available April 2014